ALSO BY CAMRYN GARRETT

Full Disclosure

OFF THE RECORD

CAMRYN GARRETT

Alfred A. Knopf
New York

nical schools for engineers, whose importance in our time need not be stressed.

In the field of adult education we have not remained idle either. With the reconstruction of our libraries we had to start from scratch.

Some years ago we built a new theater, the Schiller Theater, and it will not be long until our new opera will open its doors. Our theaters, the municipal and the private, have not yet reached the artistic level to which we aspire. But even severe critics count them among the leading theaters of Europe.

Our efforts were greatly helped not only by the Federal government but also by our American friends. The Free University would have never been born without the sympathetic understanding and the support of the American authorities. It would not have become what it is without the wonderful help of the Ford Foundation. We also owe to the United States our Memorial Library, the already-mentioned Congress Hall, the new Student Village of the Free University. And last but not least, substantial American contributions made possible our most modern hospital, one of the biggest on the Continent; the cornerstone was laid in 1959. Eleanor Dulles, the sister of the late Secretary of State, has been our loyal and staunch supporter in all these efforts.

The Berliners know that they owe a debt of gratitude to the American government, to American institutions, and finally to the American taxpayer. They also know how important the cultural contact is which expresses itself in the exchange of professors and students, or in the participation of foreign artists in our International Film Festival and the Berliner Theater Festival, which take place every summer and fall.

More than a fourth of our students come from the Soviet Zone. We also have many visitors from Eastern European countries. Among our students we find hundreds of young people from the underdeveloped countries. Here in Berlin they can study better than anywhere else the theme "East versus West" and gain a personal impression of the peaceful competition which lately has become the main topic of Soviet propaganda.

I am of the opinion that we have nothing to fear from a peaceful competition; on the contrary, I am very much in favor of it. I think we must not avoid intellectual discussions and cultural exchanges, as long as we are sure that we represent the better cause.

A special lesson of the Polish and Hungarian events, also my experience with young Germans from the Soviet Zone, has made an inextinguishable impression on me. This lesson affirms what we have already seen in many other places—namely, that the young generation cannot be molded according to the whims of certain dictators. Even under a totalitarian regime the best part of the youth languishes for greater independence, for truth and beauty and humanity. Questions of security and military defensive fronts are at present very important. Yet there are other fronts on which we can fight a successful battle, and we must fight it.

On this front of cultural competition Berlin is an important sector. It will only fulfill its real duty if through extraordinary efforts, through inspiration and courage, it becomes the intellectual center of Germany. Again and again we have to face the question: shall Berlin be only a city among many cities? A voice among many in the federalistic concert of the German states? Or will we succeed in overcoming our special position at the border of the free world?

In Berlin itself, in the German West, and also abroad I have repeatedly appealed for help so that we can make our city the cultural center from which liberal energies and great accomplishments emanate, an example for the seriousness of its scientific work, a model of what the Germans can contribute in liberty and in the fight for liberty.

4

The governing mayor of Berlin is not only charged with the administration of a big city. Since Berlin has the status of a Federal state he acts also as a kind of prime minister. Furthermore—in view of the present world political situation—he must interest himself in foreign policy much more than it would be the case in normal times. I am not only chairman of the board of trustees of the two universities, but also on the board of the Bank of Berlin and the Electric Company. In 1957–58 it was my turn to act as the President of the Federal Senate, and during the two trips abroad of the Federal President Theodor Heuss I had to substitute for him.

These many and varied tasks and duties have a strong influence on my political and on my private life.

When I was elected mayor I promised myself that I would spend at least one hour every day with my family. I could not keep this promise very often. When I reach our little house in the suburbs where we continue to live after my election, it is usually late in the evening, my boys are already in bed. Lunch or dinner together we can have only on Sunday, but many a Sunday I am out of town on official business.

It is hard for me, not being able to devote myself to Peter and Lars as much as I would like. Boys of their age—Peter is eleven, Lars eight—need the guidance of their father. I can only hope that soon there will be more peaceful times which will grant me a more normal life. Fortunately, both my wife and the boys are intelligent enough to accept the inevitable, though the boys have asked quite often why their father could not find a decent job so that he could be at home at a definite hour like all other fathers.

265

CONTENT NOTE: discussions of sexual assault and sexual harassment

THIS IS A BORZOI BOOK PUBLISHED BY ALFRED A. KNOPF

Visit us on the Web! GetUnderlined.com

Educators and librarians, for a variety of teaching tools, visit us at RHTeachersLibrarians.com

Library of Congress Cataloging-in-Publication Data
Names: Garrett, Camryn, author.
Title: Off the record / Camryn Garrett.
Description: First edition. | New York : Alfred A. Knopf, [2021] |
Audience: Ages 14 & up. | Audience: Grades 10–12. |
Summary: "A teen journalist uncovers the #metoo scandal of the decade: a bigshot Hollywood director is taking advantage of cast members." —Provided by publisher
Identifiers: LCCN 2020043217 (print) | LCCN 2020043218 (ebook) |
ISBN 978-1-9848-2999-3 (hardcover) | ISBN 978-1-9848-3000-5 (library binding) |
ISBN 978-1-9848-3001-2 (ebook)
Subjects: CYAC: Journalism—Fiction. | Sexual abuse—Fiction. |
African Americans—Fiction. | Youths' writings.
Classification: LCC PZ7.1.G3745 Of 2021 (print) | LCC PZ7.1.G3745 (ebook) |
DDC [Fic]—dc23

The text of this book is set in 10.5-point Berling MT.
Interior design by Ken Crossland

Printed in the United States of America
May 2021
10 9 8 7 6 5 4 3 2 1
First Edition

For survivors

CHAPTER 1

I've rewritten the same sentence five different times. No matter how I rearrange the words, they don't sound good enough to be published.

Clearly, Black films only receive critical acclaim when they heavily feature Black suffering. Where are our happy movies? They exist, but you don't see them winning Oscars.

I smack my keyboard. Nothing changes. I'm still on the living room couch, an episode of *Real Housewives* playing on the TV. My Word document stares back at me, cursor blinking as if daring me to rewrite the sentence for a sixth time. How am I supposed to end an op-ed like this? *In conclusion, I'm sure most of the people reading this are white and don't want to hear about race, but please don't cancel your subscription.*

I minimize the Word document, flipping to my email. No new messages. Still the same emails: one from Target, one from Spelman College confirming that I sent my application, a few from Instagram. Nothing from the contest. Nothing telling me whether I won or lost.

Ugh. I rub my forehead, staring up at the *Deep Focus*

magazine covers hanging above our TV. The Obamas, Serena Williams, and Jimi Hendrix. They've been hanging there forever, some of the best covers of my favorite magazine ever. Normally, they inspire me.

They're a little too in my face right now—while I'm waiting to hear back from the talent competition. If I win, I'll get the chance to write an actual cover story for the magazine. *Me* writing a *cover story* for *Deep Focus*.

I take a shaky breath. It's almost too much to think about.

I *should* be focusing on this op-ed I owe Monique. She enjoyed my last piece, and the one before it. That *should* make me feel better. But my anxiety doesn't pay attention to how I *should* feel. According to my sisters, I worry about everything, even the pointless, but especially the very important.

I glance at the inbox again. Still no change. The winners are supposed to hear back by the end of today. But why are they taking so long? What if they didn't like the samples I sent, or they thought my writing was too immature, or they got turned off by how much I write about race—

"Well, look here. Josie's right where we left her."

My head snaps up. Dad lumbers through the door, rolling a purple suitcase with one hand and holding his backpack strap with the other. I don't know why Alice is bringing so much stuff when she's just an hour away. She could come home every weekend, if she wanted.

Dad's still in his accountant uniform—white shirt, black tie— the air of math and numbers swirling around him. He glances at the muted TV. Blond women in sparkly dresses lunge for each other across a gigantic table. I shrug.

"I leave it on for background noise," I say.

Alice appears with an eye roll. She looks the same as she did when we dropped her off in August: ripped jeans, edges of her box braids tinged purple, her signature bored face. Looks like her first few months of college didn't change a thing.

"What are you writing now?" she asks, swinging her backpack to the floor. "Another review of *Real Housewives?*"

"Shut up." I only wrote those recaps to get my foot in the door and she knows it. "It's a serious piece."

"That's what you said last time."

I scowl, opening my email and sending the piece before closing my laptop. This piece is fine. If Monique doesn't like it, she'll send me edits, same as usual. At least it's better than a *Real Housewives* recap.

"Come on, girls," Dad says. "Where's Maggie?"

"She's at work," I say. "And the library is having a pre-Thanksgiving playtime or something, so Mom took Cash with her. She'll probably have to stay to clean everything up."

"They work her too hard." Dad shakes his head, but there's no bite in his voice. "Always have."

I stand up to hug him, but he pulls me in first. He always gives the best hugs. Eventually, I draw back to hug Alice, but she just scoffs and steps away. I don't know why I even try.

By the time she and Dad have put away their stuff, Mom is back from work, and so is my oldest sister, Maggie. She's still dressed in her apron and khakis. I hold up my phone.

"It's the rare employee Maggie," I say, opening my camera app. "Take a picture for good luck."

Maggie's eyes widen as she lunges for me. "Josie, I *swear—*"

"Mama," Cash says, worming between the two of us. "No swearing."

"You're right, baby," Maggie says, glancing down at him. "No swearing."

When he heads into the kitchen, she sticks her tongue out at me. I snort.

We haven't had a family dinner since the day before Alice left for school. It's not that we don't like each other. Our schedules just never line up. Dad works late, Maggie is always doing overtime, and Alice is usually at school. That leaves Mom, Cash, and me eating in front of the TV most nights. Cash looks a little startled to be sitting at the dinner table right now.

I tap my fingers against my side as everyone settles in, fighting the urge to go back on the computer and see if I've gotten a response from the contest yet. If Monique has replied to my email yet.

Maggie says all I ever do is search for things to keep myself anxious. I guess that's what I'm doing now. My deadline isn't until next week, and I'm pretty sure the piece is fine. It's just that when I'm anxious about one thing, it tends to bleed over to everything else. I'm already worried about hearing back from the contest, and now I can't stop myself from thinking about everything that might go wrong with the piece I wrote for Monique—the article deleting itself, Monique hating it and deciding she never wants to work with me again, my words sounding too similar to someone else's and me being accused of plagiarism, Monique calling me a racist (even though she's also Black)—and wondering what I'm going to write about next. . . .

It never ends, not unless I'm actually writing. I don't know what it is. Something about writing shuts off my brain for a little while.

"How are things at Spelman, Alice?" Mom asks, snapping me out of my thoughts. She always dresses like a hip librarian—Skechers, a T-shirt that says "All the Cool Kids Are Reading," a pair of pink reading glasses clipped to her sweater.

"Great," Alice says, grabbing another slice of pizza from the open box. No homemade food until tomorrow, when the entire family comes over for Thanksgiving. I cringe just thinking about it. "I love the psychology department. All of my classes are interesting. And I joined a sorority, actually, and it's really helping me feel like I'm part of a community."

"You? A sorority?" I raise a brow. "That sounds fake."

"Oh, come on," Maggie says, cutting up Cash's pizza. "She can try new things."

Alice flashes a smug smile. I like it better when I have Maggie to myself.

"You'll probably try a bunch of things when you head there next fall," Maggie continues. "Who knows? Maybe you'll join a sorority, too."

Alice snorts. I glare at her.

"Yeah," I say. "Maybe. I guess we'll see."

"There's a lot to do at Spelman," Alice says, rolling her eyes. "You can find something that I didn't try first."

I grip my cup extra hard. If Mom and Dad weren't here, I'd tear into Alice, and she'd probably tear right back. But now I have to force myself to be *civil*, even though none of this is my fault.

I've wanted to go to Spelman ever since I was in middle school. It's where Mom went, where Grandma went, where Auntie Denise went. It was always *my* thing, but Alice applied last year, completely out of the blue, and got in. I still applied early decision, the way I always planned to. But now, when I get in, I'll have to share the campus with my sister.

I definitely never dreamed about that.

"Auntie Josie?" Cash's little hands reach for me. "What's a sorority?"

"It's a sort of club," Dad says before I can. "But for people at college."

5

"Make sure you're eating your vegetables, Josephine," Mom says, shoveling some salad onto my plate. "It's better to eat some salad than to have more than one slice of pizza. You have to remember that we have diabetes in our family."

Alice and Maggie share a look. I force myself to stare at my plate, but I doubt Mom notices. She makes comments like that all of the time, as if I don't already second-guess everything I put in my mouth.

"Grandpa?" Cash turns to Dad. "Will you tell me a story?"

"After dinner, buddy."

I poke at my salad with my fork. Maggie always says I should tell Mom how I feel in the moment, before she forgets what she's said, but I can't now. Cash is *right there*. Plus, we'd get into an argument, since she'd say she's *only thinking about my health*. How do I respond to that without sounding like a brat?

Instead of responding, I get up and start clearing the table before anyone can ask. I want to get this over with as fast as possible.

"Josie, don't go," Dad calls from his seat. "Your mother and I want to talk to you. Alone."

Maggie scoops Cash up and disappears. Alice jogs up the stairs. Traitors.

Normally, Mom and Dad don't *announce* this sort of thing. They just start talking. The only time they make my sisters leave is when we talk about my anxiety. I actually stare longingly at the empty hallway. I'd rather babysit Cash than have a private talk with Mom and Dad.

I rack my brain to figure out what we could be talking about. I'm not pregnant. I don't do drugs or drink. I'm *boring*. All I do is go to school, write freelance articles for different magazines, and work at Cora's Chicken Stand, a dingy restaurant a few minutes away. I don't even really have a lot of friends. Everyone has *school friends*, kids you see in class and sit with at lunch and partner up with in gym. But it's almost December, which means it's almost Capstone Month, when none of us seniors have to physically show up for school. I haven't seen the girls I hang out with at lunch, Jordan and Sadie, since yesterday, and besides the two days of school we have next week, I doubt I'll see them again until the new year.

"What is it?" I ask, standing near the door. I fist my hand in my shirt. "The Spelman application?"

I did it mostly myself, but Mom and Dad had to fill out the financial stuff and pay the application fees. Oh God. Are we having money problems? What if they don't have money for college? I always knew I'd have to pitch in—my parents get a discount on my private school because Auntie Denise is an administrator, but with three daughters and relatively normal jobs, I doubt they can pay for college, too—except, what if it's so bad that my money from writing and working at Cora's isn't enough? We applied for financial aid, but what if it doesn't work out?

I want to take a deep breath, but all my air is caught in my chest.

"No, not that." Mom grabs my hand, pulling me back toward the table. I'm still irritated about the pizza thing, but it's hard to stay mad at her for long, with her warm hands and tender smile. "We've just been worried about you, Josephine. That's all."

"Worried about me?" My eyebrows shoot up. I shift my gaze to Dad. I don't think he's blinked once since this conversation began. "Why?"

"Well," Dad says, "you barely act like a teenager."

"*Oh.*" I smack my thighs. "This again?"

I've had this conversation with them almost monthly, ever since I started high school. I guess I've never been *normal* to them. I've always been shy, but they used to say I'd grow out of it, until I started locking myself in school bathroom stalls for entire periods. That ship sailed a long time ago.

"It's just," Mom says, glancing at Dad, "since the hard time you had in middle school—"

"I'm fine," I say, sitting in the closest chair. "Really, I promise. That was years ago."

The lines in Dad's forehead crease.

"Seriously," I say. "I've just been busy with my senior project and everything."

My parents switched my schools after my *hard time* in middle school. Maggie had already graduated by then and Alice didn't want to leave her friends, so I'm the only one who went to Oak Grove, a private school full of kids with bougie parents. It's weird and artsy; I get to take classes with a real journalist, and we have an actual newsroom that students are allowed to use. Capstone Month is another positive. Every senior looks forward to it because we basically get all of December off. Technically, it's for a senior capstone project; you have to volunteer, do a big project, or work in a field you're interested in. All of the kids love it, but my parents weren't exactly thrilled with the idea of me being home until the new year.

I glance between the two of them. Dad looks kind of constipated.

"It's not that," Dad says. "You've been doing a great job. But that's not what we're worried about, Josie."

"We find it difficult not to worry about you," Mom says, as if they practiced this. "Maggie was a little wild, but she was involved, and Alice flourished. I know you've been hard at work getting started on your project, but—"

"You don't have any friends," Dad interrupts. "It's just not normal for a girl your age."

"I *do*—"

Mom gives me the *look*, which means *Watch your tone before I make you regret opening your mouth,* so I shut up. But what am I *supposed* to say? Just because I'm not president of every club, like Alice was, or don't have a ton of friends, the way Maggie did, doesn't mean there's something wrong with me.

Sure, I might not have any best friends from school, but how many people do? And really, how many of these people are going to keep talking to each other once May comes around and we all graduate? Most of them don't even like each other. That's why everyone subtweets or gossips or fights in our class group chat. I want to be around people who care. If I can't, I'd rather be alone.

"Well," I say, shrugging, "I've been busy with my writing, like I said. And the holiday rush at Cora's."

There's a bit of a reaction then—the tightening of Mom's mouth, the glance Dad gives her. But they can't blame me. Writing is the only thing that helps.

"We're proud of your writing," Dad says, patting my shoulder. "But you can't put all of your eggs in one basket. You need to make some friends."

"I *have* friends," I say, sticking out my hand. "My Twitter mutuals are my friends. Jordan and Sadie are my friends. Monique is my friend."

Mom throws back her head and sighs. Dad presses his lips together.

"Isn't Monique your editor?" Dad asks. "She doesn't count."

"And neither do strangers online," Mom snaps. "You don't know them."

"Monique is literally my mentor for my senior project," I say, cocking my head to the side. "Principal O'Conner had to approve of her, remember? She's an actual person and she's, like, *impressed* by me. She only started taking my pieces because she followed me on Twitter! It leads to quality relationships."

"That's not what we mean," Mom says. "It's not normal for you to have adults as friends. You should be spending time with kids your own age."

It's impossible to understand my parents. One minute they're talking about college, and the next minute they're telling me I don't fool around enough. I'm not sure what they expect me to do. Sure, sometimes I scroll through Instagram and get jealous when I see everyone at parties or going into Atlanta together. On the other hand, I don't know what I would do if I actually hung out with them. I hear Jordan and Sadie talk about sports and dances and how much weight people need to lose at lunch. I'm lost about sixty percent of the time, and I have no desire to catch up.

"It's not that simple," I say. "I spend a lot of time with kids my own age. Lots of other kids work at Cora's, remember? Lots of kids I see in school, like Josh Sandler and Liv Carroll. You remember them?"

I leave out the fact that Josh is annoying as hell and I spend most of my shifts staring at Liv and her super-tight uniform shirt while she waits on customers, but I figure they don't need to know that.

"But you never go out," Dad says. "You don't go to school dances or clubs. You don't bring anyone home. We aren't trying to corner you. But maybe it's something we should discuss with Laura."

I press my lips together. My therapist and I have had *many* conversations about the kids at school and around town. I don't need Mom and Dad to take up a chunk of our time with whatever *this* is. We have more important things to talk about.

I've accepted that I probably won't have close friends in high school. I'm just glad I'm almost done. But there's no way to explain that to Mom and Dad without them worrying more. I don't even want to try it.

"I think I need to clear my head," I say, resting my hands on the table. "Can I go out for a drive?"

> **@JosieTheJournalist:** i figured my rebellious teenage phase would be cool but all i've managed to do is watch Tarantino movies behind my dad's back (not worth it)

CHAPTER 2

The best part of finally being seventeen is driving. I can't leave whenever I want, since I don't have my own car, but I feel better as soon as I get my hands on the wheel. Driving reminds me that there's another world out there. Life isn't just our town and high school, no matter how much it feels like it.

There's also the Dairy Queen ten minutes away from our house.

I've always loved writing, but the fact that I get paid for my articles now definitely adds to the fun. I don't have to beg anyone to buy me a milkshake and hide the evidence. I try, I really do, but this diet Mom's pushing doesn't work. I've done it all: counting points, tracking calories, cutting out dairy or wheat, and making this "healthy lifestyle change" Mom's now into. None of them work. Either I lose a max of fifteen pounds (gaining it back after two months) or nothing changes. It's not worth it. I wish Mom understood.

I'm still full from dinner, so I fly past Dairy Queen and head onto the main road. Warm Southern air flows through the open windows; the radio plays in the background. Mom hates listening to music when she drives, but when I'm behind the wheel, I blast it.

My phone's sharp ring makes my eyes snap to the passenger seat. I never have the volume loud enough for me to hear at home, mostly because I'd rather text than talk on the phone. The only reason it's up now is because it's one of Mom and Dad's rules. I pull over and park the car.

It's Monique.

For some reason, I thought it might be the contest. My heart momentarily sinks before the anxiety ramps up again. Monique probably read my last piece. Already. God. It starts again: the shallow breathing, the racing thoughts, the mental block.

It's okay. It's okay. She's going to say something nice.

Yet I can't help but wonder if she's calling for another reason. Maybe she hated what I wrote. Maybe it was so bad that she doesn't want me to write for her ever again, and then she won't write a progress report for me for school and I'll have all this horrible work and no progress report and fail senior year.

It doesn't even have to be something big and horrible. Just awkward silences make me anxious. I hate them in face-to-face conversations and on the phone. I never know what to say. I never know how to sound. And then the silence beats down on me, harder and harder, until all my air is gone.

The ringing stops. I tighten my grip on the wheel, glancing down. It barely takes a second for it to start ringing again. I force a deep breath. Before I can chicken out, I accept the call and hold the phone up to my ear. The faster we get talking, the faster I'll feel comfortable. Maybe.

"Hi," I say. My voice cracks. *Ugh.* Hopefully she didn't notice.

"Hey, Josie!" Monique's voice is big and loud. I worry so much about how I sound, but it's like she doesn't care at all. "Hope I'm not getting you at a bad time."

"No, no," I say, shaking my head even though she can't see me. "I'm just hanging out after dinner. How are you?"

"Having a lovely time at home, finally," she says, laughing. "We've been in the office for a long time, trying to finish deadlines before the holiday, and New York in the winter is most definitely not like in the movies. But speaking of deadlines, I wanted to talk to you about the piece you sent me earlier."

"Oh." Something in my stomach burns, my fingers gripping the phone a little tighter. Whenever she has notes, she's nice about it, but it's easier to not take it personally when they're written down in an email. "You finished it? Already?"

"Yup." She pops the *p*. "I couldn't stop reading. What you were saying, how movies by Black filmmakers are only valued when Black characters are suffering, it really resonated with me. I think I've always noticed the really difficult movies winning awards and the fun movies, like *Coming to America*, being excluded."

"Yeah," I say, clearing my throat. "I wish every movie came out on an equal playing field. Like, when we have coming-of-age movies about Black kids just living, people don't really pay attention, but when you have all the misery and suffering of movies like *Precious*, people eat it up. So are audiences just super interested in Black pain? I feel like we're told that stories about pain are the most important. And they can be. They just don't have to be the only ones."

"It's brilliant," Monique says. My heart soars. I always think my pieces are important, but that doesn't mean everyone else will. Monique's praise literally fuels me. "And you explored it so well. I swear, you get better and better with each essay you send me."

"Oh," I say, shifting in my seat. "Wow. Thank you so much."

Compliments are awkward because I'm not sure how to react to them. I want to be humble and sweet, but also don't want to come across like I'm surprised. Writing is my *thing*.

I know there's always room to be better, but I'm good at it. I've known that since Monique first read my blog posts and emailed me about writing film essays for *Essence* magazine. I've known that since I told her I was seventeen and she freaked out. But it's still nice to hear it.

"It has the potential to be really powerful," Monique continues. I lean back in my seat and soak it up. "I wish you were getting more attention for this work, though, especially since you're so young."

"I guess so." I pick at my jeans, not sure what else to say. "But I don't want people to pay attention to me just because of my age, you know? I want them to like my work."

"I get it," Monique says. "But between you and me, you're more talented than some of my coworkers."

I laugh, but it sounds strangled. Am I that good? It makes me giddy.

"But anyway, I just wanted to call you so that you knew what I thought," she continues. "I know I tell you how talented you are in my emails, but I need to make sure that you're really aware. It's not even a matter of potential, Josie. You're already a writer. All you have to do is keep working. By the time you're my age, you'll have people eating out of the palm of your hand, if you don't already."

"I wish." I snort. "No one cares about writing here. My parents think I'm strange, and my sister listens, sometimes, but I know she's just trying to make me feel better. And I don't talk to any of the kids at school about it. I don't think they'd get it. The only ones who really pay attention are my Twitter followers."

As soon as the words tumble out, I regret them. She called to compliment me, not to hear me complain about high school. I don't want her thinking I'm just some petulant teenager.

But Monique doesn't hang up. I didn't really think she would, but sometimes these ridiculous thoughts are hard to shake.

"Oh, high school." Monique sighs long enough for it to sound like a song. "Girl, I *definitely* don't miss that. But don't feel bad. Your people just aren't there. That's fine, all right? They could be anywhere, even the places you don't expect, and you have so much time to find them. It's the best part of growing up."

I smile up at the sky through the windshield. There's so much world I haven't seen yet—movies I haven't watched, brains I haven't picked, countries I haven't been to, people I haven't met. The real world isn't so small. Some days, this idea is what keeps me going.

CHAPTER 3

Maggie always has a *thing*. There's always a new project—putting inspirational quotes all over the walls, doula training, even starting a raw food diet (which was truly the *worst*). The rest of us always get roped into it somehow.

But Mirror Time is something I don't mind. I can't really get out of it, either, since the three of us share a bathroom. And it's just another way Maggie has tried to help. Like leaving Post-its with positive messages around the house or creating a *quiet corner* with beanbags and relaxing music for me in the room I share with Alice.

I appreciate the effort. It's just that a lot of my anxiety comes from people paying attention to me. I can't help but overthink it. Am I too much of a burden? Am I bothering them?

It seems like everyone is already downstairs helping Mom get ready. It means they're too busy to come looking for me. It means I get the bathroom all to myself. I kind of need it.

After not hearing from the contest yesterday, I'm guessing I lost. I'm used to rejections—sending pitches to different magazines will do that to you—but it still hurts.

I push my hair away from my face, revealing myself in the

mirror. There are lines under my eyes and a few crusty bits by my mouth, but I look fine otherwise. The rule is, we're supposed to start off the morning by saying something positive about ourselves in the mirror.

It took a little while, but I *do* like my face. I have dark brown skin and plump lips and what Beyoncé would call a "Negro Nose." This face is a very cute face, especially with my cheeks. Mom still likes to pinch them sometimes, like I'm a toddler. And I have been working on my hair. I don't exactly have an Afro, but there's a nice amount of follicles up there. I smile.

Honestly, I don't need this. I don't think I'm ugly. But Maggie says it's not about physical beauty. It's about *inner peace* or *self-confidence* or something. So I open my mouth and say, "You're smart and kind and talented." It sounds like something from Barney.

Liking my face is pretty easy. It's the rest of my body that can take some work. I pull up the tank top I slept in, looking at my belly as it spills out. I think it's just a habit to suck it in at this point. It's freeing and sort of disappointing every time I let go.

My therapist, Laura, and I work on framing—that's what I call it, since it sort of reminds me of TV. The idea is to look at your situation in a different light.

So I try not to frown when I see my belly. It shouldn't be so big, but it's okay, because everyone's body is different. And I don't mind my belly when it's just me. I try to think of Winnie-the-Pooh, how everyone loves him and he wears a crop top and he's generally a fashion icon. It makes me smile. I rub my hands over my own stomach, swaying back and forth in front of the mirror. There's nothing wrong with a belly. Bellies are cute, and they hold important internal organs.

"Do they hurt?"

My eyes snap up, locking on Alice's in the mirror. She's taller than me, which isn't that hard to be, seeing as I'm just barely taller than five feet. Her scarf is still on, and her sleep shirt is falling off her tiny frame. I have to shove away some of the jealousy in my gut.

"Do what hurt?" I ask, clearing my throat and moving my arms.

"The stretch marks." Her eyes dart to my stomach faster than I can pull the shirt down. "Maggie got them when she was pregnant with Cash, even though she kept using shea butter every few minutes."

"I remember." I shake my head at the memory. I was thirteen, old enough for my parents to talk to me about waiting until marriage. "And no, they don't hurt."

It doesn't *seem* like she's trying to make me feel bad, but I can never tell with Alice. Even if she didn't mean it that way, a switch has already been flipped. It's not just my voice telling me there's something wrong with my body. Normal people aren't supposed to get stretch marks unless they're pregnant. I don't even know how I got mine: deep ripples at the edges of my stomach, darker than the rest of my skin.

"Well, I guess you don't have to worry about it, then," she says, pulling off her scarf and running her hands through her braids. "Does Maggie still do Mirror Time?"

"Uh, yeah." I try not to roll my eyes. "You've been gone three months. Not much has changed."

"Hmm." Her eyes narrow as she studies herself. "I like my eyes today. They're looking hazel."

"Your eyes are brown."

"I said they *look* hazel," she says, shaking her head. "My eyes can *look* any color I want them to."

I can't tell if she's being serious or not. Alice sort of makes a joke out of everything.

I change into my Thanksgiving outfit (an orange-and-red floral dress I'm in love with) before slipping downstairs. Mom is already in the kitchen, ordering Dad, Maggie, and even Cash around with a wooden spoon. I step back, but the spoon flies up in my direction. Shit. She saw me.

"Why are you already dressed up?" She narrows her eyes. "You still have to help."

"But it's late." I glance at the ticking clock on the wall. It's eleven. "People will start showing up in an hour. You know Auntie Denise."

Dad snorts. Mom shoots him a look and he turns back to the turkey.

Auntie Denise and her new husband, a guy whose name I haven't bothered to learn yet, show up even earlier than we expected. They ring the doorbell three times. Mom gives me a pointed look. Maggie is setting the table, Cash helping, and my parents are still cooking. Who *knows* when Alice will come down? That leaves me to entertain them. I know it shouldn't, but my anxiety flares up around them, too.

"Josie!" Auntie Denise hugs me to her chest. "Oh, look at you! So big!"

I wince. It doesn't help that Auntie Denise is as thin as my pinkie. She pulls back, appraising eyes running over my body. I stare at a spot on her chest that's lighter than the rest of her body. Maybe it's a birthmark.

"How are college applications going?"

"Good." I shrug. "I applied early decision to Spelman, so waiting to hear back."

"Aw," she says, pressing a hand against my cheek. "Following in your older sister's footsteps, huh?"

"Well, actually, I wanted to go before she did," I huff. "She followed in *my* footsteps."

Auntie Denise smiles like I'm a little kid.

"Right," she says. "Of course, sweetheart."

She bustles past me, pulling her husband along. I peek into the kitchen. She's already grabbed Mom and Dad's attention. That gives me a few more minutes to hide from everyone. Before they can wonder where I am, I jog back up the stairs.

Alice and I are sharing a room while she's home. Her bags are too close to the door, so I have to suck in my stomach to squeeze through. I kick one of the suitcases over. Technically, the door could've done it.

I grab my phone off the charger. Mom hates phones at the table whenever we all sit down as a family, but that barely happens, even on Thanksgiving. Everyone ends up sitting in clusters throughout the house. We don't even keep up the pretense of sitting at the table anymore. She won't notice my phone as long as I say hi to everyone.

I've been reading this article about how *Boyz N the Hood* got made. The door stays closed while I read, even as I hear the sounds of the front door opening, of people talking and laughing. I almost miss the sound of my email notification.

There's the usual—spam emails about spying on my ex-husband, college ads . . . but.

But.

There's one from *Deep Focus* magazine. I open it, trying my best not to scream.

> *Dear Josephine,*
>
> *Congratulations! You've been selected as the winner of the* Deep Focus *Talent Search. A team of fifteen writers and editors reviewed this year's entries and took part in the judging process. We delayed making our announcement because our judges had trouble choosing*

just one out of the 400 finalists, but they finally picked
you. You should be proud of your achievement.

Oh.

My.

God.

I let out a scream. Downstairs, there's a loud thud. I look
back at my phone.

> *As you are aware, the grand prize is the chance*
> *to take part in a press tour for a new film,* Incident
> on 57th Street, *starring Academy Award nominee*
> *Art Springfield, Grace Gibbs, and newcomer Marius*
> *Canet. With* Deep Focus *partnering with Spotlight Pic-*
> *tures, you'll have unprecedented access to the cast and*
> *crew, but you will be focusing on writing a profile about*
> *Marius, who has garnered rave reviews for his perfor-*
> *mance. You will be taking part in press events for two*
> *weeks in Los Angeles, Austin, Chicago, Atlanta, and*
> *New York, where our offices are located.* Deep Focus
> *will cover all expenses related to travel and lodging. You*
> *will also receive a $500 cash prize.*
>
> *I'm so glad that you will be joining the* Deep Focus
> *team. I will be your supervisor during your assignment,*
> *which means I will organize interviews, events, and*
> *transportation during the press tour and be the first to*
> *review your final article before it's submitted to our edito-*
> *rial team. If you have any questions, please feel free to*
> *ask me!*
>
> *I've also attached a contract to this email. Please re-*
> *view and sign, along with one of your parents, as soon as*
> *possible, as we can't proceed without a signed contract.*

You will then receive an official Deep Focus *press pass in the mail, which you must wear while on assignment. After the contract is signed, we will fly you to a screening of the film in Los Angeles next weekend, with a press conference being held afterward. If you accept, I will contact you soon with more details.*

We look forward to working with you!

Best,

Lauren Jacobson

Publicity Manager of Deep Focus

My hands are shaking.

Me. I won the contest. *Me.*

When they first emailed me about being a finalist, they told me two thousand people had applied before they narrowed it down to four hundred. And out of *four hundred* people, they chose *me.* It doesn't feel real. The publicity manager of my favorite magazine just emailed *me.* I'm going to write a story for my favorite magazine. *Me, me, me.*

I don't even know how many things this could do for my career. For the past forty years, *Deep Focus* has been *the* center of popular culture. Anyone who's anyone has been on the cover, including, but not limited to:

- Classic music stars like the Beatles, Michael Jackson, and David Bowie
- Newer music stars like Adele, Kendrick Lamar, and Lorde
- The Queen (Beyoncé)
- Actors like Heath Ledger, Denzel Washington, Cate Blanchett, Natalie Portman, Keira Knightley, Andrew Garfield, Issa Rae . . .

Thinking about it all at once makes me dizzy.

I've always devoured profiles of writers and directors and actors, even though I'm sure most of them are staged. This is my chance to finally see for myself how it works. How do you even include this on a résumé? In a special box with shiny letters and glitter?

This could help me get more freelance gigs. This could lead to *bigger* things. It's *Deep Focus*, for crying out loud. I could do whatever I want after this.

I hold my hand over my mouth. Nervous laughter mixes with another scream, which makes me sound like a nervous horse. I'm not even concerned. Sure, I haven't told my parents that the grand prize entails hanging out in five different cities with a group of actors and a director and other moviemaking people. Sure, I have anxiety and hate being around too many people I don't know.

But *God*, do the positives outweigh the negatives. This is my chance to do something exciting for once. This is my chance to do what I love on a bigger scale. This is my chance to be taken seriously as a writer.

I open up two different tabs: one with the name of the actor and one with the name of the movie. I start an email reply to Ms. Jacobson. But what do I say?

"Josephine?" Mom's voice travels up the stairs. "Get down here!"

Oh, right. First things first: I have to ask Mom and Dad.

CHAPTER 4

It's torture waiting all night for everyone to leave. And when I say *all night*, I really mean it. Uncle Eddie doesn't leave until eleven. Mom has to call him a cab. I sneak up behind her as she watches him through the screen door.

"Mommy?"

She raises a brow. "What do you want?"

I pull her back into the kitchen. There's a mess: half-full containers and bottles, dirty dishes and silverware. Dad's already organizing leftovers. We'll be eating them for the next week, at least.

"Well," I say, clasping my hands together, "I've been presented with a once-in-a-lifetime opportunity."

"What?" Dad looks up. "A scholarship?"

"Uh, no," I say. "Not that kind. But it's even better."

Mom folds her arms, both eyebrows raised in expectation.

"Okay," I say, taking a deep breath. "Do you remember that contest I entered a few months ago? The *Deep Focus* Talent Search? It was for teen reporters."

"Yes," Mom says. "We remember that. Did you hear back?"

"I did," I say. "And it's really amazing news—I won. Out of two thousand people."

"Oh my goodness, Josie," Dad says, straightening. "That's *amazing*. Come here."

He pulls me into his arms, squeezing the life out of me. I laugh against his shoulder.

"*Deep Focus*," he says, shaking me back and forth. "Josie! We're so proud of you!"

"We are." Mom smiles. "So what's the downside?"

"There really *is* no downside, if you think of it." I lick my lips. "The grand prize is the chance to write a cover story for the magazine."

"I remember you telling us that," Dad says, shaking his head. "Our daughter, writing a cover story for *Deep Focus*. You know Obama was on the cover?"

"You hung the cover up in the den." I try my best not to roll my eyes. "So I'll get to write a cover story, too, about this new movie starring Art Springfield—"

"Art Springfield," Dad repeats. He glances at Mom. "Sounds like we'll have to see that one."

"Sure, honey." Mom doesn't take her eyes off of me. "Get to the catch, Josie."

"Okay." I force a deep breath through my nose. "I have to go on a press tour with the cast and crew to cover the story accurately. And the tour goes to five cities across the United States for two weeks. The first event is next weekend, in Los Angeles."

There's a heavy moment of silence as she and Dad look at each other.

"Oh," Dad says, tossing a rag over his shoulder. "Well, if that's *all*."

I flush.

"There's no way I'm sending you across the country by yourself," Mom says, shaking her head. "How many different cities? And where do you expect me to get that money from?"

Good. She's explaining herself. If Mom *really* means no, she just shuts the conversation down before it can begin. This is her way of inviting me to fight for this.

"They'll cover hotel and airfare," I say. "And I get five hundred dollars cash."

"Five hundred dollars," Dad says. "They're big spenders, aren't they?"

"The rest of it can be my Christmas present," I say. "Or I'll use my money from Cora's to help pay."

"That money is for school," Mom says.

"Right," I say. "But a press tour is way more impressive than just freelancing. And Monique can still be my mentor and everything."

I haven't even run this by her, but I'm sure she wouldn't mind. This is the type of thing capstone projects are made for. Other kids fly to different continents to do missions and build houses. I can go on a press tour that will launch my career.

"It's just—" I huff. It's hard to say everything I'm feeling all at once. "I'll do anything. This is really, *really* important to me."

"I don't know," Dad says, glancing at Mom. "It sounds like a lot of responsibility."

"I'm responsible," I say, holding out my hand, counting on my fingers. "I watch Cash when no one else can. I go grocery shopping on the weekends. I have a job. I practically did all the college stuff by myself. I can do this."

Dad nods. Mom shoots him a look.

"I understand," Mom says slowly. "I just don't feel comfortable with you being by yourself, and I can't take off of work for that long."

"Neither of us would be able to," Dad chimes in. "I really want this for you, but—"

"Maggie can go with me." The words fly out of my mouth. "She can go with me."

"Really?" Mom gives me a look. "She can't take off of work, either, and I doubt you'd want to bring Cash along."

"Well, what about Alice?"

Before my parents can even process my words, my sister comes whirling into the room. I *knew* she was listening.

"No," she snaps. "I'm not taking a leave of absence to babysit."

"It's not *babysitting*," I say. "I'm two years younger than you. And you don't need to take a leave of absence. Your winter break literally starts next week."

"Break is *me* time," she says, folding her arms. "I need to hang out with my friends."

"You can do that *any*time. Come on, Alice. I've never asked you for anything."

"That's a lie." She rolls her eyes. "How many times did I have to take you driving before you *finally* passed the driver's test?"

"That's different." My face burns. I only failed the test twice because I kept getting anxious. People would beep at me or the DMV representative would remind me to do something, and I'd completely stop breathing.

"I don't have to go just because you asked," she says, as if I'd never said anything. "What do you expect me to do the entire time? Follow you around and knit?"

"I just need—"

"If you keep this up, y'all ain't going nowhere," Mom snaps. Both of us go silent. "I can't even hear myself think."

Alice's lips are twisted into a frown. I bet she doesn't want to come just because *I* brought it up. If Mom or Dad had asked, she would've complained but gone along with it. After all, it's not like I'm asking her to poke her eyes out. I'm asking her to go on a trip with me. It's not the worst thing in the world.

"If you make sure to stay focused on your schoolwork," Dad says, choosing his words slowly, eyes locked on our mother. "And if you can convince Alice to go with you . . . I don't see why we can't make this work."

I turn back to my sister. She's still frowning.

"Alice." I settle for sticking out my lower lip. "*Please?* You'll get to go to New York and L.A., and I promise we'll go wherever you want. I'll do your chores for a year."

"I'm not here most of the year."

I groan, tossing back my head.

"Alice," Mom says, "you don't have to go if you don't want to. But it would be a nice thing to do for your sister."

Alice bites her lip. I resist the urge to pump my fist in the air. Mom's endorsement is better than anything I could ever promise.

"Well," she finally says, heaving a great and weary sigh. The twitching corners of her mouth give her away. "I *have* always wanted to go to Los Angeles. And if I get to meet—"

I yelp, tossing my arms around her. Alice usually isn't one for hugs. The limp hands at her sides prove that. I'm just so happy I can't resist. Dad laughs, but Mom bangs on the table, grabbing our attention.

"But as soon as you get back, you are focusing on *college*," Mom says, pointing a finger. I rise up on my toes. Nothing she can say will ruin this for me. "And I want phone calls. *Phone calls, not texts.* I'm talking every hour. You understand?"

I can't hear anything else she says because I'm too busy screaming and pulling her in for a hug.

> **@JosieTheJournalist:** shout out to plus sized clothes that are actually plus sized and not just average sizes that should already be carried in stores

CHAPTER 5

When I was eight, we went to a big family reunion at Disneyland, but that's the only time I've been out of the state. So I have no idea how to pack for this trip.

While Alice spends the next few days taking finals and wrapping up her first semester at college, I try to pack everything I'll need for a two-week-long tour. On Tuesday, Maggie pops into my room and frowns at my suitcase like it's an orphaned puppy.

"What?" I glance down at it. There's *enough*, even if it isn't all folded. "It's not that bad. I won't be naked."

"But this is a *big deal*. You're interviewing *movie stars*." She grips my shoulders, shaking me back and forth. "Josie, do you understand what this means?"

"I mean, the biggest star in the movie is Art Springfield, and only old people like Mom and Dad like him," I say. "I'm interviewing the newcomer, so he's not exactly what you'd—"

"Stop ruining this for me," she says. "I'm living through you."

"I wish you could come," I say. Alice isn't around, so I can play favorites. "We would have *so* much fun."

"I know." She pouts, flicking something off my T-shirt. "But you'll be with Alice. You guys will have loads of fun without me. She's really excited, you know."

I raise my brows. Maggie never picks sides when it comes to Alice and me, which means she says things no one believes. She shoves me and scoffs.

"If you can't have fun on an all-expenses-paid trip, there's something wrong with you." She puts her hands on her hips. "And you need better clothes. Something nice. Something fancy."

Ugh. I love clothes. I just hate buying them. I like looking at pictures of celebrities walking on the street during Fashion Week and watching *Project Runway*. It's this odd paradox: clothes look limp, useless when they aren't being worn, but most designers aren't thinking of bodies like mine. Even plus-sized models look more—I don't know—*symmetrical.* Their bodies look like they belong on runways. Whenever I find something I want to wear, I look wrong in it, like a gingerbread man with too much dough in the wrong places.

But I don't know how to say any of that to Maggie. She'll tell me I'm pretty the way I am. And it's not like I *need* to be pretty. It's not about being pretty. It's about the way everyone looks at me when I wear clothes that don't fit me correctly. Their mouths turn down and sometimes they even whisper. I can practically hear them thinking, *Thank goodness I don't look like her.* I just want to exist without being a spectacle. I don't want attention on me unless I ask for it.

Maggie and I talk all the time about periods and guys and bad sex she's had. But this isn't something I want to share with my sister. I've buried it deep inside me, far away from the surface.

"I have to save money for the trip," I say instead. "So the fancy actor will just have to be satisfied with normal clothes."

"Don't worry about that," Maggie says, waving her hand. "I'll treat you."

I can't bring myself to say no.

———

Later in the week, Maggie gets Mom to watch Cash so we can all go to the mall. It's thirty minutes of driving with *both* my sisters, which means I end up in the back seat while they catch up. They talk about the same things Maggie talks about with her friends on the phone: sex, guys, reality TV, hair. I tune them out and mess around on my phone.

The mall is gigantic, so there are several different stores to choose from. Maggie starts with this boutique near the entrance. I doubt she has enough money to buy us anything from this place. There's a handful of other women, and they're all white.

"This looks kind of nice," Maggie says, pulling out a long purple dress. "What do you guys think?"

"I don't think I could walk in it," Alice says. "It's too long."

"But that's kind of cool," I say. It's pretty plain otherwise, basically a long piece of fabric. "It would be like having a train behind you, almost like a princess."

Alice raises a brow but doesn't say anything. A woman behind us folds a bunch of shirts on a giant wooden table. Maggie steers us toward another rack. The white women glance at us. One whispers in another's ear. I turn to Alice. Her eyes are narrowed.

"I like this," Maggie says, pulling out a romper. "What do you think?"

It's light orange, with long, loose pants, flounce cap sleeves, and an open back. The sort of thing I imagine all of the fancy ladies in L.A. wearing. It could look like a dress or a shirt-skirt combo *and* a romper, all at once.

"I love it." I run my hand across the material. It's soft. "Are you thinking of getting it? How much is it?"

Maggie glances at the price tag, eyes widening.

"Maggie?"

"Don't think about that." She tucks the tag back. "See if you like it."

"I think that woman is following us."

Alice's voice is a whisper. Since I'm obvious, I turn my head. The same lady from the table is right behind us. She spots me looking and quickly turns toward a rack of clothes. My cheeks burn. This sort of thing *happens*, but not all the time. I want to leave and I also want the romper.

"Ugh. Ignore her," Maggie says, turning back to our rack. "Come on, Josie. Let's see if they have your size."

The biggest is an extra large and there's only one, so Maggie makes me take a large along with me to the changing room. She and Alice grab different rompers—one black and white, another with polka dots—and follow behind me. The same worker somehow ends up over there. Alice gives her a glare that could kill. She still doesn't move.

It doesn't take my sisters long to get their outfits on. Shopping is different for them. They both fit in mediums. Next to me, they look older, sexy. Maggie's had a baby and has bigger, wider hips as a result. Alice doesn't have as many curves as us, but she always looks beautiful, especially with her dark gaze pinning down her reflection in the mirror.

The large doesn't even close on me. It pinches my stomach. The extra large actually fits, but some parts look exaggerated, highlighted. I doubt I look like the models who wear this on the store's website.

My sisters are silent. I stare at the three of us in the mirror: the two of them looking like models, me looking like *me*. Alone, there's nothing wrong with that, but it's hard when I'm next to them. The world compares me to everyone else, and so now I do it like a reflex.

"Maybe we can see if there's something bigger?" Alice says, glancing at Maggie. "Maybe in the plus section?"

The plus-sized section is always hit or miss for me. Parts of my body are bigger than others—my thighs, stomach, and boobs, especially—but plus-sized clothes never take that into account. It's why nothing looks right on me.

I hate this part. I hate when they look at me like I'm a kicked puppy on the side of the road. When everyone goes quiet and all we can hear is Britney Spears playing in the store. It's easy enough to tell myself that being fat isn't wrong when I'm alone or on Twitter. Being fat in the real world, around everyone else, even family, is completely different. But what's the alternative? Never leaving the house?

I like fancy clothes that look like art. I doubt I'll ever look like I've stepped out of a magazine, because I've never seen girls like me on the glossy pages, but I can imagine while watching my sisters. I'm good at imagining.

"No." I dig my nails into my palm. "Forget it. I like it like this."

And I do, sort of. My stomach just bunches and my boobs look like they might burst out of the top. But I like the rest of it. I've had to spend a lot of time getting used to my body. I could get used to this romper. If Maggie's buying, I don't mind. I should get to have nice things.

"We look fucking awesome," Alice says. "Maggie, take a picture."

Taking pictures in dressing rooms is our *thing*. We've done it ever since Maggie first went to prom and needed to try on dresses. Back then, both of them tiptoed around the word, like they were afraid to call me fat. It's not that big a deal. Using words like *full-figured* just makes it worse. I can see how awkward people get as they search for the right word to say.

Fat is what they're thinking. *Fat* is what used to make me cry at night when I was in middle school. So it's the word I use when I describe myself. It's a word I want to strip of negativity, like how other Black people try to do with *nigga*.

Alice might be lying about how we look, but I don't mind. I don't look horrible. I just look different. At least I'm only here with my sisters. I couldn't handle being the odd one out around strangers.

Maggie's camera flash makes me blink. Alice laughs and I surprise myself, snorting.

"Okay, okay," Maggie says, shaking her head. "A few more. Come on."

She takes a few more from different angles. I used to hide in the back, but I don't anymore. From up high, all you can see is my face. I don't mind that. I hated my face back in middle school. Maybe I'll like the rest of my body one day. Right now, I don't mind being too fat in this romper. I'm glad for this moment.

LOS ANGELES, CALIFORNIA

CHAPTER 6

California is flatter than I thought it would be.

That's all I can think on Saturday after we land, after we check into our hotel, after we get an Uber to the movie theater. The sun shines down on us, palm trees gently swaying side to side, and everything seems *flat*. If there are bumps in the road, I don't feel them. Everything is smooth.

Unlike me, Alice doesn't seem interested in just looking out the window. She spends the entire ride taking pictures of everything on her phone: the car, the scenery outside, and even me.

"What?" she says. "Don't you want to remember this when it's over?"

"We just got here," I say. "You're not allowed to talk about going home yet."

She rolls her eyes and turns back to the window.

The movie theater looks like the ones used on TV as establishing shots before the camera swings to the red carpets of glitzy premieres. Alice thanks our driver while I get out and stare. It's less flashy in the daytime, but there's something charming about that, like a face without makeup.

"So this is it?" Alice glances up at the sign, squints. "I don't see anything about incidents or streets."

"I don't think they put press screenings on the marquee."

"Sure." She glances at me. "Do you know what we're doing?"

No, I want to say, I have no idea what we're doing. I haven't done this before. I'm not even sure what to expect.

"Yeah," I say, fingering the press pass in my pocket. "Come on."

I've never been to a press screening before. And, to my surprise, no one seems to be freaking out as much as me. There's a table set up in the lobby where people show their press credentials to a bored-looking woman with red hair. For a second, I'm worried she'll ask me questions—why I'm so young, why I only have one press pass when Alice is with me, who I'm writing for—or even just try to make conversation, but she barely looks up as she checks my name off the list. I breathe a sigh of relief.

"What is this about again?" Alice asks, leaning close to me as we walk into the theater. "Am I going to cry?"

"I don't know," I say, shrugging. It's almost comforting to have her so close to me. In a sea of strangers, she's the nearest thing to a lifeline I have. "You might."

The movie is about a gay kid sent to a conversion camp and the lasting impact it has on him and his family. Alice isn't really into Oscar bait, so I'm not sure if it's wise to tell her. She'll figure it out on her own.

Most of the people inside are middle-aged and white. At least there are a few women. Alice pulls me toward the front before I can linger.

"We're too close to the screen," I say, watching her throw her bag down. Her phone remains firmly in her grip. "I can't see."

"Yes, you can. That's the point of a theater. You can see anywhere."

"Alice."

"Josie," she snaps, looking up. People are staring now. My face burns. "I'm not moving. Go sit in the back if you want."

"God," I say, slumping into my seat. "I don't know why you have to be such a bitch."

"This *bitch* is the reason you're here in the first place."

I open my mouth to reply, but the lights dim. Maybe they're starting the movie early to get us to shut up.

There are the normal coming attractions—a Marvel movie, an action-adventure about cars, and a TV documentary about Roy Lennox, this director who has won about a million Oscars and has, according to the trailer, been making movies for over twenty years. Then, finally, the movie starts.

One thing is clear about ten minutes in: reading about it and seeing it are two different things. I've read early reviews raving about Marius Canet's performance as his character, Peter, but their words didn't do him justice. I'm not sure how *my* words will do him justice. He doesn't say much—his character speaks less and less as the movie goes along, as his parents force him away, as he's forced to leave his boyfriend, as he returns to a family he doesn't understand—but it's more impactful, in a way.

Watching him hurts so much that it feels like he's tearing me apart, slowly, from the inside out. The back of my throat burns with unshed tears.

Other people are taking notes, nodding, but none of them seem as choked up as me. Alice's eyes are unusually bright, though.

All I can think about is how young he is. Even though he's Black, his face seems paler in certain scenes, pale enough that I can see everything going on inside him. And he does this thing where he cries and the skin around his eyes gets red. His eyes go searching, everywhere, every corner of the frame, like he's looking for the audience to help him out. I guess I've never seen someone this young who can act and say things without opening his mouth. Not since, like, Quvenzhané Wallis in *Beasts of the Southern Wild*. Even then, there's something different about this. Something more mature.

I haven't had much time to think about interviewing Marius Canet. I've been too busy packing and fielding lectures from Mom. But now it's all I can think about. He's not established enough for me to have any idea of what he'll be like. There was an interview I watched last night before I went to sleep, but it was with the entire cast—the actors who play his parents, the counselors at the camp—and he spent more time listening than speaking.

Before I know it, the lights are up and Alice is nudging me.

"Hey," she says. Sniffs. "Are you crying?"

"No." I wipe at my damp cheeks. "Are you?"

"No." She sniffs again. "Of course not."

We walk out of the theater in silence. It's only when we're outside, staring at the pink and purple of the evening sky, that Alice speaks again.

"He didn't really talk a lot."

"I guess," I say, shoving my hands into my pockets. "But he made you feel so connected that it hurt anyway."

God, I'm supposed to go to a press conference in an hour. A press conference, with the entire cast and crew up on a dais, while the journalists sit in the audience and ask questions. How can I do that? How can I ask Marius Canet questions in front of everyone else? I don't know him, but it feels too personal. I almost wish I'd gone to the press conference before the screening. Sure, I would've lacked context, but at least I wouldn't have cared this much. Everything gets harder when I care.

"It was definitely sad." Alice shakes her head, fingers tapping on her phone. "I think his parents made it sad, though. They believed they were doing the right thing for him."

"Conversion therapy is never the right thing."

"Obviously." She rolls her eyes. "I'm just saying the movie did a good job of just—I don't know. You think these people are evil, right? But that would make things too easy. Peter—he still loves them, even though they sent him to this place to change him. That's real life."

I guess so. If we were supposed to feel bad for the parents, I failed that part. Why would I? They might've thought they were doing the right thing, but they just fucked everything up because they couldn't accept their kid. It's scary. What if my parents decided to send me away because I get too anxious? I wouldn't be able to do anything about it. I'd be stuck and messed up afterward, just like Peter.

A car pulls to the curb. Alice starts walking toward it.

"Well," she says, "the acting was really good."

I nod and get in the back seat in silence. The driver was playing something slow, quiet, but quickly switches to a fast pop song as we settle in. Alice leans forward and talks to him. I lean back and close my eyes. Now I know all the Oscar buzz wasn't just an exaggeration. I don't know how he does it, but Marius Canet can really act. Maybe it's a fluke, like first-movie luck or something, but I don't think so.

God. How do I talk to someone so talented without freaking out?

"Don't overthink it," Alice says, snapping me out of my thoughts. She's looking down at her phone. "It's just a movie."

But it's *not.* At least, it doesn't feel like just a movie. Not to me. Not anymore. It's getting harder to breathe. I force short breaths through my nose.

"It was really good," I say. Gulp a deep breath. Try to feel like I'll be okay. "You could tell it was written by a white dude, though. Because Marius's character . . . didn't act Black."

"How do you *act* Black?"

"You know what I mean," I say, even though it *does* sound kind of wrong. "I mean there wasn't really context. Like, I get that Art Springfield is white and he's playing the father, so they were trying to imply that Peter is mixed. But there was still stuff that didn't make sense for Black characters, like his mother calling the police on him for no reason."

"Oh." Alice leans her head back against the seat. "Yeah, you're right. And the way he yelled at them in the beginning. Imagine yelling at Mom like that?"

"She'd probably murder me."

"Not *probably*," Alice says. "We *know* she'd murder you."

I glance over. She's grinning. It's the first smile we've shared in a while. I'll take it to the press conference for good luck.

CHAPTER 7

I've done most of my journalism from school or our living room, calling people or spending tons of time on Google. I've never actually been around so many journalists doing their jobs before.

You could almost mistake it for a business meeting, except for the fact that no one is wearing a suit or carrying a briefcase. Some of them type frantically on phones or chat with one another. A security guard at the door checks press passes. I force myself to breathe.

"Come on," Alice says. "How long are we going to wait out here?"

I try my best to ignore her, but it's pretty difficult when she's right next to me.

"I don't know," I say. "I'm not supposed to go in until we meet Ms. Jacobson—"

"Josephine?"

I blink. In front of me stands a white lady with dark brown hair and round glasses.

I don't respond, so Alice nudges me. I let out a little squeak.

"Yes," I say. "That's me. Josephine. Or, well, I go by Josie."

"It's so nice to meet you," Ms. Jacobson says, sticking out her hand. "You look just like your picture."

We were supposed to send in pictures with our initial applications, so I chose my senior picture. I just look like me but in a cap and gown. It isn't really anything special.

"Oh," I say anyway. "Thanks."

"I read the pieces you submitted with your application," Ms. Jacobson continues, reaching into her purse. "And they were absolutely amazing. You're so talented."

My tongue seems to be stuck to the roof of my mouth. Between the compliments, meeting a new person, and having to go to a press conference only a few hours after touching down in California, I think my brain is going haywire or something. I can feel Alice looking at the two of us like we're gigantic nerds.

"All right," Ms. Jacobson says, pulling out a folder. "I know we already emailed about the itinerary and travel plans, but I wanted to make sure you got a physical copy of everything."

I take the folder and flip it open. There's a page labeled "Itinerary," listing cities and plane times and hotels. I'm supposed to interview Marius Canet tomorrow—gulp—and once in almost every city. There's another copy of the contract Mom and I signed, with a deadline of December 20 in bold letters at the top, then a guide to asking questions and writing stories. Part of me wants to laugh at it. The other part thinks I could really use some help with the *talking* part.

Alice jabs me again. Her elbows are pointy.

"Thank you," I say, looking at the folder instead of at Ms. Jacobson. "This was nice of you."

"Well," she says, pulling at her purse straps, "it's part of my job. And so is answering any questions you might have. If anything goes wrong, you can text or call me. Do you still have my number?"

I nod. She emailed it to me last week and I already programmed it into my phone. There have been a couple of moments when I wanted to text her—when I was wondering what to wear, what to say, who to hang out with. But I figured she'd find me annoying if I texted her a million times before I even got my first assignment.

"Good." She smiles, glancing between Alice and me. "And I already got approval for your sister to join you as a chaperone, so there shouldn't be much of a problem. Do you need anything else before I go?"

My stomach drops. "You're not staying?"

"Well, no," she says. "I spoke to your mother about this on the phone—I thought she would've told you. Normally I'd function as your chaperone, but since your sister is here, we figured . . ."

I glance at Alice, who is already walking toward the entrance to the conference room.

"Josie?" Ms. Jacobson snaps me out of my thoughts. "If you'd like, I could join you for this first event. I just won't be able to in the future, since I'm based here in L.A."

"Oh." I swallow, but my throat is still dry. "I didn't realize."

"It's all right," Ms. Jacobson says. "We'll mostly be communicating via phone and email, but I promise I'll be available for any questions or issues you may have."

I look over at Alice. She's lingering near the door to the conference room, arms folded, tapping her foot. Like she's waiting on *me*.

She technically is.

Like I'm acting like a *baby*.

I'm not. At least, I don't mean to be.

Like I can't even do this one thing, this thing I begged Mom and Dad for, by myself.

I swallow. My stomach is still in knots, but I don't know if having Ms. Jacobson there would even make me feel better. Do I want her watching me during the press conference? Analyzing every choice I make?

"No," I say. "I think we'll be fine."

It's pretty much a lie. But I hope it ends up being true.

———

I'm not sure what counts as "fine." If sitting in the middle of the crowd of journalists and trying my best not to be noticed counts, I'm doing pretty well. But it's probably not what Ms. Jacobson had in mind.

"Hello," a woman says, standing up and speaking into the microphone she's passed. "Art, you've spent the past few years on television. What was it like to return to your independent roots with Dennis, who you worked with on your first five films?"

Up on the dais is Art Springfield, probably the biggest star in the movie, wearing a cowboy hat. Beside him is Penny Livingstone, a former Disney Channel actress who somehow got a part in this movie. There's also the director, Dennis Bardell, and Grace Gibbs, who plays the mom and is the only Black person in the cast besides Marius Canet. He's there, too, and I can't wrap my mind around how normal he looks. Light brown skin, pink cheeks. His hair is long enough that, if my dad knew him, he'd probably bother him about getting it cut. And every few seconds, he smiles, just a little bit, showing white teeth.

I force myself not to look for too long. I focus on making sure my recorder is going, catching what everyone is saying, while I write in my notebook. Around me, some people have iPads and a few even have laptops, although I didn't realize that could be a thing.

"Come on," Alice hisses. "Aren't you going to ask something?"

I don't know what to ask. Well, that's a lie, actually. I look down at my notebook. I've been working on a bunch of questions, separated into categories—but most of them are for Marius Canet. It would be weird to stand up and ask a question that's just directed at one person, wouldn't it? Even though that's what everyone has been doing with Art Springfield and the director.

"I don't know," I whisper. "Everyone else seems to have it down."

The crowd laughs at something Art Springfield says. I wince, hoping it doesn't mess up my recording.

Alice's brow furrows. "Have it down?"

"Know what they're doing."

It's true. No one looks nervous when they stand up to ask questions. This isn't the same as when special guests, like local musicians or professors, visited my high school for assemblies and students from my journalism class got to interview them. Everyone here has a question that makes sense. Everyone here sounds official when speaking into the microphone. Everyone here has done this before.

"This film takes a very raw look at the insidious nature of homophobia," another reporter says, standing up. "Grace, your character loves her son but also sends him away to 'fix' him. How do you think she can have both of these feelings at once?"

"See," I say, frantically writing the question into my notebook. "That sounded so *good*."

I was going to ask Marius about his high school experience, since there's a sequence at the beginning where his character goes to school. But that seems stupid when everyone is asking these hard-hitting questions.

Alice shakes her head, facing forward.

"Well, we didn't just want her to be a caricature," Grace

Gibbs says, pulling her microphone closer to her mouth. "It would make things too easy. She loves her son, and she thinks she's doing the right thing because this was how she was raised, because this is how she and her husband think. But when she realizes what she's doing to him, it crushes her. . . ."

Alice leans over to whisper in my ear. "Listen," she says. "If you don't ask something, I will."

My face starts to drip with sweat almost instantaneously.

"Alice," I say. "Come on."

"I'm serious," she says. "I'm not just going to sit here in silence for an hour. What's the point of us coming here, then?"

I want to scream.

"All right, folks," the moderator says, shifting in her seat. She's a tall lady who has a microphone of her own. "We have three more minutes—enough time for *one* more question."

Alice glares at me. I almost throw up.

What would be more embarrassing: to ask my own question and have everyone look at me, or to have Alice ask something ridiculous and be associated with her for the rest of this trip?

About half a dozen hands shoot up.

"Um, hello!" Alice grabs my hand and holds it high. "She would like to ask a question!"

Heads turn in our direction as a low laugh rumbles through the crowd. My face burns and I haven't even asked a question. I was already worried about people treating me like a baby because of my age, but now Alice has made it even worse by making me look like a teenage fan.

"Well, all right," the moderator says. "Let's pass the microphone over, shall we?"

Someone shoves the microphone into my hand. Alice forces me to stand. Everything feels too hot, even though there aren't any lights shining on me. Art Springfield is looking at me, which is so weird, because I've always seen him on TV when my parents were watching his movies. They're *all* looking at me—not just the people on the dais, but all the journalists, too.

"Um." I do something wrong with the microphone, and it makes this horrible shrieking sound. "Oh, I'm sorry."

My hands are sweating. It feels like the microphone is going to slip out of my hand.

"Um," I say again. Grace Gibbs leans forward like she can't hear me—or, worse, like she's trying to get a good look at me. "So. Um, I guess I was wondering, um, how Peter's Blackness factors into his journey, for you?"

Grace Gibbs looks at Art Springfield, who looks at the director. Penny Livingstone quirks her mouth to the side. After a second, Marius Canet pulls one of the microphones closer to him, but then Dennis Bardell, the director, speaks into his own.

"I actually don't think I know what you mean," he says. "Could you expand on that?"

Oh God. I swallow. How do I expand on that? I don't even know why I asked it. I should've asked my question about high school, even if it made me seem basic.

"So, like," I say, shifting on my feet, "uh, if you watch the movie—"

"I think we all have," Art Springfield says. Everyone laughs. I try to join in, but it sounds more like I'm panting.

"Yeah," I say. "Right. But, um, Peter and his mom are the only Black people living in their town, so I was sort of thinking that maybe that would add more tension, and even if we don't explicitly see it on-screen, that could add to the way that, um, you know, the actors would play the—"

"I'm so sorry," the moderator says. "I would love to let you finish the question, but the cast has another event right after this that they can't be late for."

"Oh," I say. It echoes throughout the room.

I feel tears in my eyes, but I'm not going to cry. I'm *not* going to cry. I'm not a baby. I force myself to sit down and ignore the pitying looks Grace Gibbs and Marius Canet give me from the dais. I ignore the way Alice stares at me like she can't believe I made such a fool of myself.

"Well, everyone," the moderator continues, "let's give it up for the cast and crew for being here!"

Everyone around me claps, but I don't. I'm too busy trying not to melt into a pool of embarrassment.

CHAPTER 8

According to the itinerary, I'm supposed to interview Marius today, but I have no idea how to get through it without making an even bigger fool of myself.

"Seriously," Alice says, already waiting on the curb for our Uber. "I'm sure it won't be as bad as last night was."

I want to say something like *Gee, thanks*, but I can't really breathe. I settle for glaring at her instead.

Last night, after the embarrassment that was the press conference, I lied to Mom and Dad on the phone and told them everything was going great. I bounced between wanting to look over my questions and wanting to ignore them and pretend that today wasn't happening.

I finger my notebook in my bag. I've been buying the same type ever since I was thirteen, a classic black Moleskine, and the familiar sight has been with me through everything. Hopefully it'll bring me some sort of luck now.

When the car stops fifteen minutes later, I still can't breathe. I hate when it gets like this. I forget all the coping skills my therapist or guidance counselors or social workers have ever taught me. I'm just *there*, a tight ball of intricate knots, and I'm not sure how to untie myself.

Sometimes I try to imagine myself in the future, weeks or months from now, far away from this moment. Where will I be in six months? Will I know who I'm rooming with at Spelman? Will it be easier to breathe?

The car has pulled up in front of a line of stores. Alice doesn't hesitate. She's out of the car before I can grab my bag. I force a breath, but it's shallow. Then I follow her out the door.

I can't help but think about the negatives—that I'm already sweating, that I look backward with my long messenger bag at my side, that my tummy is already showing. Mom is always talking about how my shirts aren't big enough for me. I'm not sure if it's because of my boobs or stomach or both, but my stomach tends to peek out when I stand.

I pull my leggings up. They never stay, but I still have to try. Alice stands at the café door.

"Just texted Mom," she says in a tone suggesting *I* should've texted Mom. "She says to have fun and call when we get back to the hotel."

I nod. I can't speak. Alice frowns, opening the door.

My eyes aren't sure where to go. Inside is like Starbucks on a slow day. It smells like coffee beans and wood. A few chairs are open, but many are filled. There are abstract paintings on the walls—people twisted up into odd shapes—and pan flute music playing. I look everywhere except at the people sitting down.

"There," Alice says, nodding her head forward. "Okay, try not to look so nervous. And stop staring. Just look normal. And don't say *sort of* or *like* when you're asking questions. Be confident in yourself."

She says it as if it's easy.

I hold my breath and turn my head half an inch. Once I see

him, I can't look away. He's getting up. There's an easy smile on his face, one that's pretty hard to look away from.

I pull Alice forward, practically stumbling in my haste to move.

"Hi," I say, sticking out my hand. My voice cracks. *God.* How did I think I could do this?

"Hey," he says, grabbing my hand. The contact almost makes me jerk. At least his voice is as easygoing as his smile. "Hope you didn't have too much trouble finding this place. I know it's out of the way, but my agent took me here the first time I came to L.A., and it's just been, you know, like a home base since then."

I wish I had a home base. Alice is supposed to be a piece of home, but she just stands there, looking between the two of us. I wish she would say something. I wish time would slow down so I could catch my breath. Instead, I stare down at Marius's hands. They're bigger than mine, warm brown. I can't stop staring. It's easier than looking at his face.

"So you're Josephine?"

I can't speak. Alice clears her throat.

"Yeah, she is," she says, taking a seat. "I'm her older sister. Just here to chaperone."

"Wow." He sits, and I figure I should, too. "You were at the press conference yesterday, right?"

My throat goes dry. What do I say to that? I can't *lie.* But I don't want to admit to being that awkward kid, either. I force myself to nod.

"I thought your question was really interesting," he says. "I've been thinking about it since then. Sorry you didn't get the chance to finish."

I can't tell if he is just saying that to make me feel better or if he really means it.

Marius clears his throat.

"So you must be pretty young, right? That's so cool. When I heard *Deep Focus* wanted to do an interview, I thought it would be this journalist my dad's age asking me questions about sex scenes or something, but then they told me about the contest."

"Oh, yeah," I say, because I'm not sure what else to say. "I'm seventeen."

"Really? That's crazy."

I need something to do with my hands while we talk, so I tug at my bag, pulling out supplies—my notebook, a pen, and my recorder. Alice takes out her phone, something familiar, and it gets a little easier to focus.

"Uh, do you mind if I record you?"

He waves his hand and scoots his chair forward.

"So," he says, "how did you get started? Writing and everything?"

I blink. Most people don't ask about me when I'm interviewing them. Marius is staring at me like he actually wants me to answer, like he's not just making small talk. It's hard not to stare back.

In real life, his lips are pinker. His hair is longer—or taller, really—but still dark brown. Sunlight streaming through the windows bounces off the silver hoop at the side of his nose. That *definitely* wasn't in the movie. I make a mental note and file it away for later.

"Josephine?"

Alice steps on my foot. I squeak.

"Sorry." I clear my throat, glancing up. Brown. His eyes are brown, like the rest of him, except darker. "Uh, it's Josie. Josephine is my grandma—well, *was*, before she died."

"Right, okay." He nods, smiles. Easy. "So how'd you get started with this?"

I feel Alice's gaze on my face. Is this how this entire interview is going to go? Not only will she have *tons* to tease me about later, but it'll just make me feel like even more of a baby.

"Alice." I turn my head a fraction, barely moving my mouth. "Could you, like, sit somewhere else? Anywhere else? Just till we're done?"

Her eyes narrow. Both of Marius's brows rise, his entire face going with them. His fingers are lazily folded together on the table.

"It's no big deal," he says. "Really, I don't mind if she stays."

Alice smirks.

"No," I say, glaring at her. "She needs to go. Like, I need her to."

We glare for several long seconds. I'm not sure what this will cost me—maybe more whining when we get back to our hotel or tattling to Mom and Dad. Whatever. I just know I can't work when she's sitting right under my ass.

Eventually, she pushes herself to her feet with the most dramatic eye roll I've seen in my life. "Ungrateful," she mutters as she walks toward the other side of the room, where several young people with intern badges are clustered. It takes no time for her to launch into conversation with one of them.

"Sorry," I say, turning back to my notebook and opening to a fresh page. "It's just a little weird to have her sitting here."

"That's okay."

I pause. My eyes dart up. He's staring, expectant. I tug at my hair before forcing my arm down. Laura, my therapist, is always hounding me about self-harm, about how scratching or hair pulling counts, even if I don't think so.

"So," he says, smiling like I've made a joke. "How'd you get started?"

"Oh." My cheeks burn. "Right, right. Uh, I wrote stories for my school newspaper. Well, I don't think that really did anything, 'cause no one reads it except the parents. Then I started this blog and I posted on Twitter, and then I started pitching essays to different websites. Sometimes my blog posts went viral, so that helped me get pieces on bigger websites, like BuzzFeed and Vox. After a while, an editor for *Essence* contacted me, so I've been writing there a lot lately. But, uh, yeah, I won this contest to be able to be here, and that's sort of . . . it."

I wave my hands in the air to end the sentence. He's nodding, though, eyebrows knitted together with interest, so it wasn't a complete failure.

"I knew about the contest, but *wow*, I didn't know about the rest of it." I wish I could take notes in italics, because that's the way he sounds. "That's so impressive. My friends and I weren't doing anything *close* to that when we were younger."

"Okay, but you were *acting*," I say, not bothering to hide the laugh in my voice. "Community theater is better than writing about movies on a blog."

"*Ohhhh* no." He cocks his head to the side. The grin gets even bigger, if possible. "You *researched*."

The heat spreads from my cheeks to my chest. I glance at my recorder, the red light blinking up at me. I'm going to have to relive the awkwardness later when I transcribe this. It's already painful.

"Well, I'm supposed to," I say, shifting in my seat. "Anyway, I guess that's where I wanted to begin. You started acting when you were little, right? But you're still pretty young. So how did that start?"

He leans back against his chair, lips pressed together. It's kind of cute.

I should be taking notes on what he's doing, but I can't seem to form a sentence that doesn't sound like a fangirl admiring a crush. I scratch it down anyway.

"I mean, my parents are really into movies, so we always watched them when I was little. They were in French, you know, but still the same sort of thing," he says, bobbing his head. "And my mom is a director, so she'd take me to rehearsals with her a lot. I guess that's why acting felt accessible."

"So were you more interested in stage or film?"

"Film, definitely," he says. "It always seems—I don't know. I started off doing theater, and that always felt so normal for me, like practice for a sports team after school. But movies seemed so . . . *romantic.*"

My eyes dart up at that. The morning sun highlights streaks of gold in his hair and brings out the honey in his eyes. He's talking about *romance.* It's like he's describing himself, breaking the fourth wall. I have to force myself to look away. *Focus on the notes, Josie.*

"Romantic how?" I make myself ask.

"It's sort of like a fairy tale. It doesn't feel real, not even when you're filming." He shakes his head, tapping his fingers against the table. "It's like you exist in this alternate timeline. Normal people shouldn't be able to be in movies, but there you are anyway."

There's something wistful about his face. I need to write a note about that—how expressive his face is. I guess it's what makes him such a good actor.

"Wow," I say. It seems to fall flat after the magic of his words. I clear my throat. "Uh, does that mean you're studying film when you go to college? I mean—*are* you going to college?"

"I don't know." His mouth twitches. "You tell me. You did all this research, right?"

I freeze. It's hard to figure out how to read this situation. I don't know if he's joking or being a jerk. Journalists are supposed to research the subjects of their profiles. Would it have been better for me to walk in here without knowing anything about him?

"Hey, hey," he says, leaning forward. My breath catches. "I'm just joking. Sorry. I'm still getting used to this *on the record* thing. No one has really paid much attention to me until now."

He gestures around the sleepy coffee shop as if to prove himself. It doesn't even seem like he's lying to make me feel better, because the smile is gone, even if his mouth is still soft.

"Well," I say, tapping my pen against the side of my mouth, "I don't think that'll last that much longer. Not, you know, with all the awards you're going to get."

He actually blushes, ducks his head. It's so boyish, it feels like someone wrote it. The guys at school don't even act like *boys*. Maybe it's a French thing.

"None of it feels real," he says, voice low. "It really doesn't. It was just—*Incident* was this indie movie I did because I thought the script was awesome and I had a free summer. I was supposed to be going to Brown this year, and now I'm deferred because of awards season. It's crazy."

"Yeah." I don't know what else to say. I've never been in this position. "You deserve it, though. You were amazing in the movie. I almost died at the end, when Peter met his boyfriend again and they were like completely different people. And then you were driving away and crying and I just felt my heart . . ."

I clench my hand. The corner of his mouth turns up. The blush is still there, but he doesn't duck. He knows he's a good actor. This is something I get. When Monique tells me I'm a good writer, I don't disagree with her, because it's true.

"Aw," he says. "It wasn't just me. There was an awesome script and director, and the rest of the cast was amazing."

"Yeah, but I'm talking about you." My words surprise me. "You *made* the movie, at least for me. I cried a lot."

"Yeah?" His eyes crinkle. "So did I."

I snicker. He leans back, smile wide again. I'm struck with

sudden *want*. It pools in my chest, stealing my breath for a moment. Marius Canet is the type of guy I've only imagined hanging out with. Sure, there are cute guys back home, but none of them are like this. They don't talk about movies like they're fairy tales or express emotions as clearly as Marius does. It's like he skipped over that part of a guy's life where he learns to close himself off. I can look at his face and see everything flicker over it like a screen.

Stop. I shut my eyes. This has happened before, and it only led to hurt. Every time, I think it might be different, and it never is. Anyway, I'm supposed to be *interviewing* Marius. A crush would make this even more awkward. I glance back down at my notes.

"So, uh, you mentioned your parents. Do you think being raised by them played a role in your acting ability?"

The words are out of my mouth before I realize how formal they sound.

"Well, that's a question."

I wince.

"Are you asking because they aren't from here?" He cocks his head. "I think the different culture had an impact."

"Um, yeah." I rub the back of my neck. "It must be interesting to grow up with immigrant parents."

The only first-generation kids I know are acquaintances and aren't from Europe, but I don't mention that. He can probably already tell that I have no idea what I'm talking about.

"Yeah, a little bit," he says. "We spoke French at home and everything. I didn't learn English until school. Other than that, it wasn't exactly *exceptional*. Manhattan isn't a bad place to be different, you know?"

I nod, hurrying to jot down notes: *Manhattan theater scene???* *French parents, but not outcasts because of foreignness.*

"Everyone is different somehow," he continues. "And they're the only parents I've ever had. I'm not sure what it would be like to grow up any other way."

"Sure," I say, nodding. "I guess it's interesting because there's something so romantic about French, just like you said there's something romantic about movies."

"Yeah. Actually, you're right." He leans forward, runs a hand through his curls. I force myself to look away. "Do you speak French?"

"Uh." I bite my lip. "I can do all of Lafayette's parts from the *Hamilton* soundtrack."

He laughs. This is where he seems more like a guy from school. The noise is harsh, loud, like he isn't worried about who might hear. I guess that's something only I worry about. But at the same time, it's different. His laugh doesn't feel like a punch.

I force myself to look at my notebook. "What are you working on next? I couldn't find anything online."

"Oh." He blinks. "That's because I'm not really supposed to talk about it. I'm working with Roy Lennox."

"Wow." I shake my head. "He— They're doing a documentary series on ABC in honor of his twentieth year as a director. That's amazing."

From an indie movie to working with one of the best directors in Hollywood. Before seeing his performance, I would've doubted it. Now? I'm sure Marius Canet would slay any role he wanted. Part of me wishes it weren't a part in a Lennox movie—he *always* has all-white casts, so he must be branching out now—but it's a milestone most actors spend years working toward.

"Yeah." He nods, leaning back again. "Kinda nerve-racking, though, you know? But I feel like I can't say that. It's cool enough that it's even happening."

"I don't think you should feel bad about it." I click my pen, allowing myself to look up at him. For the first time, his expression is shy, guarded. "You're allowed to feel how you feel. I don't think you should have to lie about it. Things can be great and scary at the same time."

"I guess." His voice is soft. "Maybe."

I want to press more. I want to tell him about how I feel guilty about my anxiety when I don't have much to worry about, not with my nice house and laptop and married parents who let me travel the country to do interviews. Almost as soon as I consider it, I shove the thought down. I don't even talk to my family about this. I can't have Marius thinking there's something wrong with me.

Then his phone starts ringing. If we were having a moment, it's gone now.

"Oh, man." Marius frowns down at his screen. "I'm so sorry. I have a meeting with my agent—I totally forgot. Can we pick this up again another time? Maybe in Austin?"

I bite my lip. His publicist should've told him that an interview would take more than twenty minutes—or he could've let his agent know about this. He really *is* new to this. I should be irritated, but there's just a nervous fluttering in my stomach.

"Yeah." I suck a breath. "Yeah, we're scheduled to talk at your fitting on Tuesday, anyway. I'll keep asking questions until I'm done."

"Good." He grins, momentarily blinding me. "I'm all yours."

CHAPTER 9

"Stop it."

I peer up. Alice isn't even looking at me, has barely glanced at me since we got back to the hotel a few hours ago, even though we're lounging on the same bed.

"What?" I say. I'm actually confused. "I'm not doing anything annoying."

Alice thinks a lot of things I do are annoying, like playing music out loud instead of using my earbuds or talking to myself when I'm working. I've spent most of the evening Googling other actors from the movie so I can figure out what to ask them about Marius.

"No." Alice rolls her eyes. "I mean stop thinking about him. You have a goofy look on your face."

"I have to think about him," I say, turning back to my screen. "I'm writing a profile. And I should be working on it all the time, so I don't know what you want me to do. It's not my fault if you don't like—"

"That's not what I mean and you know it." She kisses her teeth, reaching for her scarf to wrap her hair. "You always get your heart set on these little pretty boys. That's why you can't find anyone, you know. It's not because you're not pretty or smart or whatever you're always going on about."

"Oh my *God*." I snap my head up. "Screw you, Alice."

I regret ever talking to her about the crushes I've had. Honestly, I never really thought she was listening. There was Savion, a Black guy with a gorgeous Afro, who in ninth grade told me no one wanted my "fat, nappy-headed ass, anyway" after I refused to help him cheat on a test. There was Sohail, a boy who kissed me three times sophomore year before telling me his strict Pakistani parents would never approve of me. And then there was Tasha, my sorta-kinda girlfriend last year, who didn't tell me she was moving away until she was gone. I don't always get my heart set on pretty boys. Lately, I've learned not to let my heart get set on anyone at all.

Maybe it's a *me* thing. Since I'm fat, I should probably just take whatever I can get, but I don't want to date a jerk who thinks racism is over or who doesn't read. I don't want anyone who sees my body as something to overcome. It's just hard to find people like that. I found one and she left.

"I'm just saying," Alice says. "You have to stay professional, right? So stop being weird around him."

"I'm not being weird." My cheeks burn. I very well could be acting weird around him, but I can't help it. "I *try* not to be weird."

"Well." She raises a brow. "Keep trying."

"You're the actual worst," I say.

Before I go to bed that night, I send an email to Ms. Jacobson about interviewing Penny Livingstone. Penny plays Emma, a friend Marius's character makes at the conversion camp. As the least famous, she'll probably be the easiest cast member to get a meeting with before we leave for Austin.

<hr />

When I wake up the next morning, we have a meeting set for three o'clock at a restaurant in downtown L.A. I blink a few times to make sure I'm reading correctly. I figured it'd be easy to get a meeting, but not *this* easy. Maybe Penny's Disney Channel upbringing makes her eager for any sort of press.

"Do you have the money to eat here?" Alice whispers as we walk inside. "It looks like it's out of your price range."

It isn't *that* bad. Everything is made out of wood. Flowers hang from the ceiling, and there are floor-to-ceiling windows. People eat from bowls filled with fruit of strange colors. It's like a hipster haven—a haven I probably can't afford without using a serious chunk of my prize money.

Deep Focus sent me plane tickets and hotel reservations, but I still have to pay for Alice, since she wasn't exactly part of the deal. Plus, there's the issue of food and other expenses. Ms. Jacobson told me to keep receipts from everything so they can reimburse me, but that doesn't really help right now.

"I just won't get anything." I bite my lip, looking around for Penny. "Water is free."

"She'll think you're pitiful."

"I don't care."

"Can I help you?" A woman materializes in front of us. She's dressed in jeans and boots, even though we're in L.A. "A table for two?"

"Uh, she's meeting someone," Alice says, nudging me forward. "Can I sit at the bar?"

It takes no time to spot Penny. Not only did I just see her in *Incident on 57th Street*, but she looks the same as she did three years ago, when I still watched her sing and dance her way through high school on Disney Channel. Her hair is flaming red, and there's a handful of freckles on the pale skin around her nose. Most of the baby fat from her cheeks is gone. As I get closer, I see there's something different about her nose. It's straighter.

She stands up as soon as she sees me, but instead of standing there, like Marius did, she shimmies out of her chair and actually pulls me in for a hug. I freeze. My arms hang at my sides.

"It's so nice to see you," she says. I can't tell if she means it or not. There's a polished air about her. The smile on her face is warm but guarded. "I looked at some of your writing, and it's so impressive."

"Oh, wow," I say, sitting down across from her. "Thank you."

She watches in silence as I pull out my pen, my notebook, and my recorder.

"Do you mind if I record you?"

She frowns. I blink in surprise. It's the first time anyone has hesitated when I've asked. Then again, Marius is the only person I've interviewed in person, one on one.

"I don't have to," I say, gripping the recorder in my hand. It's empty since I already uploaded yesterday's interview to my computer. "It's just easier for me. I'll be able to remember everything later and make sure all of the quotes are accurate."

"All right," she says, chewing at her lip. "As long as it helps with accuracy."

"Great," I say, setting it on the table between the two of us. "So, you know I'm working on a profile about Marius, but I'd love to start out asking about you. What have you been working on lately?"

It's just an icebreaker; I've done my research on her, too. This isn't the first movie she's done since Disney Channel, but it's the first indie movie after a stream of box-office disappointments where she didn't even have lead roles.

"Oh, that's a big question," she says, shaking her head. "I guess my biggest project would be trying to get a head start on my summer body."

I frown. She's pretty skinny. It doesn't help that the whole *summer body* thing just irritates the hell out of me, no matter who it's coming from.

"That'll be easy, then," I say, clicking my pen. "Your perfect summer body is whatever your body looks like in the summer."

Her eyebrows rise before she bursts into laughter. I want to smile. I also want her to know that I'm serious. She's shaking her head like I just said something hilarious.

"That's great," she says after a few seconds. Her face is red, making her freckles even more pronounced. "I've never thought about it that way."

That seems to get her to open up. When I ask about her time on Disney Channel, she can't stop talking.

"My parents used to drive me an hour to the Disney studio every morning for work," she says, picking at the bread in between us. "And we didn't leave until around nine at night. I spent most of my time there. All of my friends were other kids on set, but nothing was really real. Then my manager tried to push me into singing."

"How'd that work out?"

"Horribly." She smiles, sharp. "We all knew I couldn't carry a tune, but no one would tell me the truth because they were thinking about the money."

I bite my lip. A waiter comes up to the table, and I feel my stomach clench. I didn't even get the chance to scope out the cheapest thing on the menu.

"Two cheeseburgers, please," Penny says without looking at the menu. She turns to me. "I promise you they're amazing."

"Oh," I say eloquently. "Well, I— My sister has my wallet."

What a stupid excuse. I wince, waiting for her to give me an odd look. The waiter does. He purses his lips, probably seeing straight through my bullshit, before walking away.

"Don't worry about it," Penny says, waving her hand. "It's no problem."

The pain in my stomach doesn't go away.

"Oh," I say. "I mean, you can't pay for my stuff. That's— I—"

"I meant," Penny says, "that we could get your wallet from her."

I nod, pressing my lips together. Right. Of course. I stare at my notebook, trying to think of a way to smooth out the conversation.

"Oh, I guess I should probably talk about Marius, right?" she asks. "I'm so self-absorbed. Sorry about that."

"No, you're fine." I shake my head. It's a little easier to breathe with the change of subject. "But what can you tell me about working with him?"

Talking with her is different from talking to Marius. He was easy to talk to, but also more guarded. With Marius, I had to dig. Penny just gives up stories before I have to ask.

"He's really focused on set," she says, taking a sip of water. "Sometimes he messes around, because, you know, there's a lot of time between takes. But whenever he wanted to get away, he'd find some corner and wear these gigantic headphones and read a book."

"Really?" My ears perk up. "Is the movie based on a book?"

"It isn't," she says. "He'd read a lot about conversion camps, like fictional accounts and real-life ones. I read one, but I can't get through them as fast. Whenever we couldn't find him, he was somewhere reading."

I want to ask more, but then the waiter comes and we have to stop to eat. Penny's eyelids flutter when she takes a bite. I snort.

"I promise," she says, wiping her mouth, "it's really good."

And, fuck, it *is*. I almost forget to be anxious because of the way it makes my tongue melt. She laughs at me. I smile back.

We don't talk again until half her burger is gone and she's offered me the rest of her fries. I usually feel uneasy about eating in front of other people, especially skinny people, but everything is so good that I don't care.

"So," Penny says. "Any more questions?"

I glance down at my notebook. There's one I've been thinking of since she first showed up in the movie, but I wasn't going to bring it up because I wasn't sure how it would sound. But things seem to be going so well. . . .

"How does it feel to see a newcomer like Marius step into such a big role?" I ask. "Especially since you've worked so hard to get where you are?"

Penny blinks, wiping her hands on her napkin. She's silent for a long moment. Shit. Did that come out wrong?

"You should know," she finally says. "Marius really deserves all of the attention he's getting, but I'm worried he'll fall into this trap where people care more about his talent than they actually care about *him*. Do you know what I mean?"

Words stick to the roof of my mouth. Is she implying that I'm one of the people who don't care about him?

"Oh," I say, closing my notebook. I always leave the recorder going, even as I pack up, just in case I catch something important. "That's definitely not— I'm going to try my best to write a piece he deserves."

"I know you will," Penny says. "If you didn't, we'd have a problem."

Another pause. I squirm in my seat. Penny smiles, but it doesn't quite reach her eyes.

"But I'm sure that won't happen."

Then the waiter appears, and she smiles up at him.

CHAPTER 10

On Tuesday, I'm supposed to go to a fitting with Marius, but I can't focus on what to ask him. All I can think about is Penny.

I think she hates me. She's definitely wary of me after I put my foot in my mouth with that question.

"It's fine," Alice says. We're both looking in the bathroom mirror. She must notice the mess that is my hair—stuck up in all directions—and the bags under my eyes. "The second time should be easier. You don't have to be so nervous."

I stare after her as she leaves. Funnily enough, her words aren't making anything better. After I interviewed Marius, it felt like he was all I could think about, but that thankfully faded after a good night of sleep. But now I have to actually spend time with him at a fitting—I don't even *know* anything about fittings. I pull my hair back, but my curls are all over the place, so I settle on a ponytail and a hat.

It's harder to do Mirror Time when I'm away from home. There's my face I like, I guess. But I hate my mouth. I never say the right things at the right times. And I can't stand the pudgy stomach, no matter how hard I try to force myself to like it.

"Hey, Alice," I say, stepping out of the bathroom. She's

already dressed, which will probably make this harder. "What if I just went to this one alone?"

She glances up from her phone with raised eyebrows. I don't even have all of my clothes on yet, so it is kind of embarrassing to stare back at her. It's not like this is the first time I've had to negotiate. It used to be easier when she was in high school, sneaking out to parties or asking me to hide things from Mom and Dad, but I have to take what I can get.

"What's the point of me being here, then?" She folds her arms. Maggie only fights if she needs to, but Alice does it just for fun; it's exhausting. "I'm supposed to go everywhere with you. That's what Mom said."

"Since when do you care what Mom says?"

She pauses.

"Don't you want to go sightseeing?" I ask. "Go see the Hollywood sign or the Walk of Fame? Isn't that why you came in the first place?"

Alice bites her lip. I know I've got her.

"Just tell Mom I'm talking and you can't interrupt me," I say, trying to inject honey into my voice. "If you feel so bad about lying to her."

"You can't do whatever you want, you know."

"Well . . . ," I huff, "neither can you."

Alice rolls her eyes and scoffs. When the Uber comes, I go in one direction, and she goes in another.

Marius was nice the first time I met him, but we were only talking about surface-level topics. If I'm going to write a profile, I need to dig deep, to find out more about this new actor who's going to blow everyone away. I'm just not sure how to do that, especially with Penny acting like she'll murder me if I say the wrong thing.

Before I know it, the car stops. The building looks fancy from the outside: big windows revealing suits and long, flowing dresses framed by white marble. I've never seen a building like this at home. It reminds me of the store that kicked Vivian out in *Pretty Woman*. Hopefully they don't kick *me* out. I step out of the car with my notebook open.

The guy at the front desk asks for my credentials before escorting me through a pair of white double doors. Inside are a few people I don't recognize: one taking measurements, one writing things down. Marius turns and I see the warm brown eyes, the easy smile. I'd recognize his curls anywhere. I force myself to smile back at him.

"Thanks, Ethan," he says, craning his neck to see. "I was worried she wasn't gonna show up."

Shit. I'm not *that* late, am I?

Ethan just shrugs, closing the door behind me. The person with the notes stares at me. I'm not sure if I should smile or not.

"Twenty-four," the lady taking measurements says. A measuring tape is wrapped around Marius's arm, various pins sticking out of his suit jacket. "Thirty-three, forty-two."

The person with the notes writes frantically. I bite my lip, glancing around. Pink plush chairs decorate the room, which is filled with racks of clothes and long mirrors. The windows are tall, like we're in a castle, and adorned with golden curtains that drape down to the floor.

My eyes find their way back to Marius. He's still looking at me, the ghost of a smile on his face, like always.

"I'm sorry," I blurt. "My Uber took forever to come. It's beautiful here."

The woman with the tape measure finally looks at me. I already know who she is, because Past Me took the time to research her. Christina Pak is a super-eccentric designer who's dressed a lot of people for red carpets and the Met Gala. I don't understand exactly how it works, but I guess she picks actors like Marius and dresses them to publicize her designs. Or maybe he picked her.

Either way, he definitely *looks* good. His suit is dark green. Somehow, it makes his cheekbones stand out a little more. When the smile drops, he seems more like a man, even if just a young one. The suit looks like it was made to fit him, not the other way around. I guess that's what tailoring does.

"This is Josie," he says, breaking the spell. "She's a journalist. *Super* smart. Josie, this is Christina Pak, and her assistant, Meghan."

It's harder to breathe, but not because I'm anxious. Christina glances at me with an appraising eye.

"I'm just here to watch," I say, plopping down on one of the chairs. "And take notes, if that's okay with you. There's a separate person who takes pictures for the magazine."

"Yes, yes." Christina waves a hand, turning back to her measurements. "Perfectly all right. Meghan, did you get the arms? I want to move on to the pants."

I go back to my notes, trying to pay attention to the room, to the clothes, to the fabric on the racks waiting to be measured out. I'm not sure what else to talk about—the way Meghan helps him take off the suit jacket?

"We need another piece," Christina says, gesturing to Meghan. "Just in the other room. It shouldn't take too long to find."

The two of them are gone before I can say anything. Now I actually have to *talk* to him, because I'm the only person around.

Not that I don't want to. I want to know everything about him—what he thinks about right before he falls asleep, what music makes him cry, if he ever feels out of place. But I wouldn't want to put any of that in the profile. It'd just be for me.

"*So.*"

I jolt up, as if he's heard me thinking. Marius is still smiling, but this time it looks like he's trying not to spook me.

"Do you remember the last time we talked? Your sister caught up to me on my way out." He runs a hand through his hair. "We were talking a little bit."

I remember going to the bathroom right after Marius left our interview early, but I didn't realize Alice had followed him.

"Oh God." My breath freezes. "What did she say about me?"

"Nothing bad," he says, smiling like I've made a joke. "She told me about your anxiety."

My stomach drops. No one in my family talks about my anxiety to other people. It's just an unspoken promise that no one has broken. Until now. *Logically* I get that no one should look at me differently once they find out. Being awkward is one thing, but having an anxiety disorder is just—I don't know. I don't want him to think there's something wrong with me. If I had it my way, he never would've known.

The few people who know about my anxiety always say the same things: that it's okay, that they'll watch out to make sure I don't get uncomfortable, that I don't have to worry. But that's never how it works. I don't know how to communicate a panic attack in the middle of one.

"I just want you to tell me if I do anything that freaks you out," he says. "I— Well, I know I can be too much sometimes."

I don't know if I should laugh or roll my eyes. He's not overwhelming, exactly, not in the same way people at school or strangers can be. I guess he's still a stranger, but it's not the same sort of anxiety. Marius just seems different. I like being overwhelmed by him.

"You're not." I stare down at the ground. "It's— She's not really supposed to go around telling people that."

"Sorry. I don't think there's anything wrong with that, if it makes you feel better."

"No." I shake my head, glancing back at my notebook. "You don't bother me, anyway, so you don't have to worry about it."

It's just looking at him that bothers me. I'm afraid to do it for too long because I might never look away. It's not fair that I'm supposed to be professional when he seems so cool.

"Oh." He pauses. I watch him rub one thumb over the other. "That's good, right?"

"I mean, it only gets hard around people I know or really care about." I wince. That definitely didn't sound good. "Not that I'm saying I don't care about you. It's just— Usually interviews are easier because I'm interested, but it's not like I'm talking to the same person every day for the next four years, you know?"

"So school must be hard."

I glance up. There's something understanding in his eyes. For a second, I forgot he went to an actual school. I want to ask what it was like, if he knows how it feels to be so interested in something that people don't usually care about, if he was the odd one out.

I don't get the chance to say anything at all, because Christina and Meghan come whirling back in. Marius glances over at them but smiles at me again. It doesn't seem like smiling takes any effort on his part. He just gives smiles away.

"Christina, could we play music?" he asks. "It's really quiet."

"Of course." She waves a hand at Meghan, who puts down her notes and walks over to a stereo in the corner. "I have to warn you, though. I'm not sure we'll share the same taste in music."

Something light, with lots of harps, fills the room. I go back to doodling in my notebook. I realize, twenty minutes into this fitting, that I probably should've been recording. What an idiot. I guess that's one more thing to remember for next time.

"Josie."

My eyes snap up. Marius isn't yelling, but he's the only one speaking. There's also the fact that him saying my name is like catnip or something. I hate it. I'm still not sure how to get rid of the tightening in my chest when he does it.

"I like A Tribe Called Quest," he says, hands in his coat pockets. "Do you like them? Have a favorite song?"

"Of course I like them," I say. All Black parents from a certain generation play their songs at parties. "I, um, like 'Check the Rhime.' "

My favorite ATCQ song is actually "Electric Relaxation," but the entire song is about sex, and I definitely don't think that should be playing right now.

Christina and Meghan work on him for a little longer, "Check the Rhime" playing in the background. It might be because of the song, but I actually feel safe. Safe enough to get up and wander around.

"Do you mind if I look at these?" I ask Christina, gesturing toward a rack of clothes. "I won't rip anything."

She waves a hand. I take that as a yes.

Christina makes colorful clothes. They aren't bright like Skittles, more like those variety packs of twenty-dollar colored pencils. I don't think I'd wear any of them. They seem too loud, calling too much attention. Maybe that's what famous people want. I definitely don't.

There is *one* dress. It's short-sleeved, black with roses embroidered all over the place. There's also a long slit that would reveal leg, Angelina Jolie–style. I guess it's the type of dress to call attention, but it isn't as bad as the other ones, at least to me. It's beautiful. I run my hands over some of the roses. They're different colors—red and orange and yellow—contrasting against the black background.

"You should try it on."

Marius is next to me. I don't yelp, which I consider an accomplishment. He's not wearing the suit jacket anymore, just an undershirt. I can't tell if he's joking or if he actually thinks this would look good on me. Of course *it* would look good. It's a beautiful dress. But that doesn't mean *I'd* look good in it.

"I don't think so," I say, letting my hands run over it. This isn't about me anyway. "There's no way it would fit."

"Well, yeah," he says. "They never do at first. My jacket doesn't fit."

For a second, I let myself stare at him, hoping. I shouldn't. I'll expect this dress to fit me, to look beautiful, to look like it was meant for me. And then it'll hurt even more when none of those things happen.

"Christina," he says, turning around, "don't you think Josie would look beautiful in this dress?"

Oh God.

I've been called beautiful before. My parents and my sisters tell me—at least, *one* of my sisters does. Even Cash tells me, after we spend the night together reading stories about princesses, the same ones Mom and Dad used to read to me.

But it's different coming out of Marius's mouth. Maybe because it feels like he's lying. Maybe because people never say it to me unless they're trying to make me feel better: "You'd be so beautiful if you just lost a few pounds." He's just saying it to say it. I swallow down whatever *feelings* his words give me.

"Come on," Christina says, grabbing me by the hand. "I'd love to see how you look in it. I bet it would complement your skin tone and your eyes just perfectly."

I always feel uncomfortable when people who aren't Black say anything about my skin tone, but Christina is Korean American, and she seems nice enough.

She cups my face, staring into my eyes. It's oddly erotic. She smells like flowers and rich people. Then she grabs the dress, snapping at Meghan, who holds open a door across the room for me.

I'm only able to get it on because I suck in my stomach. If Meghan can tell, she doesn't say anything. There aren't any zippers, so she just clamps the dress up. The slit doesn't fall against one of my legs like it would for Angelina Jolie. It's somewhere between them, gaping wider than it's supposed to.

I don't want to look in the mirror. I don't want Marius or Christina to see. Marius will smile and be nice, like usual, but I know he'll regret even suggesting I try it on. Christina will be upset that her design looks like such a mess on me when it was so beautiful on the hanger.

Meghan does the honors of opening the door. No one gasps, like the moments in the movies or *Say Yes to the Dress*. Christina's eyes roam over me, lips moving, even though nothing comes out. Marius stares for a moment. When he sees me looking, he looks away.

Tears clog my throat. I shouldn't even be crying. A boy didn't jump up and down when I wore a dress. So what?

"I'll make the proper changes," Christina says. "I'll have to let it out, since it wasn't made with you in mind, you see. But you *make* the dress, Josie. I've found its rightful owner."

My eyebrows rise. She can't be seeing the same thing I see— how the dress practically folds under my body, like it's not enough for me.

"I don't know where I'd even wear it," I say instead, shrugging. Christina's face is nice to look at. She feels like someone I can talk to. "I don't really go anywhere that requires a dress this beautiful."

"Oh, please." She barely acknowledges the compliment. "We'll have to find *somewhere* for you to wear it. Meghan, will you grab the tape measure?"

"Maybe prom," Meghan suggests, stepping toward me. "Do you mind?"

I shake my head. As she holds the tape measure around my hips, I resist the urge to scoff. Forget the fact that I could never actually afford this dress. Marius doesn't have to worry about paying, since he's basically borrowing the clothes for some award show, but I don't have anyone to sponsor this dress. No one even knows who I am.

"I don't think so," I say instead. "I wasn't really planning on going."

"Oh," Meghan says, in a way suggesting that she's already tired of this conversation. She starts to mutter numbers under her breath.

"I never went to my prom," Marius says. I almost forgot he was here. "And I sort of wish I had. You might regret it if you don't go."

"I don't think I'll care," I say. Meghan gestures for me to lift my arms, so I do. "High school isn't a place I want to remember."

For the first time, Meghan looks like she agrees with me.

AUSTIN, TEXAS

@JosieTheJournalist: why comment on someone else's weight when you can just be quiet

CHAPTER 11

Our six a.m. flight on Wednesday is only three hours, which isn't nearly long enough for a nap. By the time we get to Austin-Bergstrom International Airport, I'm basically dead on my feet.

"Come on," I say, pulling at Alice after we've gotten our luggage. "Let's stop at Starbucks."

She groans. "I just want to go to the hotel."

"I have to do that roundtable thing today, remember?"

"Yeah," she says, stepping around me as I stumble with my suitcase. "The roundtable thing is at the *hotel*. Since you don't need me, I was gonna binge all the *Real Housewives* episodes I've missed and eat a ton of junk food."

That actually sounds like heaven right now. I shove down my jealousy as we near the Starbucks.

"Fine," I say. "You don't have to come, but I need something to help me stay awake."

"Can't we just go to the hotel?"

Jesus. My face feels weird and my entire body is just waking up after being confined to the plane. All I'm asking her to do is stand in line with me. Why is everything a fight with her?

"No," I say. "You owe me after telling Marius about my anxiety without even *asking* me first."

I don't know what I was expecting—maybe for her to at least *look* like she feels bad—but she just shakes her head.

"Oh, please," she says. "It's not like I told him you used to wet the bed. I told him something that would be helpful to know. And he wasn't mean about it. Right?"

He wasn't, but that's not the point.

"I don't care what you thought," I say instead. "It's *my* information to tell people. What if I told him about—I don't know—your heavy periods or something?"

"It's not the same thing. Don't be ridiculous."

"I'm *not*," I say. "You'd be pissed if I told him something personal about you. It's not fair of you to just go around—"

"See, *this* is why you're impossible." She slaps her hands against her thighs. "I try to do something *nice* and you're so ungrateful—"

"Whatever," I say, heading over to the Starbucks. "Forget about it."

When I was little, flying in an airplane sounded so fun, being up so high and looking down on the clouds. Now it just seems like a chore, an annoying way to get from one place to the next. I almost wish we had a tour bus. One without Alice on it.

After a few minutes waiting in the Starbucks line, Alice appears next to me.

I roll my eyes. "Did you change your mind?"

"No," she says. "Maggie wants to talk to you, or whatever."

The person in front of me walks away, leaving me as the next person in line. I step forward.

"Hello," the barista says. "What can I get you?"

I order quickly, then step aside. Alice shoves the phone in my face.

"Josie!" Maggie's face appears on the screen. She's wearing

her uniform, which means she could be at home *or* slacking off. "How was the flight?"

I fumble around for earbuds before Alice reluctantly hands me hers, fisted in her hands.

"Did you pull these out before giving me the phone?"

"Come on," she says. "Why would I do that?"

She'd totally do that.

"Josie!" a barista calls, setting my chai on the counter.

I'm not awake enough for this.

"Here," I say, giving the phone back to Alice. "Hold on."

After I've grabbed my drink, I turn back to see that Alice has somehow snagged a table, our bags strewn around it to claim our territory. She has both earbuds in and is nodding at something Maggie must be saying.

"She's back," Alice says, taking out one earbud and shoving it in my ear. "Do you see her?"

I fix the earbud, moving my head. "Hey, Mags."

"Josie!" she says again, like she didn't see me before. "Alice tells me the boy you're interviewing is really cute?"

"I didn't say that," Alice says. "I said *you* would probably think he's really cute. Josie does."

My cheeks burn. "I never said that."

"Oh, Josie." Maggie wiggles her eyebrows. "It's *bad*, huh?"

"It's not like that," I say, picking up my cup. "I'm just interviewing him."

I *should* be thinking about Marius. It's just that I'd rather not.

"Are you sure you don't have a crush?" she asks, leaning closer to the camera. "A little, itty-bitty one?"

"You're spending too much time watching *Paw Patrol*," I say. "It's not a crush."

I *refuse* to call it a crush. Maybe that'll keep one from developing. In the past, I've tried to squash my feelings before they got too big by ignoring all the fluttery thoughts and focusing on the negative aspects of a person. It's just hard to do that with Marius.

"Tell me more about him," Maggie says. "The pictures of him online are cute. Is he as cute in person?"

"Maggie," I hiss. The idea of her looking him up to appraise him is *cringy*. "He looks fine."

"He's definitely *fine*."

"Maggie."

She snickers.

"Ugh." I toss my head back, running my hand through my hair. "I'll talk about him *once* with you. Just to get it out of my system."

Gagging, Alice gets up and walks to the line.

"Excellent." Maggie nods, solemn. "A great plan."

"I can't with you." I roll my eyes, but I'm smiling. Something about Marius *is* fun to think about. Maybe it's because I've been avoiding thoughts of him since we last met. "I don't know where to start."

"I want to hear everything." She steps back, revealing the break room in the background. "You really should purge all of these feelings before you go do your next journalism thing."

"I mean, he's . . ." I shake my head, grinning. "Even his name. Like *Marius* just sounds gorgeous, you know?"

"I definitely know." Maggie smiles her *crush* grin. She looks like she's watching a romantic comedy. "What else?"

Talking about Marius when he's not here makes me feel shy.

"I don't know," I say. "He said there was something romantic about movies, but there's the same romance around him. He's . . . God, Maggie. He's stunning and beautiful and mysterious and different from anyone I've ever met."

If Alice were here, she'd make fun of me or scold Maggie for encouraging me. Maggie just squeals. I open my mouth to say more, but Alice drops back into her seat.

"What?" she says, waving around a white milkshake-looking thing with red and green sprinkles. "The line was short."

She grabs the earbud she left dangling and sticks it in her ear. I try my best not to pout.

"What are you talking about now, Mags?" Alice asks. "Still on the boy? Has Josie written any love poems yet?"

"God," I say. "You're actually the worst."

"Yeah, she is," Maggie says. "Come on, keep telling me. What's it like talking to him?"

"He's just like every other boy Josie's had a crush on." Alice holds her drink. "They all look the same."

"That's not true," I say. I can't help the anger that flares in my chest. "You act like you know everything about me, but you don't."

She folds her arms. Maggie shakes her head.

"It's fine to have a type," Maggie says. "Just make sure he knows you're better than him from the start. It should even the playing field."

"How does that make it even?" I ask. "If I'm better."

"Well, maybe *even* isn't the right word." She cocks her head. "I guess it just makes things easier."

Maggie has always indulged my crushes too much. Every time something doesn't work out, she says, "They knew you were better than them and they couldn't handle it." But I can't deal with her saying all of these profound lines about love that worked for her. I'm different. I don't look like her and I don't know how to talk like her.

"I don't know why you're always into these skinny, slinky boys," Alice says, leaning her head back against her seat. "You'll snap him in half."

"Alice, come on," Maggie barks. "Really?"

Alice says something in response, maybe an apology, but I don't hear it. My heart has already sunk. Something builds in my throat, and I struggle to swallow as I stare down into my plastic cup of tea. Out of the corner of my eye, I can see my suitcase. I try very hard not to think about the pair of Spanx I know Maggie slipped into it before I left home.

I'm sure she doesn't mean anything by it. Maybe she doesn't realize I already worry about being bigger than whoever I end up with, about people always staring at us and wondering what my person sees in me.

Being fat is hard sometimes, but especially during the holidays. It was hard when Mom kept looking at me at Thanksgiving dinner. It was hard when the websites I read started posting diet tips or "inspirational stories" about people (mostly women) losing tons of weight by starving themselves or doing a bunch of crazy eating things that I'm trying to learn my way out of.

I don't want to hear about people's diet tips or weight-loss stories. People just see my body and automatically assume that I'm dying to know how their niece lost forty pounds on Weight Watchers or the new lemonade diet.

Most of the time, I can handle myself. Sometimes I slip. It feels like everyone is trying to tear down my self-esteem and I'm barely able to hold it up.

"Josie?" Maggie says. "Do you want to keep talking?"

I shake my head. I'm trying not to blink. If I do, tears will spill over, and Alice will say she didn't mean it and that I'm too sensitive and she didn't really say anything so bad.

I *know* why thinking about Marius makes me so uncomfortable. It's not just because the movie was sad. It's because I see Marius whenever I try not to think about him. It's because I'm trying to train myself to stop wanting something I can't have. Just like being on a diet.

"Come on," I say, standing up. "We should head over to the hotel."

CHAPTER 12

I don't know why I thought I'd be exploring Austin. According to the itinerary, we're doing something called a press round-table. That means a bunch of members of the press show up at a fancy hotel—the same one Alice and I are staying at while we're here—and eat lunch in its fancy conference room and basically get treated like royalty.

"Stop looking around like that," Alice says. Somehow, I got her to come with me, despite the better plans she shared in the airport. "Try to look natural. No one looks as impressed as you."

It's hard to look natural. First, they gave us both bags of swag, even though Alice didn't have a press badge on and I had to explain to the security guard that she was my chaperone. The bags have stuff like a flipbook with hi-res photos from the movie, a bottle of alcohol (which Alice will probably steal from me when we leave), a branded notebook, a branded pen, and something called a "self-care kit," which is pretty much a little pouch filled with small containers of ChapStick, lotion, and bath salts. I guess it has to do with the fact that in the movie Peter sees a therapist who talks to him about self-care.

It's still a little weird, but I like free stuff.

Now we're eating "lunch," which arrives on plates that look like the china we have at home. It's not even normal food. We already had two courses—an avocado caprese salad and a creamy roasted red pepper and cauliflower soup with goat cheese—and now everyone has fish or chicken. Even the conference room is fancy. Gold—or what looks like gold—trims the chairs and the walls. There's fancy wallpaper with pretty flowers. The windows are wide, and we can see the fountain and green, green grass outside by the main entrance, with its towering Greek columns.

"I'm trying, but it's hard. Like, is it just me," I whisper, leaning closer to Alice, "or does this feel like a wedding?"

"I guess the director has money, huh?" She glances at my salmon. "Do you want that?"

"Not the director, exactly." I slide over my plate. "The studio. Maybe they spent a lot on this because of the combination of Dennis Bardell and Art Springfield."

Alice nods, but she's too busy tucking into my lunch to really be ingesting any of this. I turn my attention to the rest of the room. Alice is right—no one looks as impressed as I feel. Most people are typing on their phones while they eat. Some people chat with each other. A few people gather their things and head toward the door. The security guard standing there nods at them before glancing away.

"Hmm," Alice says. "Do you think they're leaving early?"

I glance back at the empty table. It isn't the only one here; there are at least two more without any jackets or chairs or backpacks.

"I don't think so," I say. "I think they're calling us to interviews in small groups."

"When do you go?"

"I don't know." I tap my fingers against the table. "When they call me, I guess."

Instead of eating, I busy myself with looking through my questions. I wrote some for the director and every member of the cast, even though I'm not sure how many I'll have a chance to ask.

The longest page in my notebook has questions for Marius. Some of them verge on being too personal, though: asking if he used any of his own experiences when playing Peter, how close he is to the material, and which scene in the movie he connects to most. But those are the sorts of things *I* want to know about him. I figure everyone else will want to know them, too.

Maybe I'll try during our next one-on-one interview.

"Excuse me." A woman dressed in a suit appears in front of us. "This section is next."

There isn't anyone else sitting at our table, but there are three other tables in this section, making about twenty reporters. Everyone gets up and grabs their stuff. I fall toward the back of the crowd as we leave the warm, bustling room, heading down the hallway.

I wish I weren't so nervous. I've already done this before—well, not a roundtable *exactly*, but something close to it. But I get scared to talk to people every time. I don't know if it'll ever go away.

"Here we are," the woman says. "Hope you enjoy."

It seems like a strange thing to say since we're all, well, working. But it doesn't *feel* like work. After all, I won a contest to be here. This—writing, reporting—is something I've always done on my own time, after school or work. But it *is* a job. I glance at the other reporters around me. No one looks excited or nervous. Does this feel like a normal office job to them?

The room has one big, circular table in the center where people take their seats. Right away, other reporters pull out their notebooks and sheets of paper and recording devices. I grab a seat on the far right, which leaves me directly facing Penny. She raises an eyebrow at me.

I'm not sure what that means.

Alice seems to notice, since she gives me a look as we're sitting down.

"Well," she whispers, "maybe this will be as interesting as *Housewives* after all."

I would nudge her, but I don't want to call too much attention to us. I force myself to take everything in. There are a few people sitting against the walls, chatting quietly to each other. They aren't sitting with us, but they're dressed pretty professionally and were already here when we got in, so I'm guessing they're PR.

I don't know why, but PR people seem scarier than other journalists. Maybe it's because they're basically *access* in human form. If you can't work with a PR person, there's really no chance of you getting the story. They're probably here to make sure everything goes smoothly—meaning they'll shut us up if we approach a topic they aren't happy with. I swallow and glance down at my questions. Probably better to stick with the "normal" stuff, then.

I glance up to see both Penny and Marius looking at me. Marius smiles. Penny doesn't.

"All right, looks like that's everyone," Dennis, the director, says, patting his hands against the table. "According to the people who run this thing, we get thirty minutes with each group. So get ready to do your worst!"

He and the cast—Art, Grace, Marius, and Penny—laugh. The PR people in the back do not.

"I suppose I'll start," a lady with a French accent says. "What do you hope audiences will take away from this movie?"

That's how it goes. Everyone has their recorders faced toward the talent and alternates between asking questions and writing things down. I mostly stare at my notebook, but I look up at everyone when I don't think they're looking.

"I really think Art and I just wanted to work together again," Dennis is saying now. "We've been getting together over the years, running into each other, and every time, we'd always say, 'Wow, we need to find something to work on together.' It was just hard to find something that wouldn't be a waste of time."

"So that's interesting," a man says, adjusting his cap. "This was a chance for the two of you to work together again, after a string of box-office successes in the nineties. But it wasn't exactly going to be fun. How did you come to the heavy subject matter?"

"It was after seeing stories like this in the news," Dennis says. He tosses a glance at Art, who nods. Without a cowboy hat, his long ponytail rests openly on his shoulder. "Not necessarily Peter's story, but seeing that conversion therapy is still legal in many states, and wanting to do something about it."

I want to raise my hand, but no one is doing that, just talking and artfully stepping around each other if they speak at the same time. It doesn't seem like the type of thing I'm made for. I swallow, but my throat remains dry.

"Um," I say. My voice sounds squeaky, so I clear my throat. "Do any of you have a personal connection to the story? Besides watching it in the news?"

Dennis stares at me like he didn't realize I was here. For a second, the table is silent as everyone seems to think. The other journalists hold on to their pens, waiting for an answer. Marius stares right at me. Silent.

"I think a lot of us have family members who are gay," Art offers up. "My son is gay, and I wouldn't want anything like this to ever happen to him."

The rest of the cast nods, seemingly pleased with this answer. It's . . . not exactly what I was expecting. I thought they'd talk a bit more. But maybe it's not the type of question anyone wants to answer in front of a bunch of people.

"So," another journalist says, "Grace—"

"I'm sorry," Marius says, cutting them off. "Josie, you asked me a question the other day, and I never got to answer it. I want to answer it now."

Everyone looks at me.

I open my mouth, but nothing comes out.

"You!" Art says, pointing a finger at me. "You're the little lady from the press conference."

I try to slide down in my seat, but Alice smacks my shoulder.

The other journalists continue writing. Something tells me they're also writing about me—the journalist who got called out by name by one of the stars of the movie at a roundtable. On the bright side, I'm not being called out in a *bad* way. At least, I don't think I am.

"Yeah, it's her," Marius says, leaning forward. "It was a really good question—if you weren't there, Josie asked me how race influenced my character's experience. She didn't get the time to finish, but I've been thinking about it for a while."

Penny turns her attention back to me. I can't read her expression.

"I think, even though it's not explicit, it influences him a lot," Marius continues. His gaze bores into me, but it's so heavy that I don't think I can look away. "Peter's pretty much the only Black person in his community, besides his mom. Between not being able to be out—or really open—about his sexuality and then being one of the only people of color, he's pretty isolated, so that influenced how I played him. I wanted him to be quiet and sort of—I don't know—"

He pulls his arms closer to his body, wrapping them around his torso.

"Closed in?" He makes a face and a few people laugh. "And that's *before* he has this horrible experience at the camp, where again, he's like the only Black person. He's with other queer kids, but they're not . . . they don't have the same experiences. Peter finds a sort of community with them. It's just, if they were to have certain conversations . . . they probably wouldn't go the way he hopes. And I think he knows that, even as he makes friends with Emma"—he points at Penny—"and everyone else."

People nod, jot things down, but I'm frozen. Alice glares at me.

"Um," I choke out. "Thank you."

Dennis glances at Marius and then at me.

"Of course," he adds, "this isn't really a story about race. Marius just happens to be Black. Peter, he wasn't—he wasn't written with any race in mind. He's supposed to be a character anyone can relate to."

Penny rolls her eyes. I bite my lip to keep from laughing.

"Right," one of the other Black journalists says. "Jumping off of that point . . ."

Her question fades out as I jot down as much of Marius's answer as I can remember. When I glance up, he's still looking over at me. He smiles. I smile back.

@JosieTheJournalist: love it when people forget about me. truly. it's the best

CHAPTER 13

The next day is more of the same. We're invited down to the conference room, but instead of lunch, we're served breakfast: fluffy little pastries and tea and all sorts of fruit.

"Is this Texas culture?" I ask Alice. She loads her plate up with everything and flags down the waiter for more coffee every time he comes within a ten-foot radius.

"I don't know," she says. "I always thought Texas culture was Juneteenth and Beyoncé."

That's . . . not too far off from what I thought, honestly.

Today, instead of breaking into roundtables, people are called for individual interviews with the talent. That means it's taking a lot longer for people to be escorted out. I've already had a full cup of coffee and Alice has had three. Now I'm even more jittery than usual. Part of it is definitely the coffee, but it's also because I'm supposed to interview Marius again.

I shouldn't be this nervous. This isn't the first time I've interviewed Marius on this trip, and it won't be the last. It's just . . . I don't think I'll be able to disconnect. If he's nice, I'll be filled with pleasant feelings, and I'll beat myself up about having a crush. If he's rude (which I sincerely doubt), I'll feel bad about that, too. And now there's even more pressure to make sure my questions are good. Is he going to be comparing them all to the one I asked at the press conference? The one I thought of off the top of my head?

Alice taps down on my phone, making me look up.

"Do you need me to come in with you?"

"Why?" I ask genuinely. "Do you have somewhere else to be?"

"I've been hanging out with some of the interns."

She points a thumb toward a table several feet behind us. Instead of casually dressed journalists with their noses in notebooks, this table is full of young people wearing suits or skirts, most of them gray. They chatter to each other and sip from coffee mugs. All of them have name tags on their lapels.

"Interns?" I repeat. "Since when . . . ?"

"I need *something* to do when you're not around."

Alice doesn't look up from her phone. At the intern table, another girl pulls out her phone, looks down at it, and laughs.

How is Alice making more friends than I am? I mean, this isn't even about making friends, but somehow Alice is doing it faster than me. She's always been like this—bonding with people after a three-minute conversation, while I struggle to even keep a conversation *going* for three minutes. I kind of hate her for it.

Chill out, Josie. I force myself to take a deep breath. Even though it sucks to admit, Alice needs *something* to do while she's chaperoning me.

"Oh," I say. It comes out harsh and awkward. "Um, so what are your friends like?"

Alice glances up, quirking an eyebrow. "Do you really care?"

"Yeah!" I say. "Why wouldn't I?"

She narrows her eyes so slowly that I feel myself squirming in my seat. Finally, she opens her mouth to say something, but she's interrupted by a man appearing next to our table.

"Josephine Wright?" he says. "You're up next."

I clear my throat and pick up my bag. Alice shoots the peace sign at me, sliding out of her seat. For a second, I think she's coming with me, but then she's grabbing her bag and going over to the intern table. The other girl with the phone glances up and smiles, saying something to the rest of the group. Smiles spread around the table. Alice grins.

How does she do that? It's so unfair.

"Miss Wright?" the man says. "Right this way."

I glance back at Alice one more time. She's leaning against the girl's chair, laughing loudly about something. No one else in the room even seems bothered by how loud she is.

I've always prided myself on being different from Alice in pretty much every way. She's tall and thin, while I'm short and fat. She wasn't interested in grades when she was in high school, but I was. She was in a ton of extracurriculars, like student council and yearbook, while I mostly stayed at home, working on articles for the school newspaper. She's always had a lot of friends. I haven't. It doesn't normally bother me, but right now I'm jealous. I'm jealous of Alice, and I hate it.

—

The room is like the one where we did the roundtable, except the table is smaller, and there are people brought in, one by one. A PR person actually sits at the table with us. As I set up my notebook and recorder, I feel her studying me. My neck starts to sweat.

Art Springfield walks in a moment later, all movie star, and part of me wants to snap a picture for Dad. He wears a big black cowboy hat, blue jeans, and a strand of leather around his neck. He actually swaggers over to the chair. I swallow.

"Well," he says, leaning back in his chair. "Been doing this all morning. I'm game for whatever you've got. Ask me anything."

Judging by the sharp look the PR person gives me, I definitely shouldn't ask anything I want. I quickly glance down at my notebook.

"Um, right," I say. "I think one of the interesting things about your character is that, like, he isn't just one thing. He thinks he's really doing the right thing for his son, and even once his wife starts pushing against the choice they've made, he's stubborn about it, even as he does his own investigation. It's like he's this macho guy who doesn't want to listen to anyone else, but he's also really loving and emotional about his relationship with his son. How do you build the layers of a character like that?"

The PR person looks up at me. Art Springfield cocks his head to the side.

I bite my lip. Did I say something wrong?

"Actually," Art Springfield says, leaning forward, "that's real interesting. When I think about it . . ."

I'm still writing notes fifteen minutes later when Dennis Bardell shows up in the room. He glances between Art Springfield and me before taking a step back toward the door.

"Oh," he says. "Am I early?"

"You're actually right on time," the PR person says. "Mr. Springfield's interview ran over."

I feel myself flush, even though it isn't technically my fault. I only asked three questions. Who would've thought that the guy would have so much to say? I'll have to tell Dad about it tonight when I call home.

"It's not a problem," Art Springfield says, waving the director over. "Just got a bit lost talking to this little lady. She really makes ya think."

I bite back a smile. When I glance up, Dennis Bardell is staring at me. I can't read his expression. He's even harder to read once he's seated at the table and Art Springfield is out of the room.

"I actually have a question about the shot at the very beginning of the movie," I say, shifting in my seat. "The one where the camera lingers on that pack of dogs as they're crossing the screen? And it feels like they're taking forever? What was the meaning behind that?"

"Wow." Dennis Bardell rubs his hand over his balding head. "I hate to say it, but that was actually a happy accident. Our cameraman happened to be rolling when we were setting up for one of the rural scenes up in Maine. I thought it was an interesting shot to pull viewers in with."

Oh. That's it? I figured there'd be more of a complicated metaphor or something.

"It definitely catches the eye," he says, as if he can read my mind. "Doesn't it?"

"Oh, yeah," I say. "Definitely."

My chest tightens as we get closer to the end of the interview. I'm supposed to talk to Marius next. What I'm feeling isn't anxiety—it's something else. Something bubbly.

"Well, thank you so much," I say. "For your time."

He nods, barely lingering long enough for me to shake his hand. I only have a few seconds to myself before I hear someone else approaching. At the sound of the door opening, I whip my head around.

"Oh," I say. "Um, Penny? Hi?"

The PR woman glances up, eyebrows drawn. "Miss Livingstone? Your interview isn't scheduled for—"

"Marius and I actually switched time slots," Penny says. She walks into the room like she owns the place. "I thought that'd be okay."

The PR woman purses her lips and stands up.

"Just one moment," she says, already typing into a phone as she walks out the door. "I need to make sure this is approved. . . ."

Penny plants herself down next to me with an eye roll.

"Louise, huh?"

I blink over at the door, cracked open a few inches, and rub my temples.

"Sorry," I say. "This is just— What's going on?"

"Well, it *looks* like the shining star didn't show up."

"Uh," I say. "Why didn't his, um, publicist call me?"

Penny shrugs. I glance down at my notebook, questions scrawled for Marius. Part of me is disappointed. But maybe his publicist called Ms. Jacobson and she just hasn't gotten the message to me yet? I pull my phone out of my pocket, but there aren't any messages waiting for me, not even in my email inbox.

Outside, Louise's sharp voice says something I can't make out. I bite my lip. Is this a big deal?

"Look," Penny says, leaning forward, "I'm not supposed to tell anyone. But the director for his next movie already has him doing rehearsals."

"His next movie," I repeat. "Uh—the one with Roy Lennox?"

Penny makes a face that looks like a grimace, but it vanishes so fast that I'm not sure if I imagined it or not. Even if it was there, it'd be understandable, since Roy Lennox is one of those directors white boys latch onto and worship and mansplain about.

"I'm not supposed to talk about it," she repeats. "Honestly? He overslept and I'm trying to buy him some time. This is his first movie, you know? Don't want him to get in trouble."

"Right," I say. "Um, you and I could talk right now. It's just that I was supposed to have an interview—"

"Yeah, that." She chews on her lip. "I think his publicist is scheduling phone interviews with all the journalists he's missed, but *you* can probably come out with us tomorrow."

Tomorrow? Everyone is flying to Chicago later today—does she want me to go out with them in the next city?

"Uh," I say. "What?"

"We're supposed to—" She waves her hand. "*Explore.* Chicago. It's, like, our one day off, so—whatever, it was his idea. But he's the one who screwed up here, so he should have to make up for it, right? So you can just interview him then."

"But . . ." My voice trails off. I've already gotten face time with Marius, so that isn't a problem, but this entire situation just rubs me the wrong way.

"What if I have plans tomorrow?" I settle on.

Penny shrugs. "Then you have plans."

My shoulders relax, but only by a fraction.

"You don't have to come," she continues, pulling out her phone. "But the offer's there, if you want. Let me give you my number, just in case. You're here for the long haul, right? The whole tour?"

The door opens and a stone-faced Louise steps back inside.

"Fifteen minutes," she says.

I barely register her words. I can't stop staring at Penny, who grabs one of my pens, leans over, and writes a phone number in my notebook. A few days ago, I thought she hated me. I'm not sure if she still does—or if she ever did.

"Josie?"

I blink. Penny is sitting back in her chair, looking at me expectantly.

"Yeah," I say, flipping my notebook to a new page. "I'm here for the long haul."

CHICAGO, ILLINOIS

CHAPTER 14

Alice and I have barely gotten settled into our Chicago hotel on Friday night when there's a knock at the door.

"Alice?" I say. "Did you invite any of the interns over?"

It's sort of a joke, but she just shrugs.

"Not yet," she says. "We were supposed to find a cool bar that doesn't card to hang out in, but that's for later tonight. Maybe one of your friends?"

I almost fire back that I don't *have* any friends, at least not here.

Another knock. I sigh and shove my suitcase out of the way before heading to the door. I don't know what I'm expecting, but it's not Penny and Marius standing out in the hallway, bundled up in jackets, hats, and gloves.

"Hey," Penny says, holding her hand up in greeting. "You ready to go?"

I blink. Marius smiles, his shoulders up close to his ears.

"Hi, Josie," he says. "Look, I wanted to apologize about—"

"Ew, stop that," Penny says, smacking his shoulder. "You can do that once we get her out. And you *are* coming out, right?"

"Oh," I say, looking back into the room. Alice is spread out on her bed, texting someone. "Yeah, I just, uh, thought you would've forgotten about me."

"I'm pretty sure that was directed at you," Penny says, glancing at Marius. He frowns.

"No," I say. God, why does she have to be like this? "No, I just— Forget it. Um, let me grab my bag, I guess."

"And a jacket," Marius calls. "It's pretty cold."

I get a jacket, then head out the door.

Despite the cold, it's beautiful as we walk around downtown Chicago. I just sort of wish we'd find somewhere to sit— somewhere warm—instead of hanging out on the sidewalk. Still, the air feels cleaner. Like I can take a deep breath.

"So," Marius says after we've been walking for a few minutes. "Am I allowed to apologize now?"

I glance at Penny and she shrugs.

"I don't know," she says. "I guess it's up to Josie now."

"Sure you can," I say. "But I'd kind of like to know where we're going first."

"Oh!" Marius looks down at his phone. "I figured we could go to the Bean—you know, that big steel sculpture?"

"Now?"

I'd normally be embarrassed at how I'm acting, and there *is* a part of me that wonders if I seem too much like a baby, but it's too cold for me to care. I can see my breath coming out in little puffs in front of me. That's not . . . natural.

"He's just being annoying," Penny says. She's wearing a knitted hat and scarf and looks like she stepped out of a J.Crew catalog. "We're looking for—or *supposed* to be looking for—this deep-dish place. Marius, did you get us lost again?"

"It was *one* time, Penny—"

I giggle, despite myself. Marius stops and looks at me. His cheeks are pink, probably from the cold. He grins back.

"Just a few more minutes," he says. "It's probably a tourist trap."

"Probably," Penny agrees. "But pizza is pizza, right?"

She's wrong. I thought this place would be dingy and dirty and sort of charming, but it looks like it was just built, with nice beige columns and sleek black furniture. I see some of the people sitting around and realize I've never seen pizza like this. It looks like one of the pies we ate at Thanksgiving, except it's filled with tomato sauce.

Marius asks for a table for three in the dining room, which again totally wasn't what I expected. At home, the pizza places are in shopping centers and have wooden tables that look like they were bought at garage sales. There's no *dining room*, at least not a real one. Not only does this place have table service, there's a gigantic menu, with sandwiches and starters or whatever, all super expensive. My five hundred dollars has already dwindled to three hundred and we're not even halfway through the tour. Isn't pizza supposed to be cheap?

Penny browses the menu for a second, but Marius doesn't open his. When the waiter comes back, he just flashes this pretty grin and asks for "Whatever you recommend" in such a flattering way that even I want to blush.

"So," Marius says as soon as the waiter leaves. "I want to apologize. Seriously, this time, even if Penny doesn't want me to."

Penny rolls her eyes, sipping her water.

"I told you about the movie I'm doing next," he says, placing his hands on the table. "Roy—he expects a lot from his actors. I've been working and rehearsing via video chat and—well, it's not your problem. I just wanted you to know that I would never blow you off on purpose. I overslept, and when I woke up, I had a dozen calls from Penny, and I felt horrible."

I bite my lip. I feel uncomfortable and I don't know why.

Maybe I should ask more about the Roy Lennox movie he's doing. Is it normal to be doing a press tour and rehearsals at the same time? How does that even work?

"Are you having a hard time?" I ask, tugging at my jacket strings. "Like, feeling, um, overwhelmed? Do you think you could talk to him about it?"

Penny makes a face down at the table. I make another mental note to ask her about this, if I can ever get any time alone with her. It could be as simple as her not liking Lennox's movies, but still, with that documentary coming out about his career, maybe I can find a way to tie it into the profile.

"No." Marius's eyes go wide. "No, no, of course not. It's, like, absolutely the biggest honor."

I don't have a notebook or a recorder out, but I'm already trying to remember everything about this, like how he looks super surprised and maybe freaked out. Like how he didn't really answer my question. Like how Penny isn't saying anything.

"Here we go," the waiter says, appearing with a gigantic deep-dish pizza. "Enjoy! I'll be back to know what you think."

Marius smiles back, but not in the same way he did before. I feel like I messed something up, and I'm not sure how to make things go back to normal.

"Anyway," Penny says, "Josie, Marius told me you're still in high school. That's incredible."

Um. That I'm in high school? Or that I'm in high school and I'm here?

"Yeah," I say, trying my best to figure out how to eat this pizza. "We do this big capstone project before graduation, so this is mine. It's supposed to look good for colleges."

Penny nods, like she understands the whole college thing, even though she never went.

"Where do you want to go?" Marius asks. There's tomato sauce on his mouth. I glance down at my own plate. Eating around other people makes me feel weird.

"Spelman," I say. "It's this all-girls school for—"

"Yeah, I know about it," Marius says, wiping his mouth. "Wow, how cool."

"Yeah."

Penny and Marius glance at each other, but I don't know what it means. I eat more of my pizza (which is actually pretty good).

"Did you have some questions you wanted to ask?" Penny asks after a few minutes. "For, you know, your story?"

Oh. I do have questions, but I'm not sure what this is—if it's a hangout or an interview or if I should be asking questions here. I already asked Marius something, and it seemed like he didn't want to answer. And what will it be like to ask them both questions at the same time?

"Um," I say. "Well, just, um, how are the press junkets? On your end, anyway."

"Oh," Marius says. I can't exactly tell, but he looks . . . relieved, I think. "It's sort of—"

"The worst," Penny cuts in. "It never stops."

I wipe my hands on a napkin and start writing in shorthand.

"Geez, Penny." Marius does this smile where he hides his lips. "You know she's going to print this, right?"

"It's okay," Penny says. "Everyone knows it's true. The studio wants you to act all excited and remember talking points and be *on* all the time. That's why your question after the screening threw Marius off."

My head snaps up. Marius's cheeks are red again.

"You didn't screw anything up," he says, leaning closer to me. "Seriously."

"Dennis just got irritated," Penny says, shaking her head.

"Like asking why you had to bring race into it when it wasn't even a story about race and stuff like that."

My stomach sinks. I don't think I asked anything wrong, but I don't want the director to hate me.

"I—I didn't mean to, like, start anything," I say. "It was just something I thought about when I watched the movie."

"Of course," Marius says. "You and every other Black person. There's nothing wrong with what you said. Dennis was just being ridiculous."

I glance at my napkin. I'm writing everything down, but I'm not sure how much of this I should include in the story. Am I writing a puff piece or something about real issues? It's hard to tell.

"Press junkets *can* be hard," Marius adds after a second. "The faces and the questions—it all starts to blur together. So that's why I remembered you. And your question."

I sneak a glance up. He's smiling, soft. I lift the corners of my mouth.

"It can be easy to get lonely, too," Penny adds. "That's one of the worst parts."

I try not to let my surprise show. It's pretty hard to picture her being lonely. Maybe that's why she and Marius seem to be friends.

"Well, we don't have to be lonely anymore," Marius says, drumming lightly against the table. "Josie's here, and now she's part of our little club, right?"

"Uh," I say. "What club?"

"The Lonely Hearts Club," Penny deadpans. "Only emotionally stunted teen prodigies allowed."

"Yeah, exactly." Marius makes a face. "Well, not exactly. I don't know about that *emotionally stunted* part—"

"No," I say. "It actually fits me perfectly."

Penny laughs, leaning over her plate. Her elbow starts to nudge Marius, who stares at me with a soft, open mouth.

"See," she says. "I *told* you."

It's weird to think of Penny telling him anything about me. I take another bite of pizza.

"Right." Marius clears his throat and lifts up his water glass. "To emotionally stunted teen prodigies."

As I clink my glass against his and Penny's, I can't help but smile.

@JosieTheJournalist: wow, men are terrifying

CHAPTER 15

"Is there anyone else from the cast you're planning on talking to?"

It's the next day, and Penny and I are in an empty Chicago hotel conference room for a one-on-one interview, sitting across from each other at a gigantic wooden table.

"I spoke to Art and Dennis back in Texas," I say. "And I sent an email to the screenwriter and one of the producers—uh, Bob something? His answer was pretty helpful."

"Okay," Penny says, counting on her fingers. "So Marius and me. You should probably talk to Grace—she's great. And maybe some of the other people who played characters at the conversion camp—they aren't here, but I'm sure you could call them or something."

I hurry to write this down. It's a great idea that I honestly didn't think of.

"That's really smart," I say, nodding as I write. "And I think maybe I'll talk to Roy Lennox, if he'll answer me. It's a long shot, but he's around promoting the documentary about his career, so he might be nicer than he's known to be."

Penny's face looks pinched. I wait for her to say something, but she's gone silent, staring at the table in between the two of us.

"What?" I want to sound lighthearted, but it's hard on a normal day, let alone when someone seems to deflate right in front of me. "I— This might sound a little weird. But I noticed you don't seem to be a fan of his."

"I—" Her eyes dart around the room, even though we're the only ones in here. "Just don't talk to him, Josie. Promise me you won't talk to him. Okay? Stay away from him."

"I don't get it," I say, pushing away my notebook. "Why?"

She sighs, her entire body slumping against her chair. I can't read her expression, and I can't think of a reason why she wouldn't want me to talk to this guy. He's a famous director and has made some pretty awesome films, according to most critics. I guess she could tell me he's racist and I wouldn't be so surprised.

In a flash, Penny grabs my arm, pulling me forward. There's something sturdy about her expression. *Too* sturdy, like she's seconds away from cracking.

"What's wrong, Penny?" I ask. "Did something happen?"

All this silence makes it hard for me to breathe. I could tell myself everything is okay, but it'd be a lie. I'm anxious for a reason, and I'm not just blowing things out of proportion. Not this time.

"It's just . . ." Her voice trails off as she shakes her head. "I haven't heard good things about him. And I've had some close calls of my own. But you have to promise not to tell anyone. This can't go into your story."

"Yeah." It's hard to think about what to say. "My story is about Marius. It's fine."

"Okay." She takes a deep breath, pinches the bridge of her nose. Her voice drops to a whisper. "It's just that I did a movie with him once. I didn't have a big role or anything. And it was one of those movies about older guys, you know, having a midlife crisis, so there were a few girls my age wandering around. He used to call me behind the camera to look at the monitor so he could tap me on the ass. It was just that, at first, and then he'd find excuses to stand behind me and, like . . . he got kind of gropey. Know what I mean?"

I don't trust myself to speak. If I open my mouth, I might throw up.

I've had guys pull at my shirt in hallways and make comments about my boobs. Maggie has complained about the jerks at her job. But it was never like this. Penny keeps glancing back and forth, breathing the way I do during a panic attack. I didn't think she was afraid of anything.

"Oh God." My voice cracks. "Did you— Does anyone know?"

"Just a few other girls." Her gaze is steely. "I broke my contract, left before I could finish shooting my part. He didn't give me a hard time about leaving. I think he guessed I would."

"But . . ." I shake my head. "Someone should know. It's not *okay*—"

"Of course it isn't," she snaps. "But it'd be my word against his. He's *Roy Lennox* and I'm just some girl who used to be on Disney Channel. I'm already fighting to get people to take me seriously. No one would even look at me again if I tried to speak about this."

"I don't even know what to say."

I've never heard anyone mention this before, but Penny is right. Why *would* anyone mention it? Roy Lennox could destroy them with a flick of his hand. But still. There's about to be a documentary celebrating his greatness. People should *know*, shouldn't they?

"I wanted you to know." She reaches for my arm, squeezes. I hate that *she* is watching out for *me*. "He scared me when I was alone with him. I don't want you to be in that position."

"But I'm seventeen." I shake my head. "He wouldn't . . ."

She gives the slightest shake of her head. I bite my lip. All of a sudden, I feel like crying, but I can't. Not if Penny isn't crying. This is something that happened to her. It's not about me.

"You're new to all of this," she says after a moment, eyes roaming over my face. "There are some things you don't understand yet."

I normally hate when people say things like that. They make me feel like I'm younger than I am, like I don't know anything, like I don't belong. But I know Penny is right. This is something I *don't* get, because I've never had to deal with it, not like she has. And it makes me anxious the way I was back in middle school, when I used to get so anxious that I'd puke in the mornings before the bus came.

"Do you—" I swallow. "Do you know other women who had the same experience? If you told them about me, do you think—"

"No." She shakes her head, folding her arms. "You're really nice, Josie. Seriously. I'm glad I met you. But there's— It's something we don't talk about. They'd all kill me for telling you."

The compliment doesn't do anything to undo the growing knot in my stomach. Will Marius notice if this happens to the women on this next set? Or will he just ignore it, like everyone else? And how many girls my age will be there? Why is this happening how can I stop it who is watching who is helping this can't happen it's not allowed it's wrong it's not *fair*—

My breaths come out fast and then stop altogether. I close my eyes, holding my breath. Penny squeezes my arm again.

"Don't worry about it," she says. "You know and you'll be okay. It's fine."

I can't tell if she's trying to convince herself or me.

ATLANTA, GEORGIA

CHAPTER 16

All I can think about on the plane to Atlanta that night is what Penny said. About Roy Lennox. About how people are still watching his movies and honoring him because they don't know what he's done.

They should. Everyone should know what a creep he is.

He shouldn't be able to keep making movies and harassing women on his sets. He shouldn't be able to go to award shows and get hailed as this great genius when he's hurting people. Other people on the plane are snuggled under blankets, eyes closed, but I'm too anxious to sleep.

"You're being quiet," Alice says. "You're not gonna ramble on about that guy?"

I don't have the energy to tell her to be quiet. I just feel sick. The plane lurches and I shift forward like I might puke.

"Hey." Alice places a hand on my arm. "Do you need to go to the bathroom?"

"No," I say, my voice almost a moan. "Alice, what would you do if you knew about something bad but you couldn't tell anyone?"

Alice frowns. "Did you do something?"

"No," I say. "You have to swear you won't tell."

She searches my face.

"Okay," she says. "What is it?"

It all comes up like vomit. I'm not sure if journalists are supposed to pour their hearts out to their older sisters, but that doesn't keep me from doing it. In a whisper, I tell her everything Penny told me about Roy Lennox, about what he did, about how there might be other girls, about Marius signing on to his next film.

"Jesus," Alice says when I'm finished. "Fuck. He always seemed like a creep, but wow."

"It's ridiculous," I say. "He's probably still doing it because no one knows."

"I don't know." Alice shakes her head. "I think—it sounds like an open secret."

"I don't know what that means."

"It means the girl—whoever told you—will probably warn other girls. I really doubt she's the only one," she says, pushing up her tray table. "And I'm sure there are executives and other men who know about what's going on. It's shit, but that's how these things go."

"It shouldn't be the girls' responsibility to warn each other, though," I say, leaning back in my seat. I hate being anxious about things I can't fix right away. "This shouldn't—it shouldn't be a thing."

"Yeah." Alice goes quiet for a second. "Maybe you could write about it."

"What?"

"You write all the time," she points out. "Doesn't that help you figure things out?"

Normally it does. I hate carrying things around in my head, but putting them on paper lifts the weight a little.

"I guess so." I tap my fingers against my tray. "It just feels wrong, like I'm in over my head. Who am I to tell their stories?"

"I mean . . ." She pauses. "This sucks, but I feel like every woman has a story. You know that guy who used to harass Maggie at the supermarket? And the really shitty boyfriend I had junior year? Stuff like that."

I've never been coerced into sex by a creepy older dude. No older dude has done anything to me, period. Sometimes guys are weird at Cora's when I'm working the counter—telling me about how I grew up pretty or asking how old I am—but that isn't the same as what Penny went through. And I've never had a shitty boyfriend, just shitty crushes and first kisses.

Middle school, though—that was definitely a different story.

It was when the anxiety first started up. I'd get sick every morning before going to school and barely slump through the day. I'm not sure how I survived it. I remember general themes of middle school, like being self-conscious, not wanting to wear the right-sized bras, and covering myself in the locker room. I used to sit alone at the lunch table. No one paid much attention to me at all, except when they were saying something rude.

Lots of kids used to tease me or make fun of me, but Ryan King . . . he was the worst. The absolute worst. He made everything horrible. I haven't brought him up since it happened. I try to shove everything from middle school to the bottom of my brain. Sometimes it works. Other times, like with my memories of Ryan, it doesn't.

"Do you remember . . . ?" I swallow. "Like, do you remember Mom coming to have a meeting when I was in middle school?"

"Mom had *so* many meetings when you were in middle school," Alice says. "So you're gonna have to narrow that down for me."

"Whatever." I flush. "Forget it."

"No," Alice says, kicking me with the tip of her foot. "Tell me. Was it about you throwing up? Or when you hid in the bathroom for a whole class period?"

God, I really hate thinking about this.

"No," I say. "It was like—there was this one kid who was, like, really into my boobs. I don't know. You remember how I grew really fast? He used to, like, track every new change and tell everyone when I was wearing a bra. And, like . . . he followed me to the bathroom once. And tried to take off my shirt."

Alice is quiet.

"I think—" My throat is dry. "I don't even know why I'm talking about it. But I keep thinking about Penny, and it's hard not to think about it. How scared I was. And he kept saying it was just a joke. At the meeting, with Mom and the principal and everyone, he just kept saying it was a joke. I was crying and I felt stupid, like everyone thought I was making a big deal out of nothing."

"Not everyone," Alice says. She rubs her jaw. "I remember now. Mom flipped the fuck out. And then Dad found out and they were both so mad. You came home and wouldn't talk to any of us. It was kind of—I don't know. Scary."

I bite my lip. For a second, I hate Penny for making me think about all of this, but I swat that thought away fast. This isn't her fault. None of it is.

"So, yeah," Alice says after a second. "There you go. Something happened to you."

I squirm in my seat.

"Not really," I say. "It's way different. Like, my thing was a kid fooling around. Hers was an actual adult man harassing her while she was at work."

"Well," Alice says, "they're both assaults."

"Not really."

"Josie." Alice gives me a look. "What happened to you is literally the definition of assault. You know that, right?"

"It was in middle school."

"So?"

Ugh. I don't know how to make her understand. What Ryan King did to me was horrible, but lots of kids were mean to me in middle school. I always got stuck with "bad" kids. That was one of the worst things about being quiet. Teachers put the guys who acted up around me, like my presence would make them simmer down.

Middle school wasn't exactly the brightest time in my life.

"You don't have to be assaulted by a creepy man for something to count," Alice says. "I hope you know that."

The Fasten Seat Belt sign lights up. I lean back and close my eyes.

"Do you know that, Josie?"

"Yeah, Alice," I sigh out. "I know."

I try not to think about it for the rest of the flight, but it's impossible. Even though I'm bone-tired when we land, I pull out my phone to search for Penny's number.

She was brave enough to share with me. I can do the same for her.

CHAPTER 17

"Josie."

I groan into my pillow. It's Alice's voice, but that doesn't give me any more reason to get out of bed.

"*Josie.* Your phone keeps ringing." She shoves my back. I barely move. There's drool on my pillow. Ew. "I don't know who it is—it's an unknown number—but you can't be that tired. You've been sleeping for forever."

I know I fell asleep as soon as we got to our hotel room, but I have no idea what time it is now. I sit up and rub my eyes. Alice frowns at me.

"Mom wanted to know where you were," she says. "I told her you were sleeping. You're welcome."

I roll my eyes. My scarf is falling off my head, the blue-and-green design blurring my vision.

"And it's noon. For all I know, you have an event or something that you're missing."

I open my mouth to say something, but my phone's shrill ringing cuts me off. Alice stares at the bed. I yank my scarf all the way off my head and hold the phone up to my ear.

"What?" I snap.

"Oh. Is this Josie?"

"Penny?" I blink. "What's up?"

Alice slips into the bathroom, closing the door behind her.

"I got your text," she says simply. "Anyway, I wanted to see if you were available for lunch or something."

Honestly, I didn't think about what would happen after I sent Penny the text about Ryan King following me into the bathroom and tearing off my shirt, the part I didn't want to talk to Alice about. It felt right in the moment. Like we were on even ground. Like I was showing her that she's not alone. But now I'm not so sure.

"Oh," I say, reaching for my computer. "Yeah, just let me check."

I open the itinerary up on my laptop. We're at the beginning of the second week of the trip, and most of the days say, "Up to your discretion." It's weird, going from being super scheduled to having to figure out what to do on my own. I'm supposed to interview Marius back at the hotel later today, but I should probably lock down more interviews with him. There's also the fact that thinking about Penny makes the anxiety in my belly flare up. It's like I should be doing something to help. Something I haven't figured out yet. That she's inviting me out—doing something for me when I'm not doing anything for her—just makes me feel worse.

"Um," I say. "Do you have anything scheduled for today?"

"I did," she says. "Some news show. It was at six this morning. I wanted to die."

"That sucks," I say, rubbing my eyes. "Um. Okay. Where should we meet?"

⌣

The best thing about Atlanta is that there are so many Black people—all shades, different hairstyles, together and apart, walking around like they own the place. I love driving out here with my family whenever we find the time. This is the closest I've been to home the entire trip.

I look up at the sign out front to make sure I'm at the right place. It's smack in the middle of a cluster of stores, all sleek and black, with signs in different fonts. Posters are plastered on the windows. One in particular makes me freeze.

It's him, with his salt-and-pepper beard, staring into the distance. ROY LENNOX: A LIVING LEGEND appears in big red letters above his head. Below are the details of the documentary: a two-day televised event featuring interviews with celebrity fans, collaborators, and the man himself. My stomach rocks like a ship at sea.

"Josie!"

Penny presses me to her chest. I blink in surprise.

"I'm so glad to see you," she says, drawing back. "How are you?"

Penny's face is open, eyes searching my face like she's actually interested in my answer. I look away.

"I'm good," I say. My eyes are drawn to the poster behind her. There's no way she hasn't seen it. "What about you?"

I want to ask what it's like. She *knows* what Roy Lennox has done. He hurt her and no one else knows. Or maybe they do, but they don't believe her.

I don't think I could stand it.

Penny's eyes dart to the poster. It's only for half a second, but I notice. She swallows.

"Come on," she says, tugging at my arm. "Let's talk inside."

It's a café like the one I first went to with Marius. That feels like it was weeks ago, even though it was only one. Penny picks a comfy-looking seat near the fireplace—why is there a fireplace in Atlanta?—and I sit in the green armchair next to her.

"So," I say before she can change the subject, "are you okay?"

"I guess so." She shrugs. There's a smile on her face, but this one is clearly fake. "But that's not what I wanted to talk about. Your text got me thinking, and now I have an idea."

I raise a brow. We're in a public place, which means either she's confident talking about this in public or she wants to make sure I don't freak out.

"An idea?" I say. "Like, for my Marius profile? Or . . . for a role you want?"

"No, no." She waves a hand. "I thought I could help you write something."

"Oh." I hesitate. "I didn't know you liked to write."

"That's—not the point," she says, shaking her head. "I want you to write something about him. About everything he's done. I want to ruin him."

My mouth opens. Nothing comes out but a croak. Penny breaks into laughter. She's inches away from my face, like she's staring into my head, analyzing every thought to gauge my response.

Good thing she can't actually read my brain. Because *what the fuck?*

I *want* to do something to help, but this is completely ridiculous. This is a job for an actual journalist. This is a job for someone with decades of experience and talent and sources. I barely know how to write a *profile*.

"Penny." I shake my head. "That's— Oh my God. It's—"

"Don't say no." She rests her hand on mine. "*Please* don't say no."

"I just don't get it." My throat is dry. "It's a great idea. Really. I think it's so important, and I'll do whatever I can to help. I just don't think I'm the right person to write about this. It's not my story, you know?"

"But it is," Penny says. "Not exactly, but you know what it's like."

I bite my lip. She makes it sound so simple.

"I could find people for you to interview," she continues. "People I've talked to."

"You're closer to them. Why don't you just interview them?"

"Even if I do, I can't write," she says. "Not like you can. I've read your work. You're talented, Josie."

Normally I tell people age doesn't matter. I don't mention mine in any of my pitches because I want people to look at my work instead of how old I am. But this feels like something out of my league. It's too important to mess up.

"Yeah, but I've only ever written soft stuff before," I try again. "What if I do this all wrong?"

"I don't know if there's a *right* way to write something like this. I can't—" Her voice breaks. It makes me go rigid. "I can't—I can't keep watching people worship him like he's some sort of saint. I can't."

I immediately squeeze her hand, surprising myself. She squeezes back.

"Please," she says. "Just tell me you'll think about it."

I stare down at our hands. Maybe I have anxiety because I always think about everything, always try to make sure everyone else is okay. It freaks me out. I never thought of it as a good thing. I *still* don't think it's a good thing. But maybe it's just a magnified part of me. The caring, so big, so amplified, that it becomes too much for me.

Can I use it to help someone else?

"Fine." I clear my throat. "I'll think about it."

CHAPTER 18

Somehow, I'm supposed to interview Marius after that conversation. He's coming up to my room for us to talk. I don't know why I ever thought it would be a good idea.

"Okay," I say after letting him into the room. "This is awkward."

Alice isn't here, which means it's just the two of us.

Alone.

In my hotel room.

"It doesn't have to be." Marius plops down on the edge of my bed, bouncing only a little. "Not every silence has to be awkward."

So far, I've been taking notes about where we are when we speak—in a restaurant, at a clothing store, in a café—but writing that he's in my hotel room feels kind of shady. God, I'm so stupid for suggesting this. Hopefully it doesn't end in some journalistic scandal that finishes my career before it's had the chance to really start.

"Do you mind if I have something out of this?"

I blink. Marius is standing in front of the mini fridge. I want to tell him not to take anything, but when I get closer, I see there are already things missing. There's supposed to be four of everything—soda, mostly—but only two bottles of beer are left. Alice must've taken the others.

It's wild. I was only gone a few hours with Penny. I wonder if Alice and the intern gang started a party here and moved it somewhere else. I'm not surprised; I'm pretty sure that's what she does at her new *sorority*. Still, I'm pissed. Who does she expect to pay for this? Yeah, the magazine covered the room and told me to save receipts to be reimbursed, but I don't think that includes extras. I don't want them to think I'm taking advantage.

"Go ahead," I say, putting my hands on my hips. Screw it. If Alice can raid the fridge, so can I. I reach for a small bottle filled with dark wine.

"Uh." He blinks, holding a can of Coke. "Are you allowed to drink that?"

"My sister's nineteen and she helped herself," I say, grabbing a glass from the counter. They're for water, but I don't care. "So I guess that sort of stuff doesn't count here. And you can drink at eighteen in France, right?"

"Well, yeah." I hear him shift behind me. "But I don't want you to get so drunk that you stop asking questions."

Right. Questions. The reason we're here. Why does that make me feel disappointed?

"I'll be fine," I say, pouring myself a glass. "Do you want some?"

He's quiet for so long that I turn to face him. I don't know why he's staring at me so hard. All I did was offer him wine. Of course, he might think I'm being childish.

When our eyes meet, I'm the first to look away, barely lasting a few seconds.

"See?" My voice is hoarse. It's embarrassing. "This definitely counts as an awkward silence."

"Sorry." His voice is low. I watch him shove off his jacket, hang it over a chair. "I'd like some, yeah. As long as you feel okay with it."

"Why wouldn't I?" I pour another glass. "It was my idea."

"I know." He stands next to me, shoulder brushing against mine. I try to ignore it. "But I don't want you to, like, feel like I'm taking advantage of you."

"No." I push his glass toward him jerkily. "It'll make us feel fancy. I always feel like Olivia Pope when I drink, and we can just pretend Olivia is interviewing a talented young actor."

He blushes, taking the glass. Some of his wine—or maybe mine—has sloshed out. I wipe it up with the sleeve of my shirt. I'm guessing he doesn't notice. It drives Mom crazy when I do it at home.

I hold the glass to my lips. To my surprise, wine is nice, a million times better than the beer I've swiped at family parties. It tastes like strong, bitter juice, cranberry without the sugar. If only we had wineglasses—then I'd really be Olivia.

"So." Marius gestures between the two of us, at our glasses. "I'm guessing this part is off the record?"

"Oh, yeah." I glance at the recorder on my nightstand. "Just for right now. I'll turn on the recorder in a little bit."

He nods, sipping more from his glass. The wine stains his lips a darker red. I watch him lick the juice off until I realize he's staring at me. My face burns. I shift my gaze to my feet.

I can't read him and I hate it. Is he messing with me? When he stops and stares, is it some sort of act? He's an actor, after all.

"I've never been drunk before," he says, breaking the silence. I must look surprised, because he shrugs. "I've been high and everything, but never drunk."

"How?" I ask. "How do you make it to nineteen without getting drunk at least once?"

I never go anywhere and I've been drunk before. It was New Year's Eve, I was sixteen, and Mom and Dad left the champagne out when we were supposed to go to bed. I was curious and drank all that was left. When Maggie found me, I was stumbling over my feet. I would probably still be grounded right now if she hadn't covered for me.

"I don't know," he says. "Guess I never really got around to it."

"But you got around to getting high?"

"Well . . ." He pauses. "I used to drink a little, with my boyfriend, but he didn't like it too much. His dad was an alcoholic, and it freaked him out. So we just smoked weed instead."

I'm not sure how to respond, since he's just told me a million things at once. He used to drink with his boyfriend. He had a boyfriend. Okay. That doesn't necessarily mean he doesn't like girls. But that doesn't tell me if the boyfriend is still around or not. And I don't know how to ask without fumbling my words.

God, I hate that this is the first thing I think of.

"What?" Something in his face steels at my silence. "Do you have a problem?"

"No, no, of course not." I grip my glass. "Wow. I, uh, don't mean to be weird. I had a crush on a girl once, last year. That's what I was thinking about."

Crushing on Tasha, the nice girl involved in every school activity, was easy. She was the only one who talked to me. She invited me to sit with her friends and always partnered up with me before I could be left for last. I didn't realize it was a crush until Alice started making fun of me—"Josie has a crush on Brooke White's little sister"—but then it didn't matter, because we were making out in her bedroom and in the locker room and almost anywhere we wouldn't be spotted by people we knew.

I'm not sure if it's harder to have crushes on boys or girls. Maybe it depends on the person. All the boys I've liked were

132

brutal. They walked away or laughed when I told them I liked them. They pretended I didn't exist, even after I'd poured my heart out. But Tasha hugged me and gave away soft touches and kisses like it cost her nothing. She called other girls *pretty* and *smart* and smelled like perfume and lotion and genuine kindness. Which is easier—someone who is too nice or someone who is too harsh?

I've tried not to think about it, but it's hard. Sometimes I go on Twitter and see nonbinary people and something tugs in my stomach, too. The world is big and wide; there are so many people to choose from. It's overwhelming.

"I didn't have a lot of crushes," Marius says, breaking me out of my thoughts. "Wes and I, we've known each other since we were little. He lives in my building—used to, before he went to college upstate."

"Oh," I say. "That's probably good—that you didn't have a lot of crushes. They never really work out. I think they just suck."

"Well, I was with him for most of high school and it didn't work out." He puts his glass down. "Maybe high school just sucks in general."

"Now you're getting the idea."

He smiles, shaking his head. I want to ask if he also likes girls. I think about telling him that I also like guys. It shouldn't matter. This is about him, not about me. We should be talking on the record. Otherwise, this is a waste of time and money.

Still. I can't bring myself to just dramatically shift subjects, not after he shared something like that with me. So I do what I'd do with Alice or Maggie—I open my playlists. I hold my breath as I pull my phone out. Marius might think I'm ignoring him or being rude and leave. I force a breath out, looking up.

"Do you like Kendrick Lamar?"

"Yeah." Marius glances up. "Why?"

There's a stack of unused paper cups on top of the cabinet. Empty cups always work well as amplifiers, so I plop my phone in. After a second, Kendrick's voice fills the room. He makes it feel *full* in a way it wasn't before. Like his voice is pushing against the walls.

Maybe it's from my glass of wine. Maybe it's Kendrick. Whatever it is, I can't explain it. I just get up and start dancing. With Kendrick ringing in my ears, I shake my head and my arms and the rest of my body the way I would if my sisters were here. Whatever Marius might think of my body is an afterthought. My eyes are shut and I'm basking in the moment. The moment when I don't have to worry about anything.

Something shifts beside me. I blink my eyes open. Marius is moving in front of me, but it looks more like someone is pulling his body in different directions. I can't help but double over in laughter. Marius is good at a *lot* of things, but evidently, dancing is not one of them. He jumps up and down and doesn't seem to care that he's falling over, even when I pull him up on the bed.

"I haven't bounced on a bed since I was little," he says, struggling to speak over Kendrick (which is almost impossible). "Oh my God, why did I ever stop?"

I giggle, shaking my head. He's holding both my hands. Part of my brain wants to stop and analyze everything. What does this mean? Is the tender feeling in my chest warranted?

Whatever. I push the questions aside. Marius tilts his head back and raps all the words. I join him, our bodies going up, down, up, down.

Kendrick isn't the only artist on this playlist, which is for rocking out—there's some Frank Ocean, J. Cole, Childish Gambino, SZA. It's hard not to look at Marius when he's right here and we're holding hands. His face blurs in front of me, but eventually, he just bounces a little in place. His cheeks—he doesn't have *real* cheeks, like me, but there's enough there—are dotted with red. I can't tell if it's from jumping or because of the drinks.

I can't stop looking at him. This isn't how getting rid of crushes works. If anything, this is the hardest I've ever fallen.

Fuck.

CHAPTER 19

I wake up the next morning without a headache, but with Alice right in my face.

"Did you drink an entire bottle of wine? By *yourself*?"

Ah, this is the reason why Mom wanted Alice to come with me. My sister is almost—*almost*—as big a nag as our mother. I groan, running a hand through my hair as I sit up. It's sticking up all over the place because I went to bed without covering it.

"Come on. It's not a real bottle," I say. "Look at it. That's a tiny little thing. And I shared it with Marius, so even less alcohol than you think."

Her brows rise so high that it looks like they've disappeared.

"You brought him back *here*? I thought you were interviewing him in the lobby?"

"When did I say that?" I ask. "No, it was always supposed to be in the room. It's not like you were here, so I don't know why it's a big deal."

"It's a *big deal* because you're supposed to be interviewing him," she says, shaking her head. "We have one more week on this trip, and instead of working, you're here drinking with your subject."

What would *she* know? Writing is my thing. She can't take it like she took Spelman.

"I— You can't just—" I run a hand through my hair. There's so much I want to say, so much anger and frustration, that my mind goes blank. "You did it *first*."

"I didn't finish an *entire bottle*," she snaps. "You did, and now the people at the magazine are gonna see the charge and we'll have to make some sort of excuse. I thought you were more responsible than this."

"Don't *lecture* me," I say, already feeling a groan rise in my chest. "I'm not a baby. I understand how things work."

"Do you?" She leans in. "Interviewing your—whoever he is— alone in your hotel room and sharing a bottle of wine with him isn't professional. At *all*. *Deep Focus* is a gigantic magazine. What would your editor say if she knew?"

God, she's right. I can only hope that Marius doesn't tell anyone about what happened yesterday. It doesn't seem like the type of thing he would share, but still, if Ms. Jacobson heard about it, I'd be toast. This is such an incredible opportunity. I'd be devastated if I ruined it over something as silly as a crush or a bottle of wine. I hate how small she makes me feel, but Alice is right.

"I guess you're right," I finally say. It sucks to admit that, but it's even worse to have to say so out loud.

"You *guess*?" Alice kisses her teeth. "I don't know why I even bother."

She stomps away into the bathroom. A few seconds later, the shower starts. I shake my head and pull out my phone. I answer several texts from Mom and Dad—Yes, I'm having fun, yes, I'll try to take more pictures, yes, I promise I'll be safe and call you tonight—before turning to a text from Penny. For some reason, she texts like she's emailing.

Hi! I know you said you'd think about what we talked about yesterday, and I was just checking to see if you made a decision?

I blink. Somehow, I'd managed to forget about our conversation. Now I'm slammed back to reality. Roy Lennox, what he did to Penny, what he's probably already done to other women. That's not the only thing that comes back—for some reason, the conversation I had with Alice on the plane starts to replay in my mind.

What happened to you is literally the definition of assault. You know that, right?

I let out a heavy sigh and rub my forehead. This isn't even about me. This is about Penny. Penny, who is completely sure of the truth, otherwise she wouldn't have told me. Penny, who wants me to help her.

God. I'm not mature enough for this.

I text back: Yeah. Let's do it.

She responds in less than a second: Oh God, I love you.

Can you meet up tomorrow? We should talk about everything.

Actually.

I already spoke to my friend Julia and she's interested in talking to you.

Here's her number.

And there's a contact attached.

I sit and stare at my phone for almost a full minute. Right now, I feel like the human equivalent of at least five question marks. Maybe an exclamation point is tossed in there, too.

How did she find someone to talk to already? Has she been thinking about this, working on this, since yesterday? My stomach sinks. Was she working on this while I danced to Kendrick Lamar? God, why am I the worst?

There are too many things going on in my head. One

comforting fact stands out: if I'm doing this—which I guess I am now—I won't be doing it alone. Penny is here and she's going to help. It makes it a little easier to breathe. Just a little.

Because her friend Julia isn't just a regular Julia. The contact below the text is Julia Morrison. I know the name—and it's not from her acting.

I'm not sure what she was ever initially famous for—a bunch of movies in the nineties, I think. A quick Google search tells me she's in her midforties and has been doing made-for-TV films lately, though they fizzled out around 2017.

What she's infamous for: kissing her brother on the lips like Angelina Jolie (though she never bounced back from that), showing up to a premiere topless, shaving her head, ranting about how the world is out to get her, and getting arrested for possession of marijuana. All part of the celebrity breakdown playbook.

I swallow, instantly feeling guilty. I've never thought much about Julia Morrison. She just seemed like a crazy person. But it feels shitty to even call her crazy, especially since I know how scared I get that people will call me the same thing if they see me have a panic attack.

Anyway, she has a *reason* for acting the way she does. I scroll through her filmography to see that one of her first movies was a Roy Lennox production. Her performance as an orphaned prodigy in *Touch of the Heart* catapulted her into the public eye. How did she deal with that? Was it a one-time thing, or did she have to keep seeing him, over and over again? What finally made her snap?

Talk to her? I text back. When?

Now, preferably. She's expecting your call. I'm so sorry to spring this on you. Do you need me to reschedule?

Shit. This is a trap.

On one hand: *PENNY, WHAT THE ACTUAL FUCKING HELL?*

On the other: She's the one most impacted by this, so I can't really judge her.

But: *WHAT THE HELL?*

I rub my hands over my arms, even though I'm not cold. There's no way I can talk to a famous woman about a powerful man taking advantage of her. God. But I have to, don't I?

I could try to talk to her another time, but we fly to New York later today for the last leg of the tour, and I really need to start piecing the Marius profile together. I can't worry about this and write a profile of Marius at the same time. I'll freak out if I talk to Julia Morrison now, and I'll freak out if I have to find some way to reschedule later. I'm screwed no matter what.

No. I'll call her now.

I glance up at the bathroom door. The shower is still running. Alice's long showers are a pain in the ass when we're both at home, but it's pretty convenient right now. What else do I need? *Questions.* I pick my messenger bag up off the floor and pull out my notebook and a pen.

I'm not sure what's too much to ask and what isn't. I figure I'll just ask some basic questions and go from there, depending on how responsive she is. This is a topic I have to tread lightly on. I've never had to do that before. It might be easier if I just pretend it's a normal conversation, but we both know it isn't one.

Thank God I still have the app I downloaded when I first started doing phone interviews a few years ago. It records calls, which I'd rather do than put her on speaker and record, especially talking about something so sensitive.

Now comes the hard part. I stare at the contact number on

my phone screen but make no move to touch it and connect the call. Then, before I know it, I'm calling.

"*What?*"

I startle at the voice on the line.

"Oh," I say, because that's a great way to start off a conversation. "Um, hi, my name is Josie Wright. I'm a freelance journalist. Penny gave me your number. I'm working on something about . . ."

My voice trails off. What can I really say?

"About Lennox." Her voice is blunt. The words don't take any more air than they need. "Right, Penny and I were talking about it the other day. You already have a place lined up to publish?"

"Uh, no." I rub the back of my head. "I thought I'd figure that out after the piece was written."

"Good luck." She snorts. "I doubt anyone will pay attention unless you have some pretty big names—God bless Penny, but she doesn't count. They'll just laugh at the two of us. I might be able to give you some more names. Maybe Penny will, too. But it'll be hard to get them to talk to you. No one wants to talk about this shit."

"Yeah." My voice is a sigh. I fold my arms. "I get it. I don't want to force anyone to bring up bad memories, but I figured they were already coming back up because of the documentary. I just don't think he should be getting awards after—you know."

"Boy, *do* I know." She snorts again. "Well, what do you want to hear about?"

"Do you mind if I record you?"

"Whatever you need."

"Uh." I clear my throat. "Can I ask what happened? When it happened?"

"The set of *Touch of the Heart*—that was more than twenty

years ago now," she says. I'm not sure whether Penny told her how old I am or not, but something about the way she says it makes me think she knows. "It was my first really big movie, and I could already tell it was going to be Oscar bait. Lennox was . . . nice, I guess, at first. He knew everything was new for me and said he'd help make things easier to handle. I was in his trailer all the time."

My stomach tightens. I don't feel good about this. And there's something heartbreaking about how clearly she remembers this, when I worked so hard to block what happened to me in middle school.

But it makes me feel like she's spent years, more than two decades, reliving this story over and over again. Like she can't escape it.

"One day, I fell asleep in his trailer," she says. "He had this really nice couch. I loved it, since it looked like it'd been made in the sixties and reminded me of home. When I woke up, he was on top of me."

My breath hitches. This conversation feels too intimate, too revealing, for us to be having over the phone. And I feel like shit for even asking.

"It's okay," I say, shaking my head. "You should only tell me as much as you feel comfortable with. If you want to take a break or—"

"I didn't just get bullied into telling you," she says, voice like steel. "I've been thinking about this long before Penny brought it up. If you don't write it into your story, I'll write it myself. This isn't a pity project. I want this guy to burn."

I force myself to breathe. She's right. It's about taking Lennox down, making sure people see the real him.

"Okay," I say. "What else do you want to tell me?"

NEW YORK, NEW YORK

CHAPTER 20

New York City is dark and slushy, not as glittery as I'd expected when we were still on the plane. Everything looked beautiful from up high.

It's even worse when we actually leave the airport. Snow blows everywhere, but it isn't crisp and white, not like in the movies. It's dirty from sloshing underneath thousands of pedestrian feet. I guess the weather isn't bad enough to keep everyone inside, because there are still crowds of people wandering around and beeping and yelling at each other. For some reason, it makes me think of Julia, and that makes me even sadder.

We spoke for a few hours on Monday before Alice and I had to catch our flight. By the time Alice had finished her shower, I'd moved out into the hotel hallway because I couldn't stop pacing back and forth. I know Julia told her costume designer right after she woke up with Lennox on top of her, and the designer told her not to tell anyone. I know everyone on set avoided her afterward, as if they knew what had happened. I know she *kept* trying to talk about it, but the more she did, the harder it became to get jobs.

"Lennox," she said. "He did it. He told me he'd make sure I never got hired again if I told, and he did."

I don't understand how one person can have so much power. But he *does*. Tons of women know it. Julia knows it. My phone call with her made everything seem more real, a gigantic weight that has settled at the bottom of my belly. It's the reason why his behavior isn't public knowledge. It's the reason why no one has written about this before. It makes me think someone smarter than me should be writing this.

But I already know I can't just toss the story to someone else. Penny asked *me*. I've already become attached to Julia. Even if part of me feels like I can't handle it, another part feels like I'm the one meant to write it.

I don't know. My head is a mess.

Today the main cast is being featured on *The Morning Show with Amy and Mike*, which means everyone is up at five in the morning, including me. I'm not sure how going with them to the show helps me write the story, but I guess the idea is that I'm supposed to follow them almost everywhere. I'm barely awake when Alice and I shuffle into the studio's greenroom. There's a TV mounted so we can see what's being broadcast to TVs across America live: the hosts, Amy and Mike, sitting at a table and chatting casually with each other.

Producers are running around and talking to Art, giggling like he's some sort of god. Someone puts makeup on Marius's face. Since Penny isn't a member of the main cast, she isn't here. I wish she were. Alice and I basically stick in the corner, barely even acknowledging each other because we aren't actually awake. I can't even bring myself to look at my phone. There's stuff to eat—pastries and fruit on a table—but I just nurse a cup of coffee instead. It doesn't seem to be helping. I'm tired enough to seriously consider dropping my head to Alice's shoulder, but I know she'd probably kill me.

My eyes fix on Marius as the makeup artist brushes something onto his cheeks. I'm too far away to hear, but he says something to make her laugh. I almost smile.

"You look a little dead."

I blink. A girl with dark hair and tan skin is standing in front of us, but she isn't looking at me. She's smiling at Alice, who grins back at her with recognition before jumping up to hug her. They do that thing a lot of girls do where they pretend that they haven't seen each other in decades when it's really only been days since they last spoke.

"I thought you weren't coming?" the girl asks, pulling away. "You said you wouldn't get up this early if I paid you."

Alice glances at me. I frown.

"I didn't make you do anything," I say. "You could've just stayed at the hotel."

"I decided to come," Alice says, shrugging. "When will I get to watch *The Morning Show* live ever again?"

"A lot, if you decide to be an intern like me," the girl says. "Is this your sister?"

Alice nods, holding her cup up to her lips. I try to smile at the girl, but it's still a bit too early and the coffee hasn't hit me yet, so I'm sure I look like I'm faking it. But she smiles back like she gets it.

"I'm Savannah," she says. "Alice has been hanging out with me and some of the other interns while you do your journalism thing. That's pretty cool, by the way."

"Thanks," I say. "Um, your intern thing is cool, too."

Alice snorts into her cup. Savannah shakes her head at her.

"If running around and getting coffee for everyone counts,

then sure," she says. "Are you staying back here during the show?"

"Um, I think so," I say. "I don't know where else we would go."

"Makes sense," Savannah says. "They usually don't have room on the soundstage for too many people at once."

Part of me wishes that I'd be out there with Art and Marius, that I'd be able to see the magic of the show as it's happening, or that I could even be in the audience. But I'm not part of the story. I'm the one who's supposed to be documenting it. At the thought, I dig around in my bag for my notebook.

"She takes tons of notes," Alice says by way of explanation. "Like, *all* the time."

I frown as I start jotting down notes about my surroundings. I'm too tired to argue with her right now.

"I mean, she should, shouldn't she?" Savannah asks. "If she's a reporter and everything."

"Thank you," I say, a little too loud.

Marius glances over at me and waves. I smile back.

"Oh God," Alice says. "Not this again."

I give her the sharpest look I can. No way I'm letting her make a *comment* about Marius when Art Springfield is getting miked up five feet away.

Savannah glances between the two of us, a small smile on her face.

"Sisters are great, huh?" she asks.

"Oh, sure," I say. "Absolutely. Completely."

Alice rolls her eyes.

@JosieTheJournalist: losing a breath when they enter a room: romance or anxiety? a novel by me

CHAPTER 21

"Let me know when you need me," Alice says as our Uber pulls up to my stop. Marius and I are having our next interview at a park. I should've asked to change it to somewhere indoors. "I can call a car for you or something. Maybe you'll get done early so we can just hang out."

I raise a brow, glancing over at her. This is the first time she's wanted to hang out with me in a while. I smile.

"Okay," I say. "See you later."

Maggie made me pack a coat and hat, but I didn't bring gloves and boots like Mom suggested. We have all of that stuff from the last time it snowed in Georgia, but I don't really use them, because they've never really been necessary. I just wish I had actually listened to her. As soon as I step outside the car, I'm pretty sure my fingers freeze.

The park is more crowded than I thought it would be on a snowy day. It is set up as a holiday market, with high black tables and stands selling waffles and bread. A faint melody plays as people murmur and huddle together. Little kids laugh and run around. Some aren't even wearing hats.

For a second, I consider calling Ms. Jacobson to see if we can move the location, but then I see him. There are snowflakes caught in his curls. He's sitting at a table by himself, somehow able to stand the cold metal chairs, reading a book. I recognize the cover without reading the title: *Sister Outsider.* I smile despite the cold.

He glances up then, mouth opening as his eyes lock on me. I remember that I'm wearing a jacket that isn't heavy enough to shield me from the weather and that I'm shaking from the cold. I shove my hands into my pockets to make up for my lack of gloves. At least Marius seems prepared—just a slight flush to his cheeks. I, on the other hand, can't feel my limbs.

"Come on," he says, standing up and bopping his shoulder against mine. Normally it would send sparks throughout my body, but I can't feel anything right now. "I know a better place for us to talk."

The café is a few minutes' walk away. I breathe a sigh of relief when we get inside, warm air enveloping us like a blanket. It seems too small for all of the people inside. People type on laptops and drink from mugs. The man at the counter, a dude with a nice Afro, smiles when he sees Marius.

"What'll it be?" he asks. "Hot chocolate?"

I glance up at the chalkboard menu hanging above us. Most of it is written in bright blue cursive. It strains my eyes.

"I usually get hot chocolate," Marius says, voice a warm wind next to my ear. "Always have. It's really good."

"Oh, um," I say. "Sure."

After we pay for the drinks, Marius asks, "Do you wanna look for a place to sit?"

I maneuver around haphazardly placed tables and chairs. There's an empty chair in the corner and I dump my bag on top, dragging another chair over in front of it. Perfect. I barely have enough time to pull out my notebook before Marius comes over with two mugs. The snow has melted in his hair, making it a little curlier. I bite my lip and stare down at the table as he pushes the mug in front of me.

Outside, snow is coming down even heavier than before. I should probably say something, but commenting on the weather is too awkward. Marius is already slurping from his mug. There's steam rising from mine.

"I like what you're reading," I say after a few beats of silence, gesturing toward the green cover. "My grandma gave me a copy when I was, like, fourteen. She used to teach it in college."

"Wow." He glances down at it. "I don't actually like reading. I just carry books around to look more serious than I really am."

I smirk. He smiles. I don't even remember what questions I was going to ask. It feels like I asked them all the first time we met.

"So how long have you been coming here?" I ask. "It's nice."

"Ever since I was little," he says. "My parents live a few blocks away. I used to come in after school."

"Oh." I hold up my recorder. "Do you mind?"

He shakes his head, sipping again from the mug.

"How did you like school?" I ask.

"A lot," he says, something faint about his smile. "I went to a performing arts high school, so it was sort of the first place where I met people who were interested in the same things as me."

"That sounds really cool," I say, writing it down in my notebook. "Do you think you'll be able to have similar experiences at college?"

"I honestly don't know." He traces the rim of his mug. "All my friends say it's so different. And Brown did seem different when I visited. At my high school, everyone was focused on the arts.

Everyone at Brown was interested in so many different things. It just— Everything feels so vast, you know?"

"Yeah." My voice is soft. That's how this trip has felt at times— like hidden parts of the world are opening up. "I know what you mean."

I'm not sure how long we talk—about favorite movies, about the plays he was in when he was a kid (not many that I recognize). He finishes his hot chocolate before me.

"So were your parents, like, strict?" I ask, pulling my mug toward me. My jacket has melted off and so has his. "Did they make you do all your homework before you went to rehearsal?"

"No." He snorts. "I usually did my homework there, at the theater. They're strict about other things, like keeping in touch with family from France and speaking French when I'm at home and keeping them in the loop about what's going on. They don't like that I've been in L.A. so much lately."

"Because it's L.A. or because you're far away?"

"My mother says it's because L.A. is *affreux*," he says, rolling his eyes. "My father says it's because they miss me. I guess it's because I'm their only kid. But I'm not staying there forever, you know? I'll be back."

"Is it ever lonely? Being an only child?" I glance down at my notebook. There are short notes that make no sense, a lot of drawings. I don't think I'll be able to understand what I mean until I'm listening to the recording. "I get lonely in my house, and I have two sisters."

"Sometimes," he admits, tracing the rim of his mug again. "But we're close. I spend a lot of time with them—or I used to, anyway. When I wasn't with them, I was with Wes and my friends, so I didn't really feel alone."

Right. That's the difference between us. He has friends and I don't.

152

I clear my throat. "So when you go back to France in the summer, what's that like?"

"We don't go to Paris or anything," he says. "All our family is in Bordeaux, so that's where we go, to see the cousins and the rest of the family. My nickname is the American."

"Wow." I shake my head. "Kids can be so cruel."

He grins, glancing out the window. The snow is still swirling, and I start to drift. I feel warm and happy and safe. Like I belong, without having to try.

"Hey."

I startle, head snapping over to him. There's something daring in his eyes.

"Do you wanna come home with me?"

CHAPTER 22

"Technically, I'm not supposed to bring a journalist home. So, uh, maybe you shouldn't touch anything."

I nod, eyes wide, as I scrunch into the corner of our taxi. It's the first *real* New York taxi I've ever been in. It's cleaner than I expected it to be. And more cramped.

"Sorry," Marius says, shifting his body away from me. "I'm not trying to take up your space. I just have long legs."

And he does. It's like he's Slender Man or a cartoon character.

"It's fine," I say, holding my bag close to my chest. We really don't need to take a taxi if his parents are just a few blocks away, but I'm grateful he hailed one anyway. I'd rather not walk in the snow anymore. "You're so skinny, you barely take up any space."

It's silent for a second. I can tell he's staring at me, and I pray he doesn't say anything about my weight.

"Well," he says eventually, voice soft, "it's not a crime to take up space."

I can't help but stare back at him. His eyes are brown and light and dark at different times. I don't know if he's talking about himself or me, but it feels like he's talking about me. It feels like he knows things no one else even tries to comprehend.

My heart clenches and so does my stomach. I *want*, I want so badly, but I know I can't have, not when it comes to this. No one ever wants the *whole* me, all of the parts, not just a few.

The spell is broken as the cab slows to a stop. Marius pays the cabdriver, and I make a mental note to pay him back at the end of all this. The building is nice, tall, going up and up and up. There's even a doorman standing outside. It's all very fancy. His mother is a theater director, but his father teaches scenic design at NYU, which I doubt brings in much. Maybe there's family money. I could ask him about it, but that would feel rude, especially since he offered to take me here in the first place. But he had to know I'd be asking questions and taking notes the entire time. I'm a journalist. It's what I'm supposed to do.

My recorder is still on, but I'm sure it's mostly picked up the sound of driving, muffled from being in my pocket. My fingers ghost over it as I follow Marius to the door.

"Eddie, this is Josie," he says, pausing in front of the doorman. He's an older man with tan skin and a cap like in the movies. "She's a journalist."

I'm sort of embarrassed, but at the same time it's kind of nice. My parents talk about my writing like it's a hobby. Technically it is, but they're more focused on college. Marius talks about me like I'm already a journalist—and I guess I am. He's one of the few people who agree with me. In any case, I'm smiling so big that Eddie must think I'm a friendly young lady.

We take the elevator to get up to his floor—sixth, not a penthouse, which would've been really cool—and I try to think of what I'm going to say. His parents aren't supposed to be home, which knocks off a ton of anxiety. I sneak a glance at him, and suddenly I'm anxious in a different way, chest tightening.

"You're so quiet," he says, glancing back at me. "I promise I'm not leading you to my evil lair or anything."

His voice, too, is hard not to melt at. I want to bottle it up. He could just *talk* to me and I'd stand there, entranced.

"I'm not scared," I say, which is a lie. "Just busy . . . buffering."

He snorts.

I've only seen New York City apartments on TV, so I'm expecting the hallway to look like the one in *Friends* or *How I Met Your Mother*. It's actually nicer than that. The colors are deeper, like someone recently went through and decided to paint the walls a rich maroon. Some people have decorations on their doors—a menorah, Christmas trees.

I always thought growing up in an apartment would be kind of sad—not having a house and trees and a backyard—but this apartment isn't sad at all. It's airy and open, without many walls. Everything is warm, yellow or red or orange, and we walk right into the kitchen.

Where two adults are sitting at the table. *Fuck.*

For a second, I'm sure Marius planned this, but then I remember his promise to avoid anything that would make me anxious. Surprise is written all over his face, anyway, his mouth dropping open and his eyes flicking between the two of them. My hand slips into my pocket, gripping my recorder. No one says anything.

It's odd to see him right next to his parents. His father has close-cropped curly hair with gray mixed into the brown, glasses resting on his nose, and dark eyebrows. His mother, on the other hand, looks more like Marius—dark brown curls tossed up in some sort of twist, brown eyes, a frowning red mouth. The lines under her eyes and around her chin seem to give her character. Unlike her son, she knows how to wear a guarded expression.

"Marius," she says, resting her chin on her knuckles. There's the French accent I was waiting for, but it's less *Beauty and the*

Beast than I thought it would be. "I did not know you were inviting a friend over. Is this Josie?"

I'm holding my breath. Actually, it's more like I can't breathe. I don't know where to look—should I make eye contact with her or the father or Marius? She might not want me to look at her, but the father might be more sympathetic.

How does she know who I am? And why are they here when he said they wouldn't be?

"Yes," Marius says, glancing at me. I can't tell what he's feeling. "This is Josie. We were just here to get out of the cold."

His mother hums. I take a random guess and force myself to stare at the father. There's a gentle smile on his face. At least he's safe, for now. I'm hoping he doesn't feel pity for me.

"Marius," his mother says again, pushing away from the table. *"J'aimerais te parler."*

I press my lips together. The father frowns, glancing at her, but she's already walking into another part of the apartment. Marius mirrors his father's face. His touch on my elbow is light but still manages to make me jump.

"She just gets grumpy sometimes," he says, glancing at his dad, as if asking him to confirm. "I'll be right back."

I watch him walk down a hallway after her. I guess this place is bigger than I thought it would be. My recorder is on. I don't know if I should turn it off, but I definitely don't want to whip it out in front of Mr. Canet.

"I am so sorry," he says, pulling off his glasses. His accent is stronger than his wife's, but there's something endearing about it. "Isabelle can be a bit brusque, I'm afraid. Sit, sit, don't just stand there. I am Henri. We know your name. Marius says it often."

My cheeks burn as I sit down across from him, holding my bag close to my body. He isn't so bad. It's just that I can hear quick speaking from the other room in a language I don't understand. I don't get it. I'm sure she's upset he brought a journalist to their home, but I still wonder if this is because I'm an American Black girl or fat or both.

"Marius has told us much about you," Mr. Canet says. The skin under his eyes crinkles when he smiles. "Your work is impressive for someone so young. Are your parents proud?"

I nod, trying to force myself to calm down. *Just breathe. Just breathe.*

"That is good." He nods, pleased. "Parents should be proud of their children."

"Are you proud of Marius?"

He doesn't hesitate. "Immensely. I see him on-screen and feel awe."

There's something about the way he says it—so intense, so eager—that reminds me of Marius. This must be where he gets it from. It's sweet. I'm glad Marius isn't one of those kids who have to weather the long, scary journey to Hollywood alone.

"Yeah," I say, rubbing my fingers together. "He seems to have that effect on lots of people."

Henri beams just as Marius appears again. His mother follows. I can't read her expression, but she seems less angry than she was before. It's Marius who looks irritated.

"Ne sois pas si fâché. Elle est belle," his mom is saying. Marius shakes his head, taking a seat at the table. *"Je veux juste que tu comprennes—"*

"Maman." He shakes his head. "Not now."

"Josie speaks English," Henri adds. Something tells me that's why she's using French in the first place. "It is not fair to her."

"I am sorry, Josie," she says, looking at me for the first time. "I just had something urgent to discuss with my son. You understand."

I nod, even though I don't really get it. What was so important to talk about that she couldn't wait until I left?

"We were just discussing Marius's accomplishments," Henri says, smiling as he puts his glasses on. "And how proud we are."

Marius groans, tilting his head as he pushes back his chair, balancing it on two legs. His mother grins, pushing the chair forward so he doesn't fall. It all seems so normal that I have the sudden urge to take a picture.

"Incredibly proud," Isabelle says, staring down at him. "You cannot possibly begin to understand."

Something passes between the two of them. Isabelle's face softens. Marius covers his eyes, smiling up at her with most of his face hidden. Henri shakes his head, fond. I don't understand, but I don't think I'm meant to, and that's fine with me. Some things are just nice to watch.

CHAPTER 23

The next day, Penny and I meet at a coffee shop.

It's sort of a gallery and an eatery where you're supposed to look at the art and eat at the same time. I get in line and Penny shuffles behind me. Standing in line normally freaks me out, because I have to know what I'm eating and how I'm going to pay for it and how much money to give all before it happens so I don't fumble and mess up, especially when I'm given change.

I clear my throat. There's something I need to ask Penny, but I'm not sure how to bring it up.

"So . . . ," I say. "How many women, um, do you think . . . ?"

"Have a story like mine?" Penny bites her lip. "I'm not sure. I've been trying to make a list of people I know."

I reach in my pocket, pulling out a messy pile of bills. There's a twenty. Will that be enough? I glance up, looking for the cheapest thing on the menu.

"How did talking with Julia go? She said it was cathartic to have someone listen."

I wonder again if I'm the right person to do this. I don't want Penny to see my uncertainty, though. Not right now.

"It went pretty well. As well as talking about sexual assault can go."

"That's so good! Julia will talk about this to anyone."

"Not anyone."

"Obviously not anyone," she says. "But you made her comfortable enough to ask around for other people who want to come forward. That's a really great step, Josie. I'm trying to think of who else to reach out to. I sent a few emails to Tallulah because we're at the same agency—"

"Tallulah Port?"

"Yeah," Penny says. "We've met once or twice. She hasn't answered yet, though."

"Next?"

We step to the front of the line. As Penny places her order, I think back to everything I know about Tallulah Port. I've always thought she was cool, but everyone did in 2011, when she won basically every award for her leading role in *Burning Heat*. She's gotten another Oscar nomination since then and she's not even thirty yet.

"And for you?"

I blink. The server stares at me.

"Um," I say, "I'll have what she's having."

After paying, Penny and I head toward the seating area. There's art everywhere—gigantic prints of plants hanging from the walls, glass sculptures and figurines encased on tables around the room, and a watercolor mural of a map.

"Anyway," Penny says, tossing her hair back and sitting down, "I'm not sure how many women there are, like, overall. But I'm sure there are a lot. We should try to include anyone who wants to talk, don't you think?"

"I don't know." I click my pen. "I've never done this before. If everyone talks as much as Julia—"

"I don't think everyone is going to talk as much as Julia."

"Yeah, well." I rub my forehead. "I don't blame them. If it happened to me, I would never want to talk about it again."

Penny pauses. I shift, my pen tumbling next to me. I don't really need my notebook. It's not like there's anything to write down. It's impossible for me to forget what happened to Julia and Penny. For some reason, I can remember their stories while forcing myself to forget my own.

"But it did, though," she finally says. "That's what your text was about."

I hold in a sigh. Part of me recognizes that Lennox hurting her and Ryan King hurting me are similar. But it still feels wrong, almost disrespectful, to call them the same.

"I mean," I say, "yeah, but not really. It's not like it's, like . . . It's not a real thing."

"What?" Her eyes snap up. "What's a *real thing*?"

"I don't know." My shoulders tense. "Like. It was in middle school. It was—I don't know. A boy being stupid."

Penny stares at me for a long time. My face burns under the attention.

"You know that's not true," she says. "I don't have to tell you that."

I stare down at my lap.

"It's . . ." She sighs. "What happened to Julia was worse than what happened to me, if you want to put it that way. But it happened to both of us. He did things to both of us. It's not—it's not like it's a contest. You don't have to hit a certain amount of points to be included. Do you know what I'm trying to say?"

Sort of. It feels ridiculous to include myself with Penny and Julia, but I get what she means.

"I get it," I say. "But it's just different. I don't know. It's

162

different when it's someone who can make or break your career with the snap of his fingers. For me, it was just a shitty kid I went to school with. It wasn't the same for you."

"Yeah," Penny says, voice soft. "That's true."

"I just kind of don't want to talk about it anymore," I say. "Let's, um, just talk about the story. Can we do that?"

"Sure," Penny says, but her expression is sour, like she drank bad milk. "We probably should anyway, because I spoke to someone and they said they might be here."

"They *might?*" I rub my temples. "Penny, you have to stop doing this to me. You can't just spring people on me at the last second."

A waiter comes over, dropping off our food. Penny goes silent. I didn't even pay attention to what I was ordering, but now I see that it's some sort of fancy salad, full of leafy greens and bright fruit.

"I'm sorry," Penny says, looking at her plate. "I'm not doing it on purpose. Eve answered last-minute, and then Julia could only talk that one afternoon—"

"Wait," I say, holding up a hand. "Who is *Eve?*"

Penny spears some salad with her fork.

"Penny?"

"Cassidy." Penny finally looks sheepish. "Eve Cassidy."

My eyes go wide. Eve Cassidy is hard enough to get *normal* interviews with. It's not surprising, since she's a member of one of the most famous families in Hollywood. James Cassidy and Alexandra Taylor, her parents, have at least two Oscars each. Eve has one of her own and a few nominations to go with it. I haven't seen her around in a few years, though. The last movie she worked on was a Roy Lennox project.

I'm pretty sure she only talks to big publications, reporters with degrees and experience. I have so many questions—does she know that this is a freelance piece, that we don't have a publication yet? Does she even know who she'll be talking to?

"Don't worry," Penny says, watching my hands on the table. "She's really nice. At least, she's always been to me when I run into her."

Somehow, that doesn't make me feel better. I'm sure rich celebrities are always nice to each other. That doesn't mean Eve will be nice to me. I don't even need her to be *nice*. I need to be able to talk to her without messing everything up before it's even started.

"It's just a lot," I say, rubbing my forehead. "I'm just thinking . . . if we're going to do—I don't know—five more women, let's say, there's going to be so much stuff to write. If we can get this published, we probably need to do it as a series. It might be too overwhelming if it's all there for people to read at once."

"I understand." Penny takes a bite of her salad, talking around her food. "We should start thinking of places to pitch to. Maybe I can ask around for some help."

"Yeah," I say. "Maybe I can ask *Deep Focus*."

It'd be weird to pitch such a huge magazine, but I already won their contest, so they must think I have at least *some* talent.

"Maybe," she says. "You're such a good writer. I'm sure everyone will want to publish it."

A couple a few tables away laughs loudly. I try not to stare, but it's hard. They look so happy. I wish that were me right now.

"I don't know. It's not exactly something that people normally like to read," I say. "What if we got everyone to talk and no one reads it? Or people read it but then Lennox calls lawyers or something?"

"If he gets lawyers involved, he's practically admitting his

164

guilt." Her face blanches and she swallows. "It won't just be me or Julia. If there's a group of us, they can't say we're *all* lying."

I know that. She knows that. But it won't matter if people don't want to listen.

My hands grip the inside of my jacket. It's all too much. I force my eyes shut, taking deep breaths. *It's okay. I'm okay. Penny is right. Everything is going to be fine.*

I reach for my water glass, draining it in one go.

"Hey," Penny says, glancing toward the door. "Eve is here."

I turn my head. Eve Cassidy is beautiful in real life, even more beautiful standing against the watercolor mural. Most famous people look different on-screen, but she looks exactly the same as she does in the movies. Her hair is blond, like most of the women in Lennox's movies, and she has dark brown eyes. Something about her demands attention, even though she isn't speaking.

She's also here by herself. I figured someone as big as Eve Cassidy would bring a publicist. Unless something else is going on.

"It's nice to see you," Penny says, moving her chair to let Eve in. "I'm so glad you came. I know this is all last-minute."

Outside, a camera flashes, a lone paparazzo taking pictures. Other customers glance over every few seconds and whisper to each other. If Eve Cassidy doesn't seem to mind, I guess we shouldn't, either.

"Of course," Eve says. She sits completely straight, hands folded on the table between us. "I respect what you're trying to do and would love to talk with you. Julia told me about your project at brunch the other day. I think it's a really valiant effort you two are making."

She makes eye contact, switching between the two of us as she speaks. I can't look away when her eyes lock on mine. It's like she's captured everyone. Maybe that's how she has commanded so many screens. I reach into my bag for my recorder.

"But, sadly, I won't be able to participate."

I freeze, eyes darting over to Penny. She's still holding her fork and blinks a thousand times a minute.

"Oh." I clear my throat. "I know it must be really difficult. If it makes you feel better, though, you wouldn't be alone. Penny and I would support you as much as possible, and Julia is already on the record—"

"But I'm not Julia." Her voice isn't loud but is definitely firm. "I can't do this. I can't talk about these things and share specifics with the entire world."

"Will you say he harassed you?" Penny asks, faster than I can. "I mean, you don't have to go into details. It's just having your support that's really important."

The laughing couple a few tables away has gone silent. For a second, I wonder if they're listening. Would it have been better to do this somewhere else?

"I'll support you from the sidelines," Eve says. She smiles, but the expression doesn't reach her eyes. "But, Penny, as much as I want to, I really can't. Just talking to Julia about it tore me up. It's been three years and I still can't reckon with it."

She clears her throat. My eyes sting. I shouldn't be getting emotional. This didn't happen to me. It happened to someone else, and I don't want to make this about how I feel. Penny reaches out for her hand. Eve grips it.

"I'm really glad you're doing this." She shakes her head, pressing her eyes closed. "Ever since they started running commercials for that documentary, it's gotten worse."

God, the documentary. The more I find out about this guy, the more the documentary burns me up.

"I know," Penny says. "I haven't been watching TV. The commercials . . . it's too much."

"He definitely knows how to curate his image," Eve says. "You should've seen my contract."

"Oh God," Penny says. "I—I can't believe so many people are *helping* him cover it up."

"Wait," I say. "What was in the contract?"

"A very intense nondisclosure agreement," Eve says. "Actors sign away their right to mention anything that happens on set or during production. If they do, Lennox will definitely sue for everything they have."

On the surface, it sounds like a famous director being particular about the way his sets are run. But knowing what I do, I think it sounds sinister.

I ask, "That doesn't make any of the actors suspicious?"

"Maybe a little," Penny says. "But it's Lennox. Everyone wants to work with him. No one's gonna give up that chance just because of an NDA."

"But . . ." I shake my head, pushing away my bowl. "Do they know? About the allegations?"

"If they don't before they sign on, I'm sure they do after," Eve says. "Just think about it. If you see that clause in your contract, you're going to have some questions. But even then, I'm not sure it's possible to work with him without knowing. It's one of the biggest open secrets in Hollywood. Everyone knows about it."

It doesn't make any sense. How could so many people know and not say anything? Not do anything? How could actors hear about this and decide to keep working with him? What about the members of the crew? Costume designers? Craft service? Is this a massive conspiracy? It's hard to fathom how many people know and haven't tried to stop it.

Does Marius know?

"But why hasn't anyone *said* anything?" I snap. "It's just—

I don't understand. How can they just stand by and watch it happen? Or know that it happens? There are other directors. Ones who don't do *this*. I can't— I don't—"

"We know," Penny says. "But imagine what you're up against if you speak out. I'm sure people want to do something. They're just scared."

She puts a hand on my knee, but it doesn't do anything to make me feel better. The fact that she's trying to comfort me when this happened to *her* just makes me feel even more useless.

"It's an ugly machine," Eve says, locking eyes with me again. "And I'm sure you'll face resistance by fighting against it. But I promise I'll help as much as I can. I just can't talk about what happened to me. Not if I want to maintain any sense of self."

She smiles again. It makes me want to cry. It makes me want to kill someone. If a woman from one of the most powerful families in Hollywood can't confront this guy, who can?

CHAPTER 24

The entire cast is supposed to go to a cocktail party at this fancy hotel today, but I've been spending all afternoon thinking of ways to get out of it. I could say that I suddenly caught the flu. Or that I don't want to be around alcohol because I'm underage—even though I'm sure no one would actually serve me. Or I could just hide in the hotel and hope that Penny doesn't notice I'm missing. Because Penny is the only one who *would* notice.

Penny and maybe Marius.

Maybe it isn't fair that I'm avoiding him right now, but I don't feel like being fair. I'm angry. Actors who work with Lennox have to sign nondisclosure agreements, but I'm sure there are stories swirling around. There have to be, if Penny and Julia know other women Lennox has hurt. Marius must have heard *something*.

I want to know why Marius would even consider working with Lennox when there are so many stories. If I got an offer to be in his movie—which I wouldn't, but still—I would say no. Even if it meant that I didn't get to be famous.

"That's not really fair, though," Alice says after I explain all of this to her. "Because you *aren't* an actor. Acting isn't your big thing, but it is for him. You don't really care like that."

"I care!"

"I mean," Alice says, "not like an actual actor does, though."

She's already dressed, wearing this fancy black dress that's so low-cut you can tell she isn't wearing a bra. It's really hard not to be jealous of Alice's body sometimes. She has curves, but in the right places—her hips and her ass and her boobs look the way they're supposed to. Or the way girls on TV and in magazines look, anyway.

I, on the other hand, am half dressed—which means I'm sitting on my bed in my underwear and have not actually put any real clothes on—my stomach and boobs and thighs too big for me to ever look like her, unless I dig the Spanx out of my suitcase. I pout.

"I guess," I say. "But it's like . . . if a gigantic magazine gave me the opportunity to write a cover on Ava DuVernay or something, but I knew the editor of the magazine had done horrible things to women, I wouldn't be able to say yes. I'd feel too shitty about it."

"But that's a hypothetical," Alice says, leaning toward the mirror to put on an earring. "You say that now, but you'd probably say something different if you actually were faced with it."

"I don't think it's that hard to say you won't work with bad people."

"It's not a contest, Josie," Alice huffs. "I'm just saying that not everything is black and white."

I stare at the bedspread. Sure, not everything is black and white, but there's a difference between working with someone who might've done something normal bad—like made a nasty comment—and someone who consistently harms other people. Yet I can't help but wonder whether I'd feel differently if I were in Marius's shoes. I don't know. I still think I would choose not to work with them. I still think I can be mad at Marius about it.

Alice tosses a skirt at me, covering my head. I grunt.

"Hurry up," she says. "I told Savannah we'd get there early."

Everyone else at the party looks like they just stepped off the runway—gowns of soft red and black and green paired with elegant high heels. I'm wearing a black skirt, because Alice made me, and a yellow blouse. That's it. I immediately stick out.

"God, where were you?" Savannah says to Alice, appearing next to her in a cute red dress. "You said you were getting here early."

I think I'm staring too long at her legs. The hard thing about being attracted to girls is that I'm never sure if I want to *be* them or be *with* them.

"Josie took forever," Alice says, an eye roll in her voice. "It's whatever. Where's the open bar?"

"In the other room," Savannah says, pointing down a dimly lit hall. Everything here is wooden floors and warm, dim lighting and the gentle murmur of polite conversation. "You're missing a rousing debate about which movie is Cassavetes's best."

"Oh," I say. This I can do. "Obviously *A Woman Under the Influence.*"

"That's what you would think!" Savannah says, turning to me. "But then one guy said *Faces*, and now no one will shut up."

"Okay." Alice stares between the two of us. "This is big nerd talk. Savannah, let's find the bar, and I'll tell you about this gorgeous guy I saw on the High Line."

Savannah grins at me and I grin back. I like talking about movies—or *films*—with other people. I don't feel like I'm the only one who cares about them.

"Is Josie coming with us?" she asks, looking at me.

"Josie is underage," Alice points out helpfully.

Savannah shrugs. "So are we."

"Yeah, but Josie is technically working," Alice says, already walking toward the next room. "And we are not."

I wish I had a great comeback prepared, but I don't. The truth is, I don't want to hit up the open bar. I don't even want to be here in general. I smile at Savannah as she follows Alice down the hall, trying to think of things I could include in my article. There will probably be speeches at some point that I can quote from. I'm sure it would be wise to . . . mingle? The only thing is, I'm not great with small talk, especially with people I don't know.

At parties, I'm usually the person standing against the wall, watching as everyone else has fun. And it's pretty much my own fault—after all, I could trail around after my sister and Savannah if I wanted to. But in some ways, it's easier to be here by myself. It's something I can handle.

I only recognize a few people in the room—a few New York–based directors of the indie variety, an actor or two. It's weird to see celebrities in real life. It's like they aren't supposed to exist off a screen. There's one woman in particular who catches my eye. I know her from somewhere. Then she turns her head and I recognize her immediately. She looks perfect: straight blond hair, blue eyes, a movie-star smile. Tallulah Port.

She's one of the people Penny mentioned reaching out to. One of the people who are rumored to have been one of Roy's victims. I watch her move around the room, a glass of wine in her hand, stopping to talk with people and flashing smiles.

Would it be ridiculous to approach her? I lick my lips. I can't ask her about the rumors, not here, not in front of everyone. But maybe I can ask her about Penny. Is that horrible? That's definitely putting her on the spot, but in a gentle way. Asking about Penny is just asking if she knows someone. That's normal small talk.

God. Why am I so bad at this?

I close my eyes. It's okay if she says no. She probably won't be mean about it. Probably. And I'm doing this for a good reason. I take a deep breath and force myself away from the wall.

Tallulah Port has just plucked a cocktail shrimp from a waiter's tray when I finally reach her, taking the biggest steps I can muster. She smiles at me in the small, bland way baristas do when you're about to make an order.

"Um," I say. "Hi."

She continues smiling. "Hi."

I swallow, willing the words to come out. She takes a sip of wine and glances around the room.

"I'm Josie," I say. "And, um, I'm friends with Penny. Penny Livingstone?"

Her face drops, just for a second, before she regains composure.

"Oh, Penny," she says. "She's the sweetest, isn't she?"

"Yeah," I say. I can't quite read her expression. "I was just, uh, wondering if you've gotten the chance to speak to her lately?"

I'm sweating. Why am I sweating? I clench my arms close to my sides so that no one can see the stains soon to form under them.

"I'm afraid I haven't," Tallulah Port says, lifting up her glass of wine. "I've been so busy."

"Sure," I say. "I just wanted—"

"I'm sorry," she says, stepping around me. "I'm afraid I see a dear friend I've been meaning to catch up with."

"Oh," I say. "But—"

"So nice meeting you," she says, flashing the same barista smile. Then she's gone.

Well, that couldn't have gone any worse.

CHAPTER 25

It takes about twenty minutes for Penny to find me, during which time I stuff myself full with spinach puffs and shrimp to suppress the guilt.

"I can't believe you didn't look for me!" Penny says. She grins so wide, I can smell the wine on her breath. "I was looking for you! So was Marius!"

I try not to frown at his name. Maybe I shouldn't be so hard on him.

"Why do you look so sad?" Penny asks, knocking her elbow with mine. "It's a party. You're supposed to have fun. This is maybe the *one* time we get to have fun this entire trip."

"I don't know," I say. "Technically, I'm supposed to be working."

Penny rolls her eyes. I smile a little.

"I'm technically working, too," she says. "It's okay to take a break. You're so serious all the time. Let me go find Marius, and maybe—"

I grab her arm before she can go. She frowns.

"Maybe not," I say. "Don't you—aren't you weirded out about him doing this movie with Lennox? I can't stop thinking about it."

"Of course." She sways a bit. "Of course it freaks me out. But I— He doesn't listen. He never wants to talk about it."

I glance around, lowering my voice.

"Never wants to talk about the movie or the allegations?"

"Both." Penny waves a hand. "All of it. He makes me want to scream. He just tells me he can handle himself and knows what he's doing."

Penny's been trying to tell him about the allegations and he just waves her off? I swallow my frustration and decide to change the subject. "I sort of tried to talk to Tallulah Port. About—you know."

Penny's eyes go big.

"Here?"

"I wasn't obvious," I hiss. "I'm not that stupid."

"I didn't say you were," she says, lowering her voice. "I just— I told you that she didn't answer any of my emails. Plus, she doesn't even know you."

"I know," I say. "I just—I don't know. She was here and I figured that I should ask her before the moment was gone. You know?"

"What did she say?"

"Nothing," I say. "Literally nothing. I just asked if she knew you, and she was kind of weird and then said she had to go."

Penny presses her lips together.

"I don't know," I say again. "I guess we can find some other people to ask, right?"

Penny rubs her eyes. Suddenly, she doesn't look so bubbly anymore.

"I hope so," she says. "I've been asking around since Eve, and it doesn't seem like anyone wants to talk."

My stomach squirms. I want to curl into a ball and watch *Real Housewives* and pretend this isn't as hard as it is. But I can't. I have to be strong for Penny.

"We got Julia," I say. "And we'll get someone else. Maybe it'll take a while, but we'll do it."

Penny glances at me but doesn't say anything.

"Come on," I say, grabbing her hand. "Let's find some spinach puffs."

I get Penny to sit with me in the corner and eat spinach puffs while we talk about our favorite members of One Direction (Harry for me and Zayn for her) and our favorite old Disney Channel movies. By the time I finally spot Marius, we're deep into conversation about our early celebrity crushes. He's across the room, wearing a dress shirt and black slacks, and he's looking right at me. Shit.

"Yeah, I know Ryan Gosling is so cliché, but I just couldn't help it," Penny is saying. "Everyone was talking about *The Notebook* and I thought he was just so . . ."

Her voice fades out as Marius starts walking toward us, excusing himself from a circle of giggling starlets in sparkly dresses and weaving between other groups of people. Someone stops him, smiling, and Marius glances back over here before engaging in the conversation.

"Anyway, I think it's really cute how he's like a family man now," Penny continues. "Because I never would've guessed that when I was little and—"

"Hey," I say, standing up. "I have to go to the bathroom. Just give me a second, okay?"

"Oh, yeah," she says, brow furrowing. "Sure."

I don't even know where the bathroom is, but I rush into the other room before Marius has the chance to come over. The open bar is extremely loud. People are laughing and almost shouting into each other's ears. I spot Savannah, Alice, and a couple of people who must be other interns dancing in the center of the room. I turn away and head down another hall.

Here it's much quieter and there are only a few lights. It's almost eerie. There are various doors—one marked "Staff Only" and another marked "Maintenance." I finally spot the bathroom symbol and am about to head over when I feel a gentle hand on my shoulder. I scream.

"Oh my God!" a feminine voice says behind me.

A familiar voice. I slowly turn to see Tallulah Port. I'm still shaking.

"Jesus Christ," I say. "You scared me."

"I didn't mean to," she says. "I saw you come here and—"

"You followed me?" I ask. Usually, you'd think this would happen the other way around. "Why?"

The lighting is so dim in this hallway, I can only vaguely make out her expression, but I see her swallow.

"If I talk to you," she says, "it has to be off the record. All of it."

I blink probably a million times. I don't have my notebook. I don't have a pen or a list of questions. I'm completely unprepared for this. I swallow my anxiety anyway.

"Um," I say, "okay. I can do that. Can I record you on my phone?"

"Not yet."

My hand freezes over my pocket.

"You need to know how serious this is," she says, eyes piercing into mine. "Penny wrote about it in her emails. I understand why she feels like this is important, and I want to help."

"Okay—"

"But this isn't a game." Her voice isn't harsh, but there's something firm about it. "You need to understand that. And if you print anything I say, I'll deny everything and send my lawyers after you. Understood?"

"Oh." I swallow. "Uh, okay. That's understandable."

"I want to believe you're trying to help." Exhaustion is plain on her face. "There just comes a point when that's not enough."

"Of course." I'm nodding like some sort of broken doll. "I know this must be difficult—there's no denying that. But I think it's really important that we do something to make sure you're all heard. And it might help to know some other people who have gone through the same thing."

"There are a lot, from what I know," she offers. "But it doesn't matter, since no one is going to talk about it."

"Right," I say. "Well, I'm glad you are."

I hold my phone up, already open to the voice recorder app. Tallulah takes a deep breath and nods.

"Can you tell me how you first met Roy Lennox?"

She's silent for a long moment. I almost want to hold her hand, but I'm not sure how she'd feel about it."

"The thing is," she starts, "well, Roy is the reason why I have an Oscar."

"Okay." I glance down at my phone, ready to Google. "It was 2011, right?"

Burning Heat," she says, more like a sigh. "It was my third movie, but it really catapulted me. A lot of people have said he made my career. That's what—what makes it—so hard."

I can't see well enough to tell if she's crying or if I'm just imagining it. I hope she isn't. If she's crying, *I'll* start to cry. Gently, I put a hand on her shoulder.

"Do you need to stop?" I ask. "We can take as many breaks as you need."

"No," she snaps. "No, I'm fine."

"All right," I say. "So on the set of *Burning Heat,* how did he behave around you?"

"He tried to force me to give him a blow job," she says. She shifts and I see tears on her cheeks. Shit. "Never when we were filming. I know it was different for Penny. But it was during the press tour—I could just never get away from him. He was everywhere."

I didn't expect her to share this so fast. I quickly scan through the list of questions in my brain to catch up.

"Was there anyone else around?" I ask. "Anyone who could've seen or overheard?"

"No." I wish I could give her a tissue. "I was drinking the first time it happened. Never did that again, because I figured something would happen—not that it made anything better. He'd go, 'Tally, what's wrong? Why are you so worked up? Relax.' And I couldn't do anything because he'd be touching my knee under the table at press conferences. If I freaked out, he'd just turn it around on me."

"What a bastard." It slips out before I can stop it. "I'm sorry, but not really, because he's such a fucking piece of shit. I don't even have the words."

Everything feels hot—my chest, my forehead—and I just want to slam my fist into a wall.

Someone laughs, loud, and Tallulah jumps. My body goes stiff. I guess we could run into the bathroom, quick, before anyone notices us—

The sound is gone almost as quickly as it appeared. We stand in silence for a few more moments. Tallulah starts to wipe her cheeks.

It's hard to swallow. I want to cry along with her. I want to tell her about what happened to me, but it's different. The boy who followed me into the bathroom was horrible—probably still is—but he was a boy. Roy Lennox is a man. Not just *a* man, but *the* man. He snaps his fingers and gets millions of dollars for a movie without even telling the studio what it's about. He makes *and* breaks careers.

When Ryan King followed me into the bathroom, I scratched his arms and his face. I tried to bite him. I kicked and bucked like a wild animal, even though I was still in middle school and didn't understand what rape was, because maybe something inside of me did. He didn't do that—he said he would, he joked, but he didn't use that word—but he touched my boobs over my shirt, and when I tried to slap him away, he tore it. After that, everything went into overdrive. Afterward, I was embarrassed, felt like I'd overreacted. I cried, I couldn't stop crying, but the principal made the whole thing go away, even if everyone thought I was a crazy girl who was making a big deal out of a joke.

Telling on Roy Lennox—that's like willingly becoming a pariah. In an industry where it's so hard to succeed, if someone got the chance to work with him, how much would they deal with? How much would they lose if they told?

I force a breath through my nose.

"Did he have you sign an NDA?"

Tallulah nods. "Before we started filming. I feel sort of guilty. Just because—well, I wish I could just come out and say something. It's not even about being sued—Julia started talking and look at what happened to her. Everyone thinks she's crazy. And he's the one behind it."

"I know." I bite my lip. "I already talked to her about it."

"And it's— I know this is horrible. But I just kept thinking I could smile and bear it and never have to deal with it again. Then I read Penny's email, and I started thinking about the stories I've heard. . . ." Her voice trails off.

"I mean, I get where you're coming from," I say. "But it's not your fault, Tallulah. He's the one who started this."

"Right." She clears her throat, though her words are still watery. "I know. It's just . . . hard to remember sometimes."

"I know." I squeeze her shoulder. "But we're going to end it. I promise."

I just hope I can keep my word.

CHAPTER 26

When I get back to the hotel, Alice is giggling on her bed with the interns. They stop laughing at the sight of me. Savannah waves. I give her a small smile back.

"I'm working," I announce, grabbing my laptop and sprawling out on my bed.

Alice doesn't say anything. One of the girls, with brown skin and long brown hair, whispers something to her. Alice nods and turns on the TV.

The clock reads 6:00 p.m. Perfect. I'm still full from all the finger food at the cocktail party, so I can work through dinner. The tour ends Monday, the same day the profile is due, but I also need to see what I can do about my project with Penny. I need to be doing *something*.

It's hard to stop thinking about Tallulah. It felt like we talked forever. She's a lot older than me, but at the same time I related to her. She told me about her addiction to Skittles and how she watches episodes of *Avatar: The Last Airbender* when she has free time. It should be comforting to know we're so similar, but it isn't. It's scary. I turn to my Marius project instead.

My Google doc labeled "Profile" isn't exactly a first draft yet.

It's more like a dump of quotes organized by topic: production on the movie, Marius's childhood, his acting, and so on. So far, I've only listened to recordings from my talk with Penny and the first few conversations with Marius. The recording from when I met his parents feels too personal. I'll check it out later.

I've barely started organizing a first draft when I get the urge to switch projects again. Marius is great and all, but I just— The story about the survivors feels more pressing. Everyone will know how talented Marius is once they see the movie. No one has talked about what these women went through. But the profile is the story I'm actually getting paid for. I hold back a groan and flip to the Word document with the Lennox story.

Maybe I'm being dramatic, but Google Drive feels too open for a story like this. It feels like anyone can hack into my account and steal Julia's and Penny's words. At least with Word, their stories are on my hard drive and not on a cloud.

Penny's and Julia's stories are already typed up. Instead of writing blocks of quotes, like I did for Marius, I wrote out their memories exactly how they shared them, in sequential order. I don't want to change anything if I don't have to. Already, I have ten single-spaced pages, but I know deep down it won't be enough for some people. They'll say that two women are a fluke or a misunderstanding or a lie. Not worth taking seriously. Even if I find a hundred women to talk to, some people will write the women off. I want to give their stories the best chance possible, and that means we need more women. I just don't know where—or how—to find them.

Alice's friends get up and start filing out the door. One waves, but I'm too focused on my work to pay attention. Alice lingers by the door after it closes. I type for another minute before realizing that she's staring at me.

"What?" I say, not looking up. "I wasn't mean. I just said I was working, which is true."

"I can help you transcribe."

I glance up. Alice is holding her phone in one hand. A reality show plays on the TV. Now that her friends are gone, she must be bored.

"I'll use my laptop," she continues. "And you can keep working on—whatever—in the meantime."

"How are you going to hear?"

She pulls an earbud out of her pocket.

I pause, fingers hovering over my laptop keys.

On one hand, it'll be humiliating if she listens to everything that happened at Marius's apartment, especially since she just lectured me about being professional a few days ago. But on the other hand, I *hate* transcribing interviews. The awkward silences, wanting to skip around but needing to listen to the full recording, even hearing the sound of my own voice . . . I want to take Alice up on her offer, but something about it makes me anxious. When she's around me, I feel like I'm always waiting for the other shoe to drop.

"I'm sorry," she says. "Savannah and Ashley and Jessica— none of them were trying to be weird when you walked in. They thought you might be mad at them. You looked a little pissed when you came in."

"Well, I'm not," I say. "It's just weird that you're hanging out with them."

"I mean," she says, "I get lonely when I'm by myself."

I glance up at her. She isn't scowling or laughing at me. She's being serious.

It's not like she's been going to events or interviews with me anymore. I figured she'd go out and explore the cities by herself, but maybe she isn't into that. Maybe she needs to be around other people. I don't know. This is the first time she's apologized in a while. I'm not even mad, so it's more than surprising.

I email her the audio file.

I've never had someone help me out with work. Alice puts in her earbuds and I go back to organizing Marius quotes. The hotel room is silent save for the sound of typing and Alice's occasional question. But it's a nice quiet.

"Hey," Alice says after a while. I don't glance up from the computer. I'm in the middle of an essay on French film theory, which doesn't exactly have to do with Marius but might make for a great opening paragraph.

"Hey," she repeats. "Josie. Did you listen to any of this?"

"No. That was the point of you typing it out."

"Yeah, whatever." She gives me the side-eye. "Anyway, they were talking about you."

"Who?"

"Marius and—I think his mom?"

I stiffen.

"I figured," I say, trying to keep my eyes on my laptop. She's shared two whole typed pages of Google docs with me. "Did they say anything horrible?"

"Shouldn't you be able to tell?"

"I take Spanish, not French."

"Maggie took French."

"And you took it because she did. I decided to branch out."

"Whatever." She rolls her eyes. "His mom said you were beautiful. It sounded like she was sort of mocking him, but she didn't say anything mean."

I pause. She can probably see the pink in my cheeks. I hate this. If she's messing around with me, I might actually cry.

"But it's not like you're fluent in French," I say instead.

"Josie." She kisses her teeth. "I've been taking French since sophomore year in high school. And I'm *minoring* in French at Spelman. Didn't you hear me talking about it at Thanksgiving?"

Oh. I must've tuned her out. Now I feel like a bad sister.

"Well," I say after a second, "what exactly did she say?"

"I told you," she says, glancing back at her own laptop. "She mentioned you being beautiful. But she told him to be careful. So maybe it's because you're obviously not French or because you look like you're thirteen. I'm not sure."

I toss a pillow at her, hoping it will draw attention away from my cringy expression; I want to smile, but my lips aren't sure where to move. I'm not *surprised*, exactly. It's a very *mom* thing to say.

"Oh my God," Alice says, tossing her head back dramatically. "This is disgusting. You should see the look on your face. I'm gonna have to tell Maggie about this."

"No way," I say. "Don't you dare."

"I'm gonna Snap her." Alice holds up her phone. "Say cheese!"

I flip her off. She takes the picture anyway, grinning as she types.

"Jesus," I say, a laugh in my voice. "Keep your mouth shut for once."

"I'm morally obligated to share. It's big-sister privilege."

I toss my other pillow at her face, and she falls off the bed with a laugh.

CHAPTER 27

On Thursday, I'm supposed to meet Marius at some old movie theater, but all I can think about is the other story I'm working on. About the interviews I went through last night.

We don't seem similar on the surface; those women are rich, white actresses who live in California. Julia is more than twice my age. Penny had a completely different childhood. Tallulah seems like she was grown in a lab, a perfect, beautiful movie star.

But we all *want*.

Penny wants to continue her career, be a *real* actress who wins awards and gets leading roles. Tallulah wanted an Oscar. Julia wanted her career. I know what it's like to be a girl who *wants*. I want *so* much that sometimes it tears me apart. I want to be a writer and to be successful, to feel *fulfilled*. I want to make things and be seen and understood, at least by a few people. What girl doesn't want that? What *person* doesn't want that?

I hit the next song on my phone. Marius still isn't here. It's cold, but I'd rather wait outside the theater than go in.

I've been trying to listen to happy music to calm myself down, but it makes me feel guilty. Should I be able to feel calm when these women are dealing with this every day? I used to tell Maggie how anxious I get about things like police brutality and institutional racism. She'd say I can't do anything if I'm not healthy myself.

She's right. But I still feel bad that I can sit here on this bench listening to Outkast while Tallulah is keeping this gigantic secret to herself. I force a deep breath. "Ms. Jackson" is playing. I rewind to the beginning, shutting my eyes as I start to sing.

"I'm sorry, Ms. Jackson

I am for realllll"

My eyes open as I hold my hands to my chest, popping and locking, but he's here. Standing in front of me. Trying not to smile. I almost fall off my seat.

"Hey, hey," Marius says, a laugh in his voice. "I'm sorry! I like 'Ms. Jackson,' too. I just didn't want to bother you because you looked like you were having fun."

"Yeah." I yank the earbuds out, shoving them into my pocket. "You could say something next time, though."

"Right." He presses his lips together, but he's still smiling. "Next time."

"It's not funny."

"I'm not laughing!" He frowns, too dramatic to be real. "I'm sorry, I'm sorry. I'm not trying to make you feel bad or anything. Hey, you've seen my horrible dancing, so we're even!"

I can't help but smile. After all, I'm still kind of pissed at him. I pull my recorder out of my pocket, waving it as I turn it on, but Marius barely takes notice.

"So." I clear my throat. "Your parents are nice."

He groans, tossing his head back. It's so theatrical, I smile despite myself.

"I'm sorry about them," he says, running a hand through his

hair. "My mom—she's protective, is all. And she knows you're a journalist and doesn't want you to take advantage of me."

"Wow." I bite my lip. "She's not a fan of journalists?"

"It's because I'm young, I think." He shrugs, looking down. "She's seen what can happen. But that doesn't mean she had to be a jerk. I'm sorry about that."

"Don't worry about it," I say, shrugging in turn. "My mom can be protective, too—that's why she made my sister come with me. Your dad is sweet, though. I like his accent."

"Yeah." He smiles like he has a secret. "I like yours."

"What?" I say. "I have an accent?"

"Yeah." His voice is soft. "A little one."

I don't know what to say. I've never heard my own accent, but I guess I wouldn't, since I've never lived anywhere but Georgia. My chest and cheeks feel warm.

I clear my throat. Now isn't the time to get tripped up by a crush. Especially since I have four days until I have to go home. I need to write a profile for my favorite magazine, but I also have to get answers for myself.

"Listen," I start, taking a deep breath. "This is—well, it's going to sound really random, but have you heard any bad things about Roy Lennox? Like, there are some allegations that—"

"No."

I glance up. His eyes are wide, his lips pressed into a straight line, jaw twitching. It's like he's seen a ghost. Penny definitely wasn't lying.

Something about the speed of his reply irritates me. I have the sinking, horrible feeling that Marius knows what Lennox has done and wants to ignore it so he can work with a great direc-tor. That's what Tallulah wanted, too, but she had to deal with weeks of sexual harassment.

"No, *what?*" I ask. The hard edge makes his eyebrows rise. "No, like you haven't heard about it?"

"No, like I don't want to talk about it." He swallows. It's no longer endearing. "We're supposed to talk about the movie."

I can barely contain my anger.

"Really?" I snap. "Is that what we've been doing? Only talking about the movie?"

"I just—" He bites his lip, eyes darting to the recorder in my hand. "We haven't even started filming the new project and I don't want to say the wrong thing. It's not worth it to upset everyone over a rumor."

I stare at him. I'm angry and disappointed, but what was I expecting? That he would denounce Roy Lennox and pull out of the movie? The internet hardly has any mentions of the allegations. Tallulah's and Penny's stories are only told in whispers. Maybe it's not fair to expect so much from him. But there's no doubt in my mind now that he knows more than he's letting on. Otherwise, why would he get so worked up?

I'm angry Marius is able to be so apathetic about this while Penny never had that choice. I'm angry we're just standing outside a movie theater while Tallulah was crying yesterday. I'm angry about everything, and it's so hard to hold back.

"We should go inside," he mumbles, shoving his hands into his pockets.

I follow in silence. I don't really feel like making an effort to fill it. After all, I don't have to *like* him. I just have to write this profile. The only reason I'm here is to get more details to pad out the story, but I have no idea how to do that while we're watching a movie. I have half a mind to leave.

At the box office, I pay for my ticket. He doesn't stop me. The hall leading to our theater is filled with old posters. I stop and stare. There's one for *North by Northwest*, the iconic scene of Cary Grant running away from a plane. When I told my English teacher how much I loved Hitchcock movies like *Psycho* and *Rear Window*, she told me about how he was a jerk to the women he worked with, controlling what they wore and how they acted off-screen. I haven't watched any of them since.

I never know how to separate the shitty things a person has done from their work. I wish we could have real heroes, perfect people who never hurt others. Einstein was a jerk to his wife. Charles Dickens cheated on his. Martin Luther King Jr. cheated on Coretta when he was on the road, and Frederick Douglass left his wife for a younger white woman. Maybe I find it all disappointing because I put too much faith in people I don't know.

I can accept whatever happened with MLK and Frederick Douglass because they were freedom fighters. They did so much good that I can deal with the bad. But I don't know if I can do the same with someone like Woody Allen. And why should I? MLK was *MLK*. Woody Allen only makes movies with white people in them.

It doesn't feel right to support the work of people who have hurt others. I don't want to watch Lennox's movies after hearing how he treated so many women. But almost everyone has done something horrible. So what's left? Alice used to nag me about my faves being problematic, and it's true. Kylo Ren could very well be a characterization of white male fragility, and a lot of rap music either doesn't mention women or treats them like objects.

But people like Lennox and Woody Allen and Roman Polanski—the things they've done are more than just problematic. Sexually abusing someone is different from cheating on a wife or rapping sexist lyrics. Sexual assault is a gigantic display of power. It's someone's way of saying, *I'm doing this to you because we both know you can't do anything to stop it.*

How do I fight against that? I don't know if I can. Survivors are all around, and their pain is real, so vivid that I can't pretend it isn't there.

"The theater," Marius says, startling me out of my thoughts. "It's this one."

I glance down at my ticket. *It's a Wonderful Life*. Perfect for the holiday season, I guess, but I wouldn't know.

"Wow," I mutter. "Never seen this before."

I really like Jimmy Stewart. Wonder if he was *regular* problematic, like a normal person, or if he harassed or assaulted someone when he was still alive. I sure hope not. I hope there are people who made good art and tried their best to be good people. It's just getting harder and harder to believe.

"Never?" He blinks. "Everyone has seen *It's a Wonderful Life*."

"I think I started it once, but I fell asleep before the ending."

"Well"—Marius's voice is soft—"it's amazing."

After a few minutes, the movie starts. Everything is in black-and-white. Jimmy's character speaks with the old-timey accent I find charming. Thirty minutes into the movie, things start going wrong for him. I flick Marius's shoulder.

"I hate you," I hiss. "This is supposed to be *happy*."

"It *will* be."

And it is, at the end, so much so that it's almost overwhelming. Jimmy's character has his wife and his family and the entire community around him, loving him. He wanted to die and now everything is better than he ever thought.

I can't believe I'm crying. But I get it. I get being completely overwhelmed with life and all of its issues. Being in New York for the holidays should be happy, but it isn't. This world feels too big for me to handle on my own. I guess I have my family, but I don't know if they can handle something as big as this.

I wish everyone in Hollywood would show up, like at the

end of *It's a Wonderful Life*, and figure out a way to make sure no one would see Lennox ever again. But wishes don't always come true.

Marius doesn't say anything as we step outside the theater, even though I'm sure he saw me blinking back tears. I realize that I don't know if he's talkative in general or if he's just been talking because I'm supposed to be writing about him.

I stop at a poster for *The Princess Bride*. It looks like it came straight out of the eighties, with faded colors and wrinkled edges clear through the frame.

"You think they've had this since it came out?"

"Maybe. This place has been around forever." Marius glances up. "It's a great movie."

"My parents love it," I say. "I don't know how many times I've seen it."

I want to reach up to touch it, just to remember it's real. *The Princess Bride* is one of the first movies that was really fun for me.

"I love happy endings," I say. I don't know if I'm talking to him or myself.

"My mom doesn't." Marius makes a soft sound. "She thinks they're contrived and unrealistic. I think she likes stories that seem more real than anything."

"I want to believe happy endings can happen in real life," I say. "I don't know. Life is just so messy. But I think I can deal with all the torture and sadness as long as it's okay by the end."

I glance at him. I don't smile, exactly, but my mouth softens. He doesn't seem like an adult who has everything together. I know I'm not.

"I understand." His voice is quiet. "But even if there isn't a happy ending, things get better after the movie is over. We just don't see it. That's what I think, anyway."

"Yeah, but I need to *know*. I can't just assume."

"Yeah." He nods once. "I get that. Sometimes things don't get better."

"I know," I say. "I just don't like being reminded of that. There are already so many negative aspects of life."

"But they're what make experiences real," he says, shoving his hands into his pockets. "It's sort of what makes life real. Otherwise you'd be dreaming all the time."

"Well." I pause. "Maybe I wish I could dream all the time."

"Yeah." He bites his lip. "Me too."

CHAPTER 28

"The front desk called."

I glance up, shutting the door to the hotel room behind me. What now?

"There's someone who wants to see you," Alice continues, barely looking up from her laptop. "But apparently, she isn't just *any* old someone. Charlotte Hart has a private room set up for you at some fancy hotel restaurant down the street."

My eyes go wide. Charlotte Hart hasn't won any Oscars, but she's still really big, running this lifestyle brand ever since she had kids. Her only good roles are from the nineties, but she's still *Charlotte Hart*. Her name is gold. I never figured anyone *that* big would speak to me. Anytime I hear a story about her in the news, it's from some big reporter.

"I thought," Alice says, very slowly, "that you were interviewing this Marius kid?"

"Um." I take a deep breath. "I mean, I still am."

"Nuh-uh." She shuts her laptop. "Talk. Now."

So I sit down on my bed and tell her everything that's happened since Atlanta, leaving out all the names. When I'm done, Alice blinks rapidly, like her brain can't compute.

"Wow." She shakes her head. "Josie, I . . ."

"You can't tell Mom," I say. "She'd make me go back home."

"I mean . . ." She bites her lip. "Do you think anything will come out of it?"

"I don't know," I say, which is the truth. "I really, really hope so."

"I . . ." She nods, slow. "I really don't know what to say."

When people say that, they usually have something in mind. Alice just sits in silence. It makes me fidget. I can't tell if she's freaked out or worried or uncomfortable. Maybe it's a combination of all three.

"You'd better head down there," Alice says, pointing at the clock. "She called, like, thirty minutes ago, and I've heard she doesn't like to be kept waiting by commoners like us."

Her joke doesn't make me laugh. If anything, it makes the knots in my stomach tighten.

"Wait," I say. "I can't go by myself. I don't even know the place. Do you wanna come?"

"Me?" Alice blinks like she's shocked. "Aren't you going to talk about, like, some really personal shit?"

We definitely will, but I'd feel more confident with my older sister by my side.

"Yeah," I say carefully. "But I think it'll be okay. And you'll get to meet someone famous. Please?"

"Like anyone would want to meet *her*." She scoffs but, thankfully, pushes herself off of the bed. "She might kick us out when we say we can't afford a three-hundred-dollar meal. Prepare yourself."

Charlotte Hart doesn't admonish us for ordering the cheapest options on the menu. I don't even think she notices. A lawyer

196

sits to her left and a publicist sits to her right. Both are dressed in gray suits and both are white women.

Honestly, I'm not even sure why she called me. I don't know what they could possibly let me print.

"Can I record this?" I ask. My hand is shaking. "Just for accuracy."

"No," the publicist says.

"Well," the lawyer says, cocking her head to the side. "It could be useful."

"For who, Jane?" the publicist asks. "Certainly not me."

"Stop," Charlotte Hart says, swishing her long dark hair over her shoulders. She didn't even raise her voice and they stop immediately. "I have to be home when the kids get back. They're never alone with the nanny for too long."

She turns to me. I swallow, but my throat is still dry. Alice grips my wrist. I shake her off.

"I hope you understand," she says. "Tallulah assured me this wouldn't take up too much time."

I blink in surprise. I wasn't expecting Tallulah to bring this up with someone like Charlotte Hart. That must've taken real guts.

"It definitely won't," I say, holding up the recorder. "So . . . do you mind?"

"Of course not." She waves a hand. "What do you want to know?"

Her elbows are on the table. I . . . I figured she'd be more tightly wound when preparing to talk about something like this. Maybe it's not the same for everyone. Or maybe she's just a good actress.

"What happened when you first worked with him?" I ask, opening my notebook. "On *Force of the Nation*?"

I make a calculated choice not to say his name, but the way her face tightens, I can tell she knows who I mean. Charlotte

Hart taps her well-manicured pale pink fingernails on the table, pursing her lips. She doesn't seem real.

"Things were normal in the beginning. He was friends with my father, so I'd met him at family dinners and events," she says, tilting her head to the side. "I told him about how nervous I was to be on his set, so he took me out to dinner. That's when he offered to father my children."

She pauses, taking a sip of water.

"I suppose he thought it sounded romantic. At first, I figured it was a joke and brushed it off. I wanted to focus on honing my craft."

Alice sighs and I stomp on her foot. My sister might find Charlotte annoying, but there's something graceful about the way she speaks and moves—even just the way she lifts her glass.

"But there were glances I noticed," Charlotte continues. "Things I tried to ignore. Toward the end of the shoot, he said I'd have to sleep with him to get my paycheck."

My eyes widen. I want to say something, but calling him a fucking asshole doesn't seem like an appropriate move around her publicist and lawyer. By the time Charlotte did *Touch of the Heart*, she was a household name. He harassed Julia *and* Charlotte on the same fucking set. Roy Lennox preyed on all sorts of women, regardless of whether or not they were already famous.

"That's pretty much it." She reaches for her water, and her hand is shaking. "I've spent a lot of time trying to make sure other girls don't work with him."

"Did you sign an NDA?"

"Don't answer that," the lawyer says.

"Okay," I say. "Did you tell anyone else? Like friends or family?"

"Charlotte." Her publicist leans over. "You don't have to answer that if you don't want to."

I glance at Alice, who presses her lips together. This feels like a police interrogation—one where *I'm* the cop Charlotte needs protection from.

"It's fine," Charlotte says. "I told my brother. He was the only one."

I nod, jotting it down in my notebook. "And—"

"I'm afraid that's all the time Charlotte has today," the lawyer says, already getting to her feet. "She's a very busy woman."

"Uh—okay." I blink. "And you're comfortable with your name being printed?"

"Well, yes." Charlotte looks straight into my eyes. "If it's going to help other women, I don't mind taking the risk."

It's a much smaller risk for someone like her than someone like Penny, who is still trying to be taken seriously, but that's not Charlotte Hart's fault. It's not her fault, or Tallulah's, or Julia's, or Penny's. It's not even just Lennox's fault. There are people who know what he does, people who choose to keep their mouths shut. People who let him continue.

"Thank you." My voice wavers, so I clear my throat. "Thank you so much."

CHAPTER 29

"What do you think about working with problematic people?"

It's Friday and we're sitting in the back of Marius's favorite café. I hope I don't sound as confrontational as I did when we last met. With time to think it over, I've realized that I'm presenting an inaccurate version of Marius in the profile. My story makes him sound like a talented young actor who got lucky.

It's just surface level. It's not real. Maybe talking about this again, approaching it from a different angle, will help me move forward with the piece.

"Problematic?" The dim lighting does nothing to hide Marius's tense shoulders. "What do you mean by that?"

"I don't know," I say. "Like, if you know the director of a movie did something horrible, are you still gonna watch it and love it and call it your favorite?"

"Wow," he says, breathing out. "That's a big question."

"I know," I say. "It's something I've been thinking about. Like how I used to really love Tina Fey before I realized she makes weird racist jokes in almost all of her work. It's hard, because I'm sure I could find out something bad about everyone."

"Yeah, that *is* where it gets hard." He runs a hand through his hair, glancing down at the recorder between the two of us. "It's like Hitchcock did a lot of shitty things—"

"Yup."

"And I don't know." He forces out a sigh. "I'm gonna sound like a jerk, but I don't stop watching movies or TV shows just because some producer or some actor screws up."

I close my eyes. Force myself to count to ten.

"Okay," I say. "What's your definition of *bad*?"

"That's the thing," he says. "I don't know what my definition of *bad* is anymore. I used to think, like, if someone got drunk and said something stupid, I wouldn't hold it against them. Or, like, if someone called something *gay* in 2003, I wouldn't boycott their work."

"But not everything is like that," I say, leaning forward. "Like, there are murderers or whatever—"

"Murderers?"

"I'm pretty sure this record producer from the eighties killed someone," I say, waving a hand. "But if there's a director who has, like, raped people or abused their wives, can you still watch their stuff?"

He pauses. Swallows. I would've felt bad for pressing him so hard before, but not now. I need to know this.

"I don't think so," he says finally. "That wouldn't— I don't think I could."

"Yeah." I stare at my hot cocoa. I've barely touched it. "I think that's a basic human response. But there are lots of people who hear about these things and act like nothing happened."

"I guess people might just feel so far removed from this stuff, you know?" He's doing what he did when we first met: talking with his hands. "Actors and directors and singers and just— I don't know—anyone you see in the news, it's like you don't really *know* them. So if you hear an allegation, you don't know whether or not it's true, and it's in a different universe, so it doesn't feel real. Does that make sense?"

"I *guess*," I say. "But there are people who stand up for those men when they hear an allegation, even if they don't know the truth. I just don't understand—like, when women get raped, a lot of people call them liars. And I don't know why someone's first response would be to assume a woman is lying about something like that."

"It's easier, I think." He stares into his mug. "It's easier to think someone is lying than to think about something so horrible happening."

"Yeah."

"Or," he says, "they just don't care."

It seems like too simple an explanation, but it still adds up. At school, a lot of kids pick maybe three things to care about—prom, sports, and maybe student council or yearbook—and they blow off everything else. I guess it's not *wrong* to focus on what's important to you, but I feel like I care about *everything*. It seems like Marius does, too, so much that it bleeds out into his expressions. So why doesn't he care about *this*?

Asking these questions was a chance to retrace my steps, but his answers aren't helping. There's no magic quote to pull the story together. It feels like I'm missing something. With a sigh, I glance down at my notebook.

"I have another question," I say, pulling my mug toward me. "Completely different. Can you just get into character right away, or does it take you a while? I was reading about how some actors stay in character during the entire shoot."

"Oh." His whole demeanor perks up, tension fading from his shoulders. "It's sort of both for me. There's a general mood for the day, usually. I wanted to take time to get into the headspace for each scene, so sometimes I'd isolate myself. But I wasn't in character all of the time. It'd be cool to explore that, though, maybe on another movie."

"That's interesting," I say. "So you need time to prepare before you can immerse yourself in a character? Like, if I just gave you a scene right now, would you be able to do it?"

"Well, yeah, that's kind of what auditions are," he says. "You practice as much as possible, but you become much closer to the character when you're actually cast."

"What are auditions like?"

"I'm pretty close to the character and the scene, because I've probably been reading it over and over again," he says, gesturing with his left hand. I scoot his mug back so he doesn't knock it over. "But there's a deeper kind of immersion that happens once you've spent some time in the role. I don't know if that makes sense."

"No, it does, it does," I say. I like hearing him speak, especially about things like this. "I've never really thought about this sort of thing. I just pictured people walking onto the set and acting or, like, snapping out of it as soon as the director yells 'Cut.'"

"Sometimes," he says, tilting his head to the side. The silver hoop in his nose catches the light. "In high school, I had this one teacher who made us memorize a monologue and perform it in front of the class. It was, like, freshman year. And people were talking and laughing, I guess because they were nervous, but I had to sit in the hall the entire period before it was my turn so I could get ready."

"Wow."

"I get nervous," he says, blushing like the subject of an Italian painting. "But I also need time to just—transform. I don't know. Maybe that sounds stupid."

"It doesn't sound stupid." I force myself to stare down at my notebook. "I like listening to you."

It doesn't make sense. I'm frustrated with him because of Lennox, but he doesn't seem *evil*. Most of the time, he seems compassionate. And he's still the same person I like to look at and listen to and try not to think about too often. I want to know what he thinks about Lennox, if he really knows what's happened, or if he's just scared. I want to know what he thinks about everything.

I glance up. He's staring at me. I can't read his expression—it almost seems like he's surprised. Like the idea of someone caring what he has to say is a shock. But I know I'm not the only one. He's *Marius*, after all. People from Indie Movie Twitter talk about him all the time. And once this movie goes big, he'll have even more fans.

"Anyway." I clear my throat. "Sorry about all of the hardcore questions. This is probably the last time we'll sit down together—"

"Wait, what?"

"Yeah, I mean, I'll go to the LGBTQ event with you, but the story is officially due on the twentieth," I say, suppressing my panic over the looming deadline. "And I fly home after that. I guess we could do more one-on-one interviews if you think I—"

"No, I— Whatever you think is best." He's frowning. "I— Wow. I just didn't think today would be the last day."

I don't know why it matters. I'm not sure what else to say, so I just stare down at my notebook. We sit in silence for a few moments, looking at everything but each other.

"Well," he says after a while, "you can always call me. If you need to ask more questions."

"Yeah."

"Do you have my number?"

I freeze. This whole time, I've been communicating with Ms. Jacobson, who has communicated with his publicist. Part of me thinks that calling his personal cell would be unprofessional. The other part is thrilled. It's the second part I'm trying to push down.

"Uh, no," I say. My throat is dry. "But I can just call my contact and maybe—"

He shakes his head. "No, I'll just give you my number. Can I use your pen?"

I slide my notebook and the pen over just enough for him to write at the very top of the page.

"You always have this with you," he says as he writes. It should take only three seconds to jot down a number, but it feels like he takes an hour per digit. "I'm going to press the pen down really hard so you don't forget."

Something in my chest freezes. It's like a panic attack caused by hopefulness. And I can't let myself be hopeful. Hoping for things like this only works out badly for me. It only leads to going into Maggie's room and trying not to cry, even though I always do.

"So I won't forget what?"

I shouldn't get my hopes up. I *know* I shouldn't. But being with him is like when we danced on the bed together: everything else in the world went silent for a little while.

"I've been thinking," he says. It's slower than usual. "I don't know what I'm gonna do when I don't have an excuse to talk to you anymore."

My mouth opens, but no sound comes out.

I don't know how it happens. Maybe I'm the first one to move. It could've been him. I know for sure it's him who kisses me first because I register everything about it a few seconds too late—his chair scraping forward a little, the fact that his lips are warm and taste like chocolate. It's almost funny, the idea of this boy with chocolate skin tasting like chocolate. But then I remember what's happening.

I jerk away.

"No." My voice is trembling. His face is inches from mine and I can't even look at it. "You can't— No. Don't *play* with me."

His lips pucker and his brow furrows. I *wish* he didn't look so confused. He's supposed to understand this. Marius *has* to know that pretty boys, especially skinny ones who can speak French and have nice smiles and hair and eyes, aren't supposed to want awkward fat Black girls. It's just how things have always been. I refuse to get my hopes up. If I do, it will be different than Tasha moving away or the boys at school laughing at me. It'll be worse than falling off a horse. It'll be like falling off a cliff.

"I'm not playing," he says, lowering his voice. "I've wanted to do that for a long time. And I thought you . . ."

I'm staring at his mouth instead of his eyes. After a moment, it stops moving. I allow myself a quick glance up. I'm looking at his face, how open it is, like he's laid all this in front of me and is waiting to hear what I'm going to say. Technically, *I'm* not the vulnerable one here. He is.

"I like you," I say. My voice is scratchy. "I really like you. So I can't do this if you're just going to fuck around. I can't. I won't."

He nods once. I reach a hand out, tracing my thumb along his chin. It feels like touching a door handle after zipping around a rug in socks. Electric. I've always made fun of people for saying shit like that. But I can't believe I'm touching him. He's putting his face in my hands for me to touch and isn't pulling away. I can take, if I want, because he's giving.

The thing about thoughts is they don't take as long as saying sentences out loud. So I can think about a ton of things— like holding his hand and kissing him for *real*, running a hand through his hair, actually *looking* at him instead of fleeting glances. It happens quickly, the thoughts blurring together like they're being fast-forwarded.

Even now, it feels scary to touch him, like he'll disappear if I press too hard. I only trust myself to ghost over his face. I'm focused on remembering this moment, *being* in this moment and grounding myself the way my therapist taught me, instead of dwelling on my fears—what if he thinks I'm weird, what if he's just doing this to be nice, what if he just wants me to write something nice about him? And *God*, this must be the most unprofessional thing in the world.

"Josie?"

I move my thumb under his bottom lip. He goes still—almost still. I feel him shaking. It's odd that I could make someone else shake. I've thought about it in abstract moments, like when movies show people kissing for the first time, with big, dramatic scenes like in *The Fault in Our Stars* or *Bridget Jones's Diary*. But I didn't think this would happen for me. Not for a while. Not with someone like Marius.

I still can't really process that this is actually happening. Like, these are the lips I spend so much time trying not to look at. These are the lips I just kissed. The softest lips I know.

"Josie?"

I kiss him deeply, and this time, it lasts longer than a few seconds.

CHAPTER 30

New plan: instead of finishing the interview at the café, we go back to Marius's apartment. The interview is all but forgotten; I just want to spend time with him. That sounds so corny, but it's true.

He hugs me when we reach the apartment, catching me off guard. It takes a second for me to really hug him back. I'm trying to remember everything about this moment so I can file it away for later. He's soft and solid in my arms at the same time. He smells like too many different things for me to pin down one scent; there's soap and sweetness and warmth.

And then I'm kissing him, without any warning. Unlike me, Marius doesn't hesitate in responding. I know I cry too easily, and although I'm not crying now, there's something about the way Marius throws himself into everything he does, even something like a kiss, that makes me want to. I like his laugh, his pink lips, the narrow shape of his face, the soft hair at the nape of his neck. I like touching it. I like looking at it. I don't know how I was going to convince myself that I didn't want this. I would've gone home still wanting this. The ache in my chest would've only gotten worse.

"Come on," he says, pulling me inside. I draw back, pausing on the threshold. It feels wrong to be in his apartment without his parents around.

"What's wrong?"

I blink, realizing that I've been staring at him. I've been doing it a lot lately. It's like looking at an artsy photograph. I like the way he moves through space, the way his face rises and falls, the way his eyes are full of emotion. Everything about Marius feels so alive, like vivid colors in a painting.

"Nothing," I say. "I just like watching you."

He smiles. I love it when he smiles. My heart warms when he smiles.

"I like looking at you," he says, leading me over to the couch. It's less like a real couch a regular family would have than a leather sculpture featured in a photo shoot for *Architectural Digest*. "And talking to you. And listening to you."

"I like listening to you, too," I say. If we spend the rest of today listing the things we like about each other, I'll have absolutely no problem with it. "Especially when you speak French. You should do that more often."

"You won't even know what I'm saying," he says. "My dad gets so pissed when my mom does it just to get out of conversations."

"Well, I like it," I say, sitting on the couch. It's not comfortable, but I didn't expect it to be. "Sometimes the things I don't understand are more beautiful than the things I do."

God, that was sappy. Everything about this is sappy. I'm not complaining.

He stares at me again. I might feel like I'm doing all of the staring, but he does some, too. I look away after a while, cheeks burning, and feel his eyes on me. And when I look back, he's still staring at my face, and I let my eyes roam over every part of him—long, slender fingers, the socks on his feet when we walk around his apartment, the mole on the back of his neck, the sharp curve of his cheekbones—everything.

"Le jardin dans mon coeur fleurit pour toi," he says. "The garden in my heart blooms for you."

Fine. He takes the prize for most sappy.

"You're beautiful," I say, not to be outdone. "So, so beautiful."

"Shush," he says, even though he's still smiling. "I'm trying to look at you."

"You can look at me while I'm talking."

"I feel bad."

"Why?" I lift a shoulder, reaching for one of his curls. It's soft in my fingers like it's something delicate, something that could break easily. "For looking at me?"

"No." He scoffs. "Did you get the chance to explore the city yet?"

"That's not really what I'm here for," I say. "It doesn't matter. I'll come back one day."

"But you're here now." He pushes himself up. I blink in surprise. "We should go somewhere. Do you feel like walking around?"

———

I've been to plenty of parks before, but they're nothing compared to Central Park. It has a million different entrances—I'm not sure how the Uber driver picked one. There are people ice-skating, trees everywhere, and the smell of dog pee and roasting chestnuts. People stop to take pictures in the middle of the path or in front of statues of dead guys. Beyond the skating rink, there are dark hills everywhere. The edges of the park run away from my gaze. I doubt I could see the entire thing in a day.

"In the spring and summer, people race little boats," Marius says, pointing toward the ice-skaters. "And there's a restaurant at the edge of the park."

"It's gigantic." I can't stop staring. "I didn't think you guys had this much free space."

"*Hey*," he says. "There are tons of parks in New York. This is just the biggest one."

There's a grin on his face. I can't really get over how much I love it when he smiles. I really do. His face already makes him look young, but when he smiles, it's even better, like this rash expression of boyish joy I've always found annoying on everyone else. It makes me want to smile, too.

We probably look odd to everyone walking past. We're standing in the middle of the path and people have to step around us to get by and we're both smiling like idiots. When I stare at Marius, he doesn't look away like I do. He's not uncomfortable with attention—giving it or receiving it.

I grab his hand and start walking again. Something about holding Marius's hand feels really intimate. It's like the most I've ever touched anyone. Before this, I was so conscious of the way I touched him, trying to stay clear of every single accidental meeting of skin. It feels like electricity shooting through my fingertips.

There's a huge amount of space in Central Park, but that doesn't stop some random woman from trying to walk right between us. Marius pulls me to the side. I'm still pissed off.

"People are so rude," I say, loud enough for her to hear. "We're obviously walking here. I don't know why they can't just wait or walk around or something."

"Oh my God."

A group of white girls stops next to me, clogging up the path even more. There are about four of them, and they all have a variation of the same dirty blond hair. The one in the front clutches a pink phone in her hand. They're staring, but not at me. I glance up at Marius. His eyes have widened slightly.

"Uh, hi," the girl in the front says. "You're Marius Canet, right?"

Someone grumbles as they shove through us. I step to the side, up onto the grass, but no one follows me until Marius does the same.

"Yeah," he says, smiling. He can't even say anything else before the other girls squeal.

"Oh my God, okay," the girl in the front says. "We saw some clips of *Incident on 57th Street* online and you were *amazing*."

"Oh, wow," Marius says. His cheeks are pink, but I'm guessing it's not from the cold. The smile on his face gets wider. "Thank you so much."

"Could we have a picture?" a girl in the back asks. "All of us together?"

"Oh." Marius glances at me. "Do you mind?"

One by one, each girl looks at me. My stomach tightens and my air constricts and I'm immediately sure they're thinking the worst things about me: trying to figure out what Marius is doing with me, what I'm wearing, why I'm standing the way I am.

"You can be in the picture," one of the other girls says to me. "If you want."

I stare at her. These girls look perfect, like they walked out of a glossy magazine ad for the Beautiful College Student Store. I don't see any blemishes or scars or pimples. When they smile, they look like they could be models. They look like sisters. Meanwhile, everything about me is different—my hair, my skin, my belly, my thighs. At the back of my mind, I know being different doesn't mean I'm ugly. Staring at them just makes it harder to believe myself.

These girls are everything I always wanted to be. Even when

I started complimenting myself in the mirror, a big part of me wanted to look like these girls. I wanted straighter hair and a flat stomach. Looking at them makes me want to be like them, but I know I can't. All of the diets I've tried—Weight Watchers, Atkins, drinking nothing but lemonade for an entire day, counting calories until I was eating nothing at all—only kept the weight off for a few weeks. My hair doesn't look like theirs, even after I straighten it. I'm never going to be them. I'm never going to be skinny or have good hair or be white. I've *known* this, but it still hurts, especially looking at them next to Marius.

"It's fine," I say, shoving my hands into my pockets. "You guys go ahead."

"Actually, could you take the picture for us?"

I take the pink phone and hold the screen up so I can see. They all look like they belong together, especially with Marius in the center. As time goes on and Marius's career takes off, there are going to be more and more people coming up to him and asking for pictures. Will I still be around, standing behind the camera, taking pictures of people who belong in them?

"Smile," I say. One of the girls blinks. I take the picture anyway.

@JosieTheJournalist: queer kids are the coolest

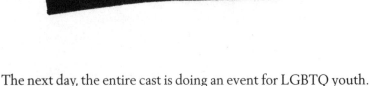

The next day, the entire cast is doing an event for LGBTQ youth. It's in a big auditorium with flyers advertising after-school programs and different Pride flags all around. There are tons of teenagers here. It's kind of weird. At almost all of the events up to now, everyone has been adults, but these people are my age and younger, waiting in line when everyone is ushered into the screening room. There are people with braces, green hair, pins on their jackets, backpacks. It's almost jarring how much it feels like I'm back at school.

"We have a very special treat for you," the guy on the small stage up front says. "I'd like to welcome you all to an advance screening of *Incident on 57th Street,* hosted by GLAAD and The Center! Sit back and enjoy!"

The cast sits in the very back while the movie plays. I wonder what it's like to watch yourself on-screen, seeing the same scenes over and over. I hate hearing the sound of my own voice; seeing your entire body up on a gigantic screen must be a thousand times worse. I wish I had another interview with Marius so I could ask about it.

As the closing credits roll, the lead actors get up onstage to

214

thunderous applause. It's loudest when Marius walks on. I can't tell if it's because he's the best one in the movie or because he's the youngest person there—or just because he's *Marius*. Kids in the audience line up behind a microphone to ask questions. It looks like a ton of people from back here, but it must not be, since they're letting every single person go up.

There weren't enough seats on the stage for Penny, so she's sitting in the front row with me. If she's feeling slighted or pissed about the mix-up, she doesn't show it, smiling widely and clapping along with the rest of the crowd.

"Do you ever feel jealous?" I ask. I'm not sure why; it just jumped out of me. "That you aren't called up to stuff like this with them?"

Cameras are flashing all over—professional cameras with big, dramatic gear and smaller phones. A young kid stands next to Marius, saying something that makes him grin. On the other side of the stage, Art Springfield talks to an older audience member.

"Yes," she says almost instantly. "Not all of the time, but definitely during stuff like this."

I'm not surprised that she feels that way, but I'm surprised she told me.

"It'll get better," I say, even though I'm not sure. "You'll get another movie, right?"

"I don't know." Penny shrugs. "That's what I tell myself."

I can't read her expression. Before I can think of something reassuring to say, she changes the subject.

"Listen," she says, lowering her voice. "Do you know when you'll have a draft of the story ready?"

My stomach squirms. With the murmuring and laughing, it's hard for anyone to hear what we're saying. Still. Talking about this in a public place makes the hair on my arms stand up.

"I don't know," I say, which is the truth. "I still feel like we need more people."

"We do," she says. "But we also have to start figuring out where we'll get this published. We can show them what you have already, right?"

What I have already is a bunch of interviews that I've only halfway typed out. I don't think she needs to know that, though.

"It's pretty rough," I say instead. "I've been kind of busy."

Penny looks back onstage. Marius is signing a kid's arm, laughing. I smile.

"Right," she says. "Busy."

"I'm supposed to write a story about him!"

"I didn't say anything," she says, folding her arms. "But is it so much to ask that you write a draft? Even if it's just a rough one? And then maybe I could—"

"Do you think it's safe?" I ask. "To, like, have the draft floating around? Especially with the stuff that's in it?"

Penny bites her lip.

"I don't know," I say. "I'm just saying. You don't want the wrong people to see it. Especially with the names."

"You could remove the names?" she says. "Just for now?"

"Maybe."

"I'll just send it to one person," she says. "Or I won't even send it right away. I'll pitch it first."

Part of me wants to bring up pitching to *Deep Focus* again, but it doesn't seem like such a great idea anymore. Then the magazine will know exactly what I've been doing on the side. What if they tell me to stop?

"That makes sense."

"Great. We have that done." Penny grins, looking extremely similar to the little sister she played on Disney Channel a few years ago. "Now spill the details on what's going on with you and Marius. He won't tell me."

My heart does a weird floppy thing. I feel like one of those fair maidens from old books who fainted at the mention of violence. I really need to deal with that.

"It's . . ." I don't know what to say. "It's kind of embarrassing."

"Why?"

"It's . . ." My voice trails off. I'm not sure how to articulate what I've been thinking about. "I don't know. Thinking about all this stuff with Lennox and then the guys at my school, it just makes me feel like guys are bad. And it makes me feel, like, irresponsible for liking them. Like I shouldn't be attracted to guys because of what can happen."

"Oh." She frowns. "I—I don't—I really don't know, Josie. Maybe it's just guys with a lot of money. A lot of the guys I worked with were really sweet when we were younger and then went through horrible phases when we were teenagers. But they're better now. At least that's what I think."

She sighs like an old woman. It's hard not to feel for her. Penny is only a few years older than me but has already had so many different experiences. I wish she hadn't had some of them. Girls have to deal with so many things boys don't even have to think about.

"I guess the problem is that you don't *know*," she says. "Guys are a case-by-case thing. On the whole, they're horrible. I guess there are nice ones. I'm just not willing to risk it, so I don't date."

"What if you *do* meet a nice guy?"

"I don't know," she says. "I would wait to see what he's like when he's not nice."

CHAPTER 32

"It's just weird. Like, they all know each other and have talked about what's happened with each other and everything. But they didn't notice the same thing happening to women of color?"

"I mean, white women pay attention to each other most of all," Alice says, leaning back against my pillows. "I don't know. There's no way I'd tell a white woman if something like this happened to me. At school, there's a reason I only hang out with Black girls."

"Alice," I say, taking a deep breath, "you go to a school that's *only* for Black girls." I try to ignore the mild sense of panic that sneaks up my neck. Mom and Dad are supposed to let me know if I get a letter from Spelman, but I haven't heard anything about it yet.

It's Saturday evening and we have two more days until we fly back home. I'm trying to put all of the Lennox story pieces together—both for Marius's profile and for the story I'm working on with Penny—and I have no idea how I'm going to finish when, as it stands, it's all about privileged white women.

It's hard to articulate why it bothers me so much. Obviously, the women I've spoken to have suffered and been hurt by Lennox; it's not a contest. But I know how easily—and how often—Black women and other women of color are left out of conversations about "women's issues." If there's even one woman of color who went through this and I don't get to talk to her, I won't be telling the full story.

"Yeah, for a *reason*," Alice says, glancing up. "Look. We both have white friends. Our town is pretty white. Sometimes you just don't want to be the odd one out. It's nice to be in the majority."

"I get that," I say. "But that doesn't help me with the article. I've been searching literally every single corner of the internet and haven't found any women of color he might've worked with. I tried to ask Penny and even *she* didn't know. That's impossible, right?"

Alice snorts. "Definitely not impossible."

My phone buzzes and I glance down, hoping for a lead. But it's just Marius texting me again. Well, not *just* Marius. I barely saw him at the LGBTQ event earlier, and I haven't answered any of his messages since then. I know it's kind of mean. It's just hard to focus on this Lennox story and him at the same time, especially when it's not just *him* I have to focus on, but my *feelings* about him, too.

"I don't know," I say. "I just have a gut feeling. There *must've been* women of color affected. It's crazy that we can't find them."

"I mean, if something like that happened to me, I don't think I'd wanna tell anyone. Let alone someone I didn't feel close to," Alice says.

"Yeah," I say. "I just—I don't want other women to be left out, you know? Because Penny was telling me about how this is making her feel better, and if it helps another woman feel better—"

Alice is making a weird face. It's the face she makes when Cash farts or when Mom gets disappointed in her.

"Wait," I say. "Do you know someone?"

I try to think back to all the times I saw her hanging out with different interns, if they were all white or if there were women of color. Would any of them know anything about Lennox? Have any of them worked with him directly?

"Why would I?" she asks, but it's a little too fast. "Even if I did, I wouldn't tell you."

"Why not?" I scoot closer to her. "Don't you see how important this is?"

"Of course I do," she says. "But I don't think you can just call up brown ladies and ask them about sexual assault allegations. Especially brown ladies I like."

"So you *do* know someone."

"*Josie,*" Alice huffs. "Listen. I'll ask her. But if she doesn't want to talk, I'm not badgering her about it, and neither are you."

"Who says I'd badger her?"

Alice ignores me and starts typing on her phone. I feel like I should keep working on the stories, but now that I'm waiting to hear back from this girl, I can't focus. I write a line and then erase it a minute later. I fool around on Twitter. After a few minutes—it feels like an hour—my phone buzzes. I'm expecting it to be Alice's friend, but it's Ms. Jacobson.

Hi, Josephine! I wanted to check in and see how your profile of Marius is coming along. I really don't want to rush you, but you should keep in mind that I'll need your draft by Monday so we can edit together before sending off to our editors. Is there a time a phone call would work for you? Thanks!

It feels like I don't know how to breathe anymore. *I really don't want to rush you?* But what else would I do except rush when Monday is just two days away?

It shouldn't be such a big deal. I've written pieces for Monique in less than a day. But those were always different. If

I needed quotes, it was usually from some film expert at a college somewhere, and I could do it over the phone in thirty minutes. This is a celebrity profile for a major magazine. That should have my complete attention, but the piece I'm working on with Penny keeps pulling me away. It's more serious than anything I've ever written.

"*Ugh*," I say, tossing back my head. "I hate *everything.*"

A phone starts to ring. I glance up to see Alice holding it to her ear.

"Hey," she says. "Are you sure?"

After a second, she nods, silently handing me the phone.

"What?" I say.

"Just do your thing," Alice says. "And don't be obnoxious."

I want to tell her that I'm never obnoxious, but I put the phone up to my ear instead.

"Hi," I say. "This is Josie Wright."

"Um, yeah, I know," Savannah says. "Alice told me you wanted to talk? About Lennox and stuff?"

I glare at my sister. She's turned on the TV and seems intent on watching an episode of *Real Housewives* I'm sure she doesn't really care about. I cover the phone speaker, pushing it away from my face.

"*Alice,*" I hiss. "Are you fucking serious? Savannah?"

"You said you wanted to talk to a woman of color!"

I stare at her in response. Alice shakes her head, making a face that says, *What were you expecting?* I honestly don't know what I was expecting. Alice has been spending time with so many of the interns during this entire trip; I didn't think it would be one I knew. I didn't think it would be Savannah. I guess we aren't exactly friends, but this feels personal, closer to me than talking to the other women did.

"Josie?" Savannah says. "Are you still there?"

"Oh God, yes," I say, clearing my throat. "Savannah, thank you so much for talking to me. You really don't have to if you don't want to. I don't know if—"

"I wouldn't have said yes if I didn't want to," she says. "But I have a condition."

"Of course." I sit up straighter. "What is it?"

"I need you to change my name."

"Oh, that's totally fine." I chew my lip. "But are you okay being on the record?"

There's a long pause. I feel like I can't breathe, like all the air has been sucked out of the room, while I wait for her answer.

Alice glances over.

"I'll have to call you back."

"Wait," I say, but she's already hung up. Shit. She was my best chance so far. It seems like this is the day everything goes wrong for me.

I toss myself on the bed next to Alice. She looks at me with raised eyebrows.

"Why didn't you tell me it was gonna be her?"

"I don't know," she says, looking down at her phone. "I didn't want you to be weird about it."

"I wasn't weird."

"You were, a little."

"I don't know how to act when it's someone I actually know," I say, resting my head on her shoulder. She usually moves when I make displays of affection like this. Surprisingly, she lets me stay. "I keep wondering if I'm doing the wrong thing. Like, Penny is into it and I care about her and I don't want to let her down. But what if I'm not doing it the right way?"

"What's the right way?"

"I don't know." I groan again. "I know this is going to be

something big, something we might not be able to handle once it's out, and I don't know what to do with that."

"It sounds like a big story," Alice says, muting the TV. "But you've been working really, really hard on it. If the people in your story trust you, then I think you're okay. And it'll probably get better once you have an editor behind you."

I don't have the chance to reply, because Alice's phone rings. I recognize the number from a few minutes ago.

"Okay," Savannah says when I pick up. Her voice is fast. It reminds me of someone from an Aaron Sorkin movie. "I'll be on the record, but we can't talk on the phone. I'll send you my address and we'll talk here. Okay?"

I'm already putting my coat on.

———

Most of what I've seen of New York has been from movies— Times Square and the Plaza and Union Square, Christmas decorations, Central Park. The address Savannah gave me is in a completely different area. We could take the subway, like Marius says he does, but I would get lost. For once, I'm actually glad Alice comes with me.

The longer we drive, the more things change. I already know this isn't a white neighborhood. There aren't doormen standing outside buildings or fancy cupcake shops or clothing stores. It's almost like our neighborhood at home: people with brown skin walking on sidewalks, more brown than I've seen since we've been in New York, with only a handful of white people scattered around.

"It used to be a lot different when I lived up here," our driver says when Alice brings it up. "Look, over there, you see that white lady with her baby? You never would've seen that up here when I was here. Probably why I can't afford it anymore."

Alice nods like she's had the same issue and completely understands. I guess she's putting that psychology major to use.

Savannah's apartment is on the fifth floor. I have my recorder and my notebook in my bag, but it feels intrusive to be meeting Savannah in her home, a place that tells me so much before she's even said a word.

It's not a bad building, but I know it's not as expensive as where Marius lives. There's no doorman, and the chipped beige paint looks like it hasn't been touched up in at least twenty years. It just looks like a place to live. And it's filled with comforting sounds: someone speaking Spanish, little kids talking loudly, a TV playing *Judge Judy*, and one lady who sounds so much like Mom that Alice and I have to bite our lips to keep from laughing.

I knock on the door, even though I want Alice to, because I have to fight the anxiety somehow. I force myself to breathe. In and out.

The door swings open to reveal an older woman with tan skin and dark hair pulled up in a bun. She's wearing a pair of scrubs, which I definitely didn't expect. Before I can say anything, she turns her head and starts speaking Spanish to someone inside. I see people move past—a kid around my age wearing a hoodie, two little kids who duck at the sight of strangers, and finally a younger woman.

Immediately, Alice wraps her in a hug. Savannah grips her hard. I bite my lip.

"Come on," Savannah finally says, nodding at me. "We'll talk in my room."

Inside is cozy with bursts of color everywhere, almost like Marius's apartment, except with more people. Three of them sit on the couch in front of the TV. While we walk past, the little kids stare at us, but only when they think we aren't looking. The older woman watches us for a moment before leaving.

"She has to head to work," Savannah says once we're in her room. There are two twin beds. Half the room is decorated with dozens of movie posters, while the other is cluttered with JoJo memorabilia. "I'm supposed to be watching the kids, but I figured this wouldn't take too long."

"Thanks again," Alice says. "Josie has a couple of questions, but we should be out of your hair soon."

Then she glances at me. I guess this is my deal.

"Right," I say, reaching into my bag. "I just wanted to record this, if it's okay—"

"Where are you putting this again?" Savannah's eyes are narrowed, hair pulled back in a ponytail. She looks much more serious than I've ever seen her. "Are you putting my voice up on some website?"

"No," I say. "It's just easier for me than taking notes, and it's good to have solid proof to refer back to."

"Okay." She glances at Alice, then back at me. "So where *are* you gonna put it?"

"Well," I say, "I'm not sure yet."

"Wait a second." Savannah holds up a hand. "Josie."

"It's just—"

"I don't understand," she says, talking over me. "You're seventeen. You want to write a story about Lennox groping people. And you don't even have a place to publish it? You think that's gonna work? Does *Deep Focus* even know you're doing this?"

I swallow, forcing myself to stay calm. I can't help but feel defensive when people talk about my age. I know I can write. I've been doing it my whole life.

"*Deep Focus* doesn't own me; it's not like I have to tell them everything," I say, even though my tongue feels heavy and dry. "And I think we have a real shot at getting this published. I've gotten four other people to talk—two of them are Oscar winners."

I wince as soon as I've said it.

"Josie." Alice smacks my side. "What's wrong with you?"

"It's fine." Savannah folds her arms. "I knew that. I'm asking if your age is going to keep the story from being seen."

"I have a background in journalism." I force myself to hold eye contact. "Before I won this contest, I mean. They don't need to know my age. I have contacts already, and then some of the women I've spoken to can help get the story out. It's an important story. I'm sure it'll get attention."

Savannah rubs her thighs. "Come on, sit down. Sorry there aren't any chairs. I didn't want to talk about this in front of them."

"In front of your siblings?" Alice asks. I glance at her in surprise. I figured she would just sit back like normal. "I used to lock the bathroom door to keep Josie from coming in and spying, but she always found a way."

"Yeah, little brothers and sisters can be like that." Savannah snickers. I set up my recorder, trying to take notes with my brain. "But yeah. I—I'm the first one to go to college. I worked two jobs to get myself through City College. And I wanted a job in film production, but it's not real practical, so I picked business."

"I feel that. I worry about what I'm gonna study," I say, flipping open my notebook. "Before you keep going, can I just ask your full name and age? I'm not gonna use it—I know you want a fake name—but it's just so I can fact-check and everything."

"No using it." She raises a brow. "If you do, I'll deny everything."

"Promise."

"Okay." She takes a deep breath. "Savannah Rodriguez. I'm twenty-two."

"So is our sister," I say, leaning back. "And she's going to college next year, but I'm not sure what she'll major in."

"Running her mouth, probably," Alice says.

Savannah smiles, but only a little bit.

"Okay," I say, pressing the recorder out on the bed between us. "So you go to a state college and study business. How did you get in touch with Lennox?"

"It was an internship two summers ago." She rubs her arms. "Like the one I'm doing now with Spotlight Pictures. I wanted to get experience in film and there was an opportunity to work with his production company. I was basically another assistant— I did the coffee runs and answered phone calls and made copies. I was really excited when I heard he'd be shooting in New York. I thought the job meant he could be, like, a mentor. I thought I'd learn from him."

"Did you?" I glance up. Her lips are pressed tightly together. "Learn from him, I mean. But take your time."

"He wasn't really in the office a lot," she says. "But I still thought it was a great opportunity to get my foot in the door."

"But that's not what happened." My voice is soft. It's hard to see the emotions flickering across her face, almost as hard as the silences on the phone.

"No." She shakes her head. "I wasn't the only one—there were other women in the office, but they wouldn't want to talk about this sort of thing. I don't know when it started. Maybe when scenes were getting more complicated and we were over budget? I don't know. But he'd always come in when there was just one of us in the office."

"Just you."

"Yeah," she says. "Just me. And that's why it feels like I imagined it sometimes. He'd come in around lunchtime and tell me not to work so hard, call me *sweetheart* or whatever. I didn't think it was a big deal."

Her lower lip trembles. My throat goes dry. I don't know what to do, so I grab her hand in mine. She startles, staring down at our intertwined hands, but doesn't pull hers away. Alice puts hers on top. I guess I won't have written notes for this interview, but it doesn't matter.

"I'm so stupid, but I liked him a little bit. He seemed nice." She shakes her head, biting her lip. "So stupid. When he kissed me, I thought it was a little forward, but I didn't tell anyone or anything. But then he wanted to do more and he didn't know my name and wouldn't listen when I said no."

"I'm sorry," I say, shaking my head. "You're not stupid."

"I don't know." She squeezes my hand. "He didn't rape me or anything. Just started groping me, pulling down my shirt, and I told him I'd yell if he didn't stop. He said he'd make sure I never worked in the industry again."

"Did he stop?" I ask. "After you told him to?"

"After he threatened me? No." She grimaces. "He only stopped pulling down my shirt because one of the other workers came in. But everyone just pretended like nothing ever happened. I told my manager, but she pretended like nothing happened, even when I quit."

"I'm so sorry," I say, gripping my pen uselessly in my other hand. "I'm so sorry, Savannah."

"I'm glad I'm talking about it." She looks up at the ceiling. "I just told my mom today. Before then, it felt like I made the whole thing up. It's scary. I don't know. We prayed about it."

"I'm glad you could talk to your mom," I say. "You're so brave for talking about this. Seriously—so fucking brave."

I glance at Alice, but her eyes are red-rimmed, and it just makes it harder to swallow down my own tears.

"Thanks," Savannah says. "I want to be. I try to be. I mostly fucking hate him for ruining my experience, you know? My brothers make fun of me for liking his movies because they're boring and super white and everything, but he was a poor kid from the city like me. I figured I could be like him."

"Yeah," I say. "I never thought I'd be like him, but I never thought he'd be such a fucking douchebag. Like, I thought only having white people in his movies was bad, but this is different. This is—*taking* from other people."

That's the difference between being problematic and assaulting or harassing women. Savannah was lucky enough to get another internship, but Julia's career is a mess, and even Tallulah, who is still getting roles, has had something taken from her. When that boy followed me into the bathroom, he took something from me. That's what happens during harassment and assault and shitty touching of other people when they don't want it.

"I feel like he ruined that whole experience for me," Savannah says. "My whole, like, initial love for movies was based on Roy Lennox's work. It's been hard to deal with."

"He stole something from you," I say. "So we're gonna take something from him. Okay?"

"Yeah." She squeezes my hand. "Okay."

CHAPTER 33

I wake up on Sunday to the sound of a phone ringing.

"Alice," I say into my pillow, "can you get it?"

She groans, but I hear her bed creaking, so I snuggle deeper under the covers.

"It's your phone, Josie," Alice says, dumping it on top of me. "Not mine."

"Ugh. Can't you just answer for me?"

"Oh, hey, Marius."

I shoot up. Alice is standing on her bed, wiggling her eyebrows.

"Alice," I say, "give me the phone."

"I don't know why she hasn't been answering you," she says, ignoring me. "I'm sorry. That's horrible of her."

"Alice." I lunge for her, but she easily avoids me.

"Oh, I know." She steps to the side as I jump on her bed. "It sucks that we're leaving tomorrow."

"Alice," I say, reaching for the phone. She shoves her elbow in my face. "Alice, come on!"

"Oh, yeah," she says. "I'm sure she'd love to meet you at your apartment to discuss the profile."

"Alice."

I launch myself onto her back. We collapse onto the bed in a heap.

"I *hate* you," I say, jabbing my shoulder in her side. "Why are you so obnoxious?"

"Trouble in paradise?" She shakes her head. "It's such a shame."

"Shut up." I hide behind my hands. "I don't know what you're talking about."

But I obviously do. That's what makes me so nervous to talk to him.

———

On the way to Marius's apartment, I decide I'm going to ask thoughtful, professional final follow-up questions that will allow me to complete my profile on time. But he opens the door to his apartment, with his golden-brown curls and his brown eyes and the most open expression, and all I can do is kiss him.

His hands cup my cheeks, and I lean into his touch. For once, I'm not worried about anything. I just want to kiss him. I just want to enjoy this, to live in the moment without thinking about what will come next. Eventually, he pulls away.

"You haven't been answering any of my messages," he says. "I thought you were gonna leave without talking to me again."

"Yeah, well." I stare at his mouth. "I'm not—not very good at this."

He bites his lip. I can't tell if he's thinking about the ignored texts or the kissing or my sister's embarrassing phone call. My fingers twitch at my sides, anxiety returning. *I could be the one to end the silence.* The problem is, I have no idea what to say. None of my plans seem appropriate anymore. I don't want to talk about being professional or even Lennox. I want to look at him as much as I want, without it being creepy. I want to kiss him again. Kissing Marius in an empty apartment, everything silent except the sound of our breathing, should count as a form of therapy.

"Did I do something?" he asks, breaking my trance. "To bother you?"

"No," I say. "Not at all."

I watch him nod, just the slightest movement of his head. There's still a worried crease between his eyebrows. I want to smooth it away.

"I just . . ." My voice trails off. There are so many reasons and I don't want to get into any of them. "I saw your texts. I'm sorry I didn't answer. It's just—I'm supposed to work on the story. I thought I'd have a few days to finish it and that I'd never see you again. If I answered, I thought I'd miss you more."

I've shown more of myself than I meant to. I stop breathing. A panic attack is coming. He's going to think I'm weird, because normal people answer texts, because it shouldn't be a big deal, because we only kissed a few times and holding hands doesn't even count and—

"Hey." He tugs on my hand. "Come on. Sit down."

I nod. Marius sits first, and I slowly lower my body next to his, as if the couch will collapse under my weight. He's warm. It releases some of the tension in my shoulders. This time, he leans in, almost in slow motion. I pull him forward by his hair and kiss him again.

My first kiss was during a game of Truth or Dare in seventh grade. I don't remember the boy who kissed me, and it only lasted for a second. My lack of experience means I don't really know the difference between good kissing and bad kissing. That hasn't stopped me from worrying—about open mouths, and tongues, and, God forbid, herpes.

232

It's different with Marius. I don't worry about much of anything when I'm kissing him. I tangle my fingers in his hair, so soft, and pull him closer to me. He bites my lip and a moan escapes my mouth. He moves back a little more with each kiss. One minute we're both sitting up, and the next he's spread out underneath me. It doesn't really hit me until I come up for air, fear—and something else—pooling in my gut.

You'll snap him in half.

I freeze.

"Josie?" Marius stares up at me. "Are you okay?"

I rest my weight on my knees so I don't squish him, but I don't think he notices. His lips are stained red, shining like someone just put gloss on them. His eyes are a little hazy and his hair is fanned out around him and he's beautiful. Incredibly beautiful. As much as I tell myself I'm beautiful, I know Marius doesn't have to speak into the mirror every morning to remind himself. It's obvious.

He reaches out for my hands, pulling them close to his chest.

"You can touch me," he says. "If you want to, I mean."

I always want to touch him—his face and his neck and his hands and his arms, the smooth skin, the mole, everything. This is something I want and have wanted almost since the day I met him. I force myself to stop thinking for just a second, running my thumbs over his hands. They're warm, soft. These are Marius's hands and no one else's.

Then I run my hands up his arms. I feel his gaze on me the entire time. I'm pretty sure our arms are the only parts of our bodies that match, at least in width. He doesn't have any marks anywhere, just light, faint hairs I have to squint to see. I push up the sleeves of his shirt as I go, but by the time I'm up to his elbow, he's already pulling it off.

"You don't have to . . ."

My voice trails off as he drops the shirt to the floor.

He's skinny. Not like he's been starving himself, but he's smaller than me. Smaller than I'm ever going to be. And that's *fine*, because I don't mind being fat, because this is my *body*. It's just that our bodies are so different. I want this to *work*, but we're already different—different ages and genders and people. . . .

But I can't stop looking. There are miles of skin. His nipples are pink, just like his lips, just like his tongue. It makes me tingle. It makes me want to touch, so I do, stroking his shoulders and getting closer. There's just the sound of his gentle breathing. I formulate a plan: touch every bit of him with my hands before following the same pattern with my mouth. I feel light-headed, but in a good way, like after I finish an impromptu dance party.

I kiss his shoulder. I'm not sure if my brain is processing like normal.

Marius turns his head.

"Josie?" he says. "Can I see you?"

It's a simple request, but enough to make my palms sweat. I'm not the same type of beautiful as him. There are no smooth miles of skin. I have stretch marks everywhere.

"You don't have to," he says when I don't say anything. "I just—"

"No." I reach for the bottom of my shirt. "It's just—I want you to know that I won't— There are stretch marks on my stomach and on my legs. They're darker than the rest of my skin. And my stomach is bigger, just . . ."

I can't read the expression on his face. Disbelief? Surprise? Whatever it is doesn't make me feel any better.

"You don't have to tell me," he says, kissing my chin. "I want to see."

"I want you to be prepared."

I pull the shirt over my head before he can say anything else. My stomach pools in between my legs, and my back is straighter than usual. I force myself to imagine the bathroom mirror at home, how good I look in it. It's easier to feel like I look good when there's no one else around.

After a second, I let myself glance at his face. His smile is so tender that it makes me want to cry.

"You're beautiful," he says, shifting so he's sitting up. "Why were you so scared?"

"Not everyone else thinks so." I swallow. "They're wrong, obviously."

"Obviously." He flashes a boyish grin. "You're gorgeous."

My cheeks burn. He tilts my head up and kisses me. I let myself fall into it, wrapping my arms around his neck, pulling him closer to me. He doesn't feel like he'll snap. He feels warm and solid and here. This is real. I'm not imagining it.

But then he's pulling me closer to him, almost on his lap. I jerk away.

"Marius, no," I say, shaking my head. "What if I crush you?"

"Then I'll be crushed," he says. "What a lovely way to go."

"It's not funny," I say. "You're acting like—like I'm not fat, but I am, and you obviously know it. You don't have to pretend like it isn't the truth."

"I'm not trying to ignore anything, Josie." Surprise flickers across his face. He shifts forward, our knees touching. "I know you're bigger than me, but I also know you aren't gonna crush me so much that I won't be able to handle it."

"How?"

"Because I can talk." He kisses my cheek. "And if I need to stop, I'll tell you. Just like you'll tell me, right?"

"Yeah."

He makes it sound so simple. Maybe it is to him, but it isn't to me.

"I like your body," he says, leaning forward. "It's my favorite person's body. And it's not like I didn't notice that you're, you know, bigger."

"It's okay for you to say *fat*," I say. My voice comes out as a whisper. "I'm fat."

"Yeah." He smiles, soft. "I know."

"It's just that . . ." My voice trails off. What am I trying to do here? Convince him that he shouldn't like me? I've spent all this time telling myself that I'm beautiful, but now it's like I don't even believe it. "I don't know. People I like don't really like me back. Not usually, anyway. I think it's because they don't like the way I look. And I'm pretty sure everyone likes the way you look. I don't want you to do anything just because you feel bad for me."

He snorts. "People are stupid. I like you and the way you look and I don't care what anyone else thinks."

"It's just a lot," I say. "Sometimes I have trouble with the way I look, but I like everything about you."

He takes my hand.

"I think I understand," he says. "I don't think anyone really likes the way they look. At least, not all the time. Sometimes I look in the mirror and feel like I'm still fifteen. I hate it."

My eyes snap up. He shrugs a little.

"Are you serious?" I say. "You shouldn't. You're beautiful."

"Are you just saying it because you feel bad for me?"

Now I know he's mimicking me. I roll my eyes and look away.

"Not everyone looks the same." He moves closer, placing a hand on my cheek. There's something so intent in his eyes, so earnest, that I can't just laugh it off. "And not everyone is— Look, Paris and New York are both beautiful cities, right? But they're different. People love them for different reasons. It's like us."

"You make it sound so *sappy*," I say, ducking my head into the

236

crook of his neck. "I must sound more insecure than I thought if you're doing big-city metaphors now."

Instead of laughing, he leans closer.

"But I want you to know that I'm here because I want you," he says. "You know that, right?"

I think I do. I fight back a smile.

"Well, I want you, too," I say, cheeks burning. "I just haven't done this before."

"Kissing?"

"Not without shirts."

"Ah." He moves down, kissing my chest. "It's a little different for me. The last time I did this was with a guy—that was, like, two years ago."

"Oh," I say. It's another thing for my brain to worry about—how different my body must be from his ex-boyfriend's. "Is it weird? To be with a girl this time?"

"I don't think so," he says, cocking his head to the side. "Kissing someone new is always *different*. You're different from him, but it's not just the gender. I don't know if that makes sense."

"I think it does."

Marius runs his hands over my stomach. No one has ever been this nice to my belly, touching it with gentle hands and grinning up at me every few seconds. Then he moves lower and I let him, both of us reaching for the buttons of my jeans, pulling them down.

I always thought of sex as the thing straight cis people do to make babies, but Marius leaving kisses on my thighs feels like sex, too.

"Is this okay?"

"Yeah." I close my eyes and let myself forget everything else but his lips. "It's perfect."

CHAPTER 34

I'm giddy when I get back to the hotel room a few hours later, but my grin is wiped off my face when I see Alice waiting for me by the door with her arms folded. There's no reason for her to be waiting for me outside the room unless something bad happened.

I glance down at my phone. There's a call from Maggie, but also an email and three calls from Ms. Jacobson. Shit. I didn't look at my phone once while I was at Marius's, and I didn't think to check it while I was on my way back. Why would I? I've been floating on air.

My steps slow as I get closer to Alice. Her eyes are wide as she glances up at me.

"What took you so long?"

"Um," I say. "Marius and I hung out a little longer than I thought. . . . Why does it matter?"

"You— It's—" She runs a hand over her forehead. "I don't know what's going on, but someone left you a bunch of messages on the hotel phone."

I push past her and into the hotel room, my stomach sinking. Was it Ms. Jacobson again? Maybe she wanted to get in touch with me about some notes, but I wasn't picking up. I'm just grasping at straws. My stomach is all twisted up as I head to the nightstand between our beds. The phone flashes red.

"Did you listen to them?" I ask. My throat is so dry that it's hard to swallow. "Do you know who was calling? Did they sound mad?"

"I only listened to the first one." Alice pauses by the door. "It was Ms. Jacobson, asking you to call her about something urgent."

It feels like there's a large stone in my throat and I can't swallow around it. All of the things I've been doing wrong jump to mind: spending time with Marius when I'm not supposed to, kissing him, doing things you aren't supposed to do with interview subjects. But how would they know about that? He wouldn't have told them, would he have? I don't even think he knows people at the magazine.

I stare at the phone like it's going to bite me.

"I would get it over with," Alice says, interrupting my thoughts. "You should know what you're dealing with."

Like it's that simple. Like knowing what I'm dealing with will make anything any better. I take a deep breath and pick up the phone, pressing the button that plays back messages.

"Hello." The word is practically barked into the receiver, but I know it's a woman's voice. "I'm looking to reach Josie Wright. This is Lauren Jacobson. It's urgent. If you could call me back, that'd be great. Thanks."

"Hello again," the second message starts. "This is Lauren Jacobson looking for Josie Wright. It's really important that you call me back."

"Josie," the third message starts, "it's Lauren trying to reach you again. I sent you an email, but it would be really helpful if you could call me. There's something urgent we have to discuss."

I frown down at the phone. The idea of calling her back definitely is not appealing. I hold my breath as I dial the number she gave on the hotel phone.

"Josie," Ms. Jacobson says on the other end of the line. "I've been trying to reach you. How is the press tour going?"

"Oh," I say. She doesn't sound as angry as I expected her to. "It's fine. Um, we're spending a lot of time in New York, like you said we would. I just got back from interviewing Marius, actually. Just, you know, wrapping up loose ends."

It's only partially true. But there's no way I'm going to get into everything with Ms. Jacobson.

"I figured," she says. "But I'm glad you're finishing up. Will you still be able to get me a draft by tomorrow?"

"Yeah, I should be able to do that."

Alice glances at me and I shrug at her. I honestly don't know what this call is about. Ms. Jacobson could've emailed all of this to me. I bounce on my toes. If she's calling, it has to be about something important. But what?

"Great," she says, brisk, like she's crossing things off a list. "And there's something else I wanted to talk to you about. Look, Josie. I don't want to scare you."

Saying that is the easiest, fastest way to scare me. My stomach instantly flips.

"Oh," I say. What else *can* I say?

"I've been hearing some things," she says. "Well, the entire office was hearing things all week. And we know they're probably rumors—about a bunch of women getting together to accuse Roy Lennox of assault. Honestly, we've been hearing rumors like those for a while."

My mouth goes dry.

"Obviously, I'm not calling to tell you about the rumors," she continues. "I wouldn't waste your time with rumors. But

I'm calling specifically because we got a call from Mr. Lennox today."

My entire body freezes. It feels like my throat is locked up, like I'm having an allergic reaction to the news she's sharing with me. Why would he call? He wouldn't call unless he knows about me. I figured . . . I don't know what I figured. That he wouldn't know about my involvement until the article was published. But of course I was wrong. This whole time I've been hearing about how powerful and connected this guy is, how he can make or break women's careers, and I'm writing a story accusing him of sexual assault. Of course he found out.

"He's accused you of collecting lies about him," she says. Her voice is unusually gentle, like she's telling me someone just died. "He claimed you're working on a story about him, intending to publish some sort of slander from a bunch of angry, vindictive former actresses. We told him you're completely focused on a profile of Marius Canet at the moment."

My brain short-circuits. I'm not sure what to say. I could deny it. I definitely could deny it. But part of me, the hopeful part of me, wonders if I could tell her the truth. If she would have my back.

"Between you and me, I think this is a case of a big man with loads of power getting paranoid," she adds. "I don't know what it is, exactly—maybe he's asked around, noticed that you're working with Penny Livingstone, assumed a few things. But I assured him that you aren't publishing any story like that with us."

"Right," I say. My voice sounds weak. I think I'm about to throw up.

"We told him you aren't a professional journalist," she continues. "That you won our contest and you're a high school student who loves to write. That's it."

Something about her words makes me unfreeze.

That's it. Like I don't have an entire portfolio of online writing I've been working on since I was fifteen. She makes me sound like I'm a little kid. Like I don't know anything. Like . . . the only reason why he doesn't have to worry about me is because of who I am.

I don't like it.

"I just wanted to bring it up to you," she continues. "I consider the matter handled, but on the very, *very* small chance someone from his camp reaches out to you, I wanted to make sure you knew what was going on."

My body drops to the bed. I'm not sure how to deal with any of this at all.

"Josie?" Ms. Jacobson says. "Are you still there?"

"Um, yeah," I say. "Just a little, um, shocked."

"I completely understand," Ms. Jacobson says. "It truly is ridiculous. Lennox is an amazing filmmaker, but he's so out of line to go around accusing teenage girls of doing things like this."

"Yeah," I say. "Um. Is there actually a story? Like the one he thinks?"

"I doubt it," she says. "Everyone knows not to cross him. I mean, you didn't even do anything, and he accused you of slander. Imagine what would happen if an actual reporter tried to write the story?"

An actual reporter. I swallow the emotion rising in my throat.

"Anyway, I didn't mean to freak you out." Ms. Jacobson laughs. "People like Lennox are just crazy. If you decide to go into this industry when you get older, you'll definitely see."

"Right," I say. "Yeah. I see that."

I can't bring myself to laugh along with her.

"I'll let you go now, Josie," she says. "Have a great time finishing out the tour. I'm excited to read your draft."

"Yeah," I say, but my voice sounds distant. "Thanks."

I hang up before I can hear what else she has to say. When I glance up, Alice is looking at me, frowning. I'm still clutching the phone in my hand.

"Josie?"

I see Alice's shape in front of me, but my breaths are coming out so quick, it's hard to focus on her.

"Josie," she says again. "Come on. It can't be that bad."

But it is that bad, actually. Because Lennox knows. He called them to get me to stop. Does that mean he's called Penny? Has he called the other women who talked to us? Does he know about all of them?

I want to throw up.

And there's no way I can ask Ms. Jacobson for help. She sounded so sure that it couldn't have been me. But it *was* me—and Lennox knows. He must have people watching me. People asking around. He *knows*.

I imagine what Ms. Jacobson would do if she found out the truth. *Deep Focus* would probably ask me for the prize money back. She could probably tell me to stop writing the Lennox story—and I'd have to do it. If she finds out I'm actually writing it while on assignment for *Deep Focus*, they could probably take me to court, right after Lennox does.

"Josie?" Alice says again. "Listen—"

I don't hear the rest of what she says. Instead, I push past her and into the bathroom and throw up.

@JosieTheJournalist: do you ever want to yell at yourself

CHAPTER 35

I still feel sick when I show up at Marius's apartment an hour later. I don't even know why I'm back here. Maybe I'm just looking for a fight. I've spent these last few days trying to ignore Marius's complicity. Not anymore.

"Hey," he says when he opens the door, smiling in the same way that always makes something tighten in my chest. And it does. It just doesn't feel good. "Haven't seen you in a while," he jokes.

I think he's about to kiss me, but I slide past him and into the apartment.

"Is something wrong?"

I turn to face him, keeping my eyes on his socked feet instead of his face.

"I know you've heard the rumors," I start, forcing my voice to remain level. "But did you know that Roy Lennox has sexually harassed and assaulted at least six of the women he's worked with?"

Silence.

I sneak a quick look at him. His eyes are wide as he shakes his head, blinking too much. It's like the first time I asked him.

I always thought Marius was genuine, but I can't tell if this is a real reaction or not.

"I think you do," I continue. "Because I tried to bring it up with you before and you brushed me off. But you can't brush me off again. Not right now."

"I don't—" He falters. "Josie, I've heard rumors, but I told you, I can't—"

"They're not just *rumors*," I say. "No one would make up *rumors* about something this serious. Women know that no one would believe them. I just don't get it. Everyone knows, but I guess you guys trick yourselves into thinking they're just *rumors*, and that's how Lennox keeps getting away with it. I don't know. You tell me."

"You don't know what you're talking about."

"*I* don't? Of course not. I've only been interviewing women about it for the past week." My eyes snap up to his face. "Don't bullshit me, Marius. You can't just brush this off because you want to be in one of his movies. You could be in *any* movie you want after *Incident on 57th Street*, but you chose to work with Lennox."

I don't know what I'm expecting, but it isn't his eyes growing glossy with tears. He's breathing steadily, chest slowly rising and falling, nostrils flaring. I take a step back. I've never seen him angry. Penny's words echo in my head: *I would wait to see what he's like when he's not nice.* Maybe this is what he's like. Maybe he's about to yell.

"I don't—" He looks away, swallowing. "It's not as simple as just *talking* about it. And if I told anyone, I'd never get work again. I don't know why we have to keep *talking* about it."

"What are you talking about?" I fold my arms. "I'm sure it's so hard for you to have to be asked about it when there are women who—"

"It's not just *them*," he snaps. "Everyone who works with him has to deal with something. I just didn't know before I signed on, okay? And now there's nothing I can do about it."

"Wait." My heart sinks to the bottom of my stomach. "You mean . . ."

Oh my God.

"Marius—"

"Don't believe me? Do I have to tell you every detail for it to be true?" His breathing is faster now, frantic, like he's just run a marathon. "Do you want to know how he took me to his hotel room for a 'full cast reading'? But I was the only one, and—"

"Marius." Acid burns at the back of my throat. I'm going to be sick. "Stop. You don't have to tell me anything. I shouldn't have—"

"And halfway through," he continues, hands trembling at his sides, "there still wasn't anyone else there, and I thought it was just something that would happen when I did more films, but no, it was just this guy my dad's age who whipped out his dick and started jerking off right in front of me."

I hold a hand to my face. I can't stop shaking. All of the people we spoke to were women. I never thought—I figured— *God.* I'm such a fucking jerk. I want to make this better, but I don't think I can.

"I don't understand," I say. We're both breathing frantically now. "Marius, do you know how talented you are? You could work with *anyone.* Why wouldn't you just leave the movie after that?"

"It's not that simple." He shakes his head. "It's not like I'm some white kid. I—I have to take opportunities I get. My parents are so proud of me, and so is everyone else. If I pulled out now, everyone would think something happened. I'm not allowed. He said no one goes against Roy Lennox without killing their career. He said things *wouldn't go so well* for me if I told anyone. I don't even *want* to. I'll just shoot the movie in February and go to press events and never work with him again."

"No." I feel guilty and mad and angry and I want to punch Roy Lennox in the face until his eyes fall out. "You shouldn't have to keep working with him when you don't want to, when he did something like that to you. Maybe you could talk about it with—"

"*Josie.*" His voice sounds strained, like he's spent the night screaming. "Talking about it won't solve anything. All it's going to do is make sure everyone knows. Half of them won't believe me. And—fuck, then my *parents* would know. My mother already doesn't want me acting. She thinks I'm going to lag behind in college. Can you imagine what this would do to her?"

"But you can't just *work* with him." My mouth is dry. "Marius, you can't."

"I have to."

"Maybe . . ." My throat hurts and I'm going to be sick and I just need to make this better. "Maybe the article I'm writing will come out before he starts production and you won't have to go because everyone will get mad at him and the studio will take away his budget."

"That isn't going to happen," he says. His eyes are red. "The women you're interviewing for whatever you're working on, they're gonna get called liars. They might never find work in Hollywood again. Talking about it won't help. We just have to pretend everything is normal."

"We can't just *not* talk about it."

"We can't *talk* about it," he says. "It won't fix anything, Josie. He has the power. He can end any of us in a second. It's fine. I just won't get in a room alone with him again."

"But what about the people who don't know?" I ask. "What about the people who are new to the scene and think Lennox is gonna give them their big break? Somebody has to warn them. We at least have to *try.*"

"There's no point in trying," he says. "I'm not telling anyone what happened. You can't just force people to talk about it. He can deny it all he wants and turn around and fight dirty. I know exactly what people would say if I ever told: that I wanted it because I'm bi."

His words hit me like a slap. It hurts because I know it's true.

"Marius—"

"So why should I try?"

"For other people!" I'm waving my hands now, just like he does when he talks. "You aren't the only one wrapped up in this. God, Marius, think about *them*."

His face looked horrible before, but it fucking crumples. It makes me want to cry. Before it was because of what Lennox did. Now it's because *I* made him feel this way. I yelled at him and pushed him into telling me what happened and now I'm treating him like shit. I feel like dissolving into a puddle of tears.

He steps away, arms folded so tight, they look like they're the only thing holding together his narrow frame.

"Marius," I say again. "I—I want to make it better. Tell me what to do."

"I think," he says, not meeting my eyes, "you should go."

His words make my chest ache. I've never fucked up this badly before. I want to fix it. I want to erase Roy Lennox from history. I want to go back in time and make sure none of this ever happened.

But this is *my* fault.

I can't just run away, and yet that's what my body wants me to do. I still feel sick. It's the worst sort of panic attack. This isn't because someone was talking too loud or because I had to give an order at a restaurant. This is because I fucked up. I hurt Marius, the nicest person I know, by stepping on an open wound.

He told me to go, so I do.

CHAPTER 36

"Fuck."

I'm pretty sure this is the fifth time my computer has shut down and deleted my draft. I don't know whether to scream or cry. It's not like it was a good draft, anyway. I have no idea how to combine all six of these women's accounts in a way that makes sense. Normally, I make a story as good as I can before sending it to an editor, but I need this one to be *perfect*. I need to make sure whoever edits this story immediately wants to take it on and defend it to the ends of the earth. It needs to be amazing. Most of all, I need to make sure these women are represented well.

It's early Monday morning, and since our flight is tonight, I have to get everything done now. It doesn't help that I'm not even sure I should be writing this story. Every time I reread the sentences, I picture it happening: the groping, the fear, being trapped in a corner. Then I think about Marius and want to puke. After what happened at his apartment yesterday, how can I be the best person to write this story? How can I be the right person to write a profile of Marius, for that matter? I keep ignoring Penny's texts, keep ignoring everyone and everything, plugging myself into my computer. It doesn't help.

"Hey." Oddly enough, Alice's voice is soft. "Having trouble over there, Bernstein?"

"I want to be Woodward," I mutter, slamming the restart option on my computer again. "And yeah, I think I'm dying. I want this to be perfect before I send it out."

Even though I owe Ms. Jacobson a draft of my Marius profile, I can't bring myself to open the document. It literally hurts to look at it. Instead, I've been working on the Lennox story. I already have three other drafts. Maybe I should add a personal anecdote about what happened to me in middle school at the beginning. The plan was to send it to Penny, but I don't even know if I should do *that* anymore.

"You mean the profile?"

"I—well, no, I was working on the Lennox piece. But I'll get started on the profile as soon as I'm done."

If I'm *ever* done. My computer is moving along at a glacial pace. I run a hand through my hair and yank at it, hissing. There are tears in my eyes. I honestly shouldn't have committed to either one of these things. I'm not mature or talented enough. I should just go back home and hang out with Maggie and Cash and never leave the house again.

Alice walks over, bending down next to my chair. I don't know why I force myself to write at the desk in our hotel room. At home, I write on the couch. Maybe it's my form of self-inflicted punishment.

"I think you should take a break," my sister says. "Working on the same thing for hours won't get you very far if you're just frustrated the entire time."

"I *can't*, Alice," I say, scrubbing at my face. She pulls one of my hands away. "I have deadlines and people counting on me."

"You can't get anything done like this, though. That's what I'm trying to tell you," she says. "You're literally pulling your hair out. What does your doctor tell you to do? Those breathing exercises, right?"

"I *know*," I snap, even though I hadn't thought of doing them. I couldn't tell that this was anxiety. It feels more like a million emotions blended together and a lack of sleep and the feeling I had on the math portion of the SAT. I force myself to take deep breaths and count.

Alice moves to the other side of the room, shoving things into her suitcase. I close my eyes. The article is fine. It has to be. I've been working on it for what seems like a month now. I'll send it to Penny and hope Lennox hasn't threatened her, and we'll see what she wants to do next. And then . . . the profile, I guess.

It was already hell to go through the recordings where women talked about being sexually assaulted and harassed. I don't want to listen to all the conversations I had with Marius. I can't listen to his voice. It'll just make me feel bad. Maybe I *should* feel bad. It was wrong for me to assume. I thought Lennox only targeted women, but I was wrong. Now I can't stop wondering. Did Lennox pick Marius because he knew he was bi? Or was it just because Marius was the youngest person on set? Are there other boys?

All I can think about is what he said. *Talking about it won't solve anything.*

This *has* to work. It just has to. I don't know what we'll do if it doesn't. I'll spend the rest of my career making sure that people call Lennox out for being one of the worst people in existence. If I have to spend the rest of my life making sure directors can't harass workers on the job, I'll do it. I'll do it without a second thought.

My phone beeps and I frown down at it. There's a new email from Spelman. I feel a flutter in my chest, despite everything. I open my email up on my laptop so I can see. It's not like I need to see the acceptance letter now, but it might make me feel a little better, make me feel like less of a failure who has no idea what she's doing.

Dear Josephine Wright,

Thank you for your interest in Spelman College. We received many interesting and excellent applications, only some of which we were able to accept. We reviewed your application very carefully and noted several strong features. That said, there was rigorous competition for entry into our undergraduate programs this year, and your application was not among those that we were able to accept.

We wish you every success with your studies and beyond.

Yours truly,

I don't see the rest because my eyes have blurred with tears.

How could this have happened? I had it all—top grades, great SAT scores. Is it because I wasn't in enough clubs? But I had all my writing stuff. I thought that would stand out. And I'm a legacy applicant. Everyone in my family has gone: Grandma, Auntie Denise, Mom, Alice—

Alice. How the hell did she get in when I didn't?

I toss my computer to the side. Alice glances up at me. She's still packing clothes away in her suitcase.

"Did something happen?" Alice asks. It sounds more like a statement. She already knows.

"Shut up, Alice," I snap. "God, why do you have to be the worst?"

"Is this about the boy? Marius?"

I clench my hands into fists. I still feel shitty for hurting him. How am I different from the people who called Julia a liar when she first came out with her story years ago?

"No," I say, even though it is, partially. "It's about you applying to Spelman when you didn't even want to go and taking my spot."

I know it's stupid—there wasn't a spot reserved for me—but it feels really good to say.

I'm expecting her to yell at me, but her eyes just widen.

"Fuck," she says. "You didn't get in?"

"I know." I laugh. "As if this trip couldn't get any worse, right? I have no future. I got rejected from my dream school. I messed up everything with Marius. I don't know how to stay objective anymore—I don't know if I ever *was* objective. I've spent all this time on this story I probably won't even be able to publish. I'm failing everyone."

Alice presses her lips together, closing her suitcase.

"I wouldn't call you a *complete* failure."

"Right." I laugh again, but my throat is clogged with tears. I try my best to hold them back. "Thanks, Alice. You're super inspirational."

"You don't have to be a bitch to me, you know," she says, sitting at the edge of my bed. "I'm trying to help. Look—you're gonna figure this out."

I don't say anything. I might start crying if I do.

"I'm sure you're not the only one who has gotten too close to a subject," she continues. "It's not just Marius. It's all these women you're writing about—I don't know. I'm not a journalist."

"Wait," I say, leaning forward. I'd rather listen to her speak than be stuck inside my own head any longer. "Tell me what you were gonna say."

"I don't think you have to be objective all the time," she says, shrugging. "I don't know what's going on with Marius. I told you to leave that boy alone, didn't I?"

"Forget it." My stomach sinks at the thought of another one of her lectures. "It's not about Marius being too pretty or too skinny for me, okay? It's about me messing up. And I don't want to talk about it anymore."

"What?" Her eyebrows rise. "I never said he was too skinny for you."

"Well," I say, "it was implied when you said I'd snap him in half."

"I—" She opens her mouth but seems to think better of what she was going to say. I almost flinch away when she places a hand on my shoulder. It's awkward in a way that only Alice could be.

"You're full-figured," she says. "And you're gorgeous."

I roll my eyes. "You can just say *fat*."

"Fat. Whatever," she says. "But pretty boys—especially skinny pretty boys—usually can't handle Black women at all, let alone fat ones, even if they're Black themselves. That's the only reason why I said anything."

She's not *wrong*. But that was never the issue with Marius.

"I don't know," I say. "The way you and Maggie talk sometimes makes me feel like you think I'm not as good as you because I'm fat."

We're moving into different territory now, something I wasn't prepared for when we first started talking, but I keep going.

"And I know you probably don't mean it—"

"I don't," she says. "And I know Maggie doesn't, either."

"Yeah, well." I shrug. "It can just be hard to remember when it feels like the world is telling me I'm not."

"I'm sorry." She bites her lip. "I don't know what to say. You're amazing and you know we don't think any less of you because of your weight. I guess we could mention those things more."

"Thanks," I say, picking at my pajama pants. "I'll remind you, I guess. I just don't want to seem like I'm . . . fragile or something."

"What do you mean?"

"You know," I say. "Because of my anxiety."

Alice narrows her eyes.

"Lots of people have anxiety," she says. "It doesn't mean you can't have *feelings*. You should tell us things. I'm always level-headed and you're the same way."

"Really?" My brows rise. I'd say I'm the furthest thing from *levelheaded*. "Am I?"

"Why do you think you're so good at getting people to talk to you?" She folds her arms, like this has been too much tenderness for one day. "Anyway. This all feels like the end of the world, but I promise that it isn't."

I snort. "Have you been threatened with legal action from a gigantic director and major company before?"

"Well, no," she says. "But I know you're going to figure it out."

"Sure."

"I'm serious." She pulls her knees to her chin. "You know, Spelman wasn't my first choice."

"Geez, thank you for sharing that." I roll my eyes. "It's not like it's the school I wanted to go to ever since I was in eighth grade. It's not like it's the only school I applied to."

"Can you stop feeling sorry for yourself for a second?" she says. "First of all, you literally applied early decision. You still have more time to apply to other schools. And second, I'm telling you so you feel better. I wanted to go to Emory."

"Ew. Where all the white kids go?" I wrinkle my nose. "Why?"

"*Josie*," Alice says. "I don't know. I just did. I figured I'd be farther away from home. They have such a beautiful campus. Ava and Chloe and I decided we'd all go together."

Her best friends from high school. I haven't heard her talk about them since she went away.

"Oh," I say.

"Yeah." She makes a face. "It was the worst. I thought my life was over. Ava got wait-listed and Chloe was the only one who got in. So we had to figure out a new plan."

"Oh," I say again. "Um. That sucks."

"Yes, it totally did." She smirks. "But I love it at Spelman. I'm not saying that to make you sad, I swear. I'm just saying—it works out. You end up where you're supposed to be. Maybe you weren't supposed to be there."

"But it's tradition," I say, staring down at my lap. "You all did it."

"Maggie didn't."

"She could."

"But she's not going to," Alice says. "And she's still part of the family."

"I'm not—" I huff. "I know I'm not, like, excommunicated if I don't go. I just really wanted to. That's all. I wanted it for a long time."

"I get it," she says. "But you'll make your own tradition somewhere else."

"I guess." I bite my lip. I feel the tiniest bit better. "I could take a gap year, maybe."

"That sounds good," Alice says. "Work on your writing."

Writing sounds like the last thing I want to do, but I nod anyway. Mom and Dad won't give me a hard time about a gap year if I'm working. I just don't know if I'll ever be able to get freelance work after this whole mess. I sigh.

"Um," I say after a second, "do you have advice about the whole *I might get sued* thing?"

"Hell no." She leans back. "Maybe you should talk to another journalist. I have advice for dating and prom, but not this. Getting advice from someone who has gone through it can help. Because, for real, I just don't have any suggestions."

But that gives me an idea. I reach for my phone and open up my contacts list. Monique's number is on my "Favorites" list.

CHAPTER 37

Monique's apartment isn't like Marius's. There isn't a cute café around the corner or a doorman in the lobby. She lives in Harlem in an apartment the size of a shoebox, but it's cozy, and there are Lena Horne posters that make me smile.

Monique has a curly Afro, one that looks like it should be a wig because every curl is so perfect. She's a little plump and has a big smile. As soon as she pulls me in for a hug, I'm reminded just how much I love her.

When I called to ask if I could hang out at her place to finish a story, I think she could tell I was a mess. I still *am*, even though I've gotten myself set up at her desk and have opened all my writing on my laptop. Something about the change of setting helps. This isn't the place I've spent hours daydreaming about Marius.

I can't stop replaying the last time I spoke to him, the way his face crumpled and he immediately closed himself off to me.

All this time, I've been freaked out about speaking to survivors of sexual assault the correct way. I didn't want to imply I didn't believe them or make them relive things any longer than necessary. But I didn't even try with Marius. I didn't even think something like this could've happened to him.

Once Alice and I got settled at Monique's, I switched back over to the profile, but it's not like writing it is any easier; I'm pretty sure I've written only a few lines in two hours. I groan.

"Josie?" Monique says. "It sounds like you need to take a break."

Alice looks over from her spot on the couch. The two of them have spent the last few hours pretending to watch *Living Single* while secretly watching me.

"I can't take a break," I say. "I need this done, Monique. It's due today and I only have two hundred words."

I run a hand over my eyes. They're burning. Usually, I don't mind this feeling. It comes after I've spent the entire night writing something amazing or reading the best book ever. That's definitely not the case now.

"Hey." She places a hand on my shoulder, forcing me to meet her fierce gaze. "*Deep Focus* wouldn't have given you this project if they didn't think you could do it. The only person who doesn't believe in yourself is you, and honestly, I think it's the saddest thing."

I force a breath through my nose. Before I started this, I was nervous but definitely thought I could do it. That was before I realized what I'd be getting myself into. Monique doesn't even know about the investigation.

"It's not about thinking I can't do it," I say. I don't know if that's true or not. "I just—I feel like I'm doing it all wrong. Have you ever gotten too close to a subject? I've never spent this much time with one. It's always been fast for me."

Monique studies my face. It's almost like she knows what happened without my saying it. I feel like Black ladies always know what I'm talking about, even when I don't come right out and explicitly say it.

"I don't think it's possible to ever be completely objective," Monique says slowly. "We should always try to, but I don't think it can happen. There's something that pulls you to the story in the first place. And the best stories are the ones where the writers really care."

"I always care," I say. "But sometimes I think it's too much and it doesn't even help. I just care and care and don't know what to do with it."

"I don't know, Josie," she says. "It doesn't have to be all or nothing. You can't take on all of the responsibilities of the world. We can't control everything. You can only control your own actions. That's where you start."

I stare down at my hands. The best I can do for Marius is write the profile he deserves. I know this isn't any way to make up for what I said. I signed up to write a profile before anything happened, and that's what I'm going to do.

So I write.

It's not clean at first. I write out everything—the way Marius looks when he smiles and talks about acting, how he can't dance, the way he watches people when they speak. He's kind and talented and smart. He deserves everything that's happening *for* him right now and none of what Lennox did *to* him.

I have to go through and edit it, clear out the parts that sound like a love letter. People reading this will be able to tell I like him. Profiles sound like that sometimes, though. It'll be fine.

When I'm finished, I take a moment to close my eyes, leaning back in my chair. I did it. It's actually done. For a second, I wonder if I should ask Monique to read it, but then I remember Ms. Jacobson said her editors would work on it. I pull up her email address, trying not to stare too hard at the words *Deep Focus* in her address. Then I hit send.

"There," I say. I sound like I've just climbed a mountain. "It's over."

Alice and Monique cheer, wrapping me in a hug from both sides. I barely register it. I should be happy. Two weeks ago, I would've been ecstatic. But things aren't as simple as I thought they would be.

"Stop *thinking*," Alice demands, pulling away. "So what, you made a mistake with Marius? Everyone makes mistakes. You can't beat yourself up over it. Come on. You're watching *Living Single* with us."

She doesn't even *like* the show—at least, she always makes us turn it off when we're at home. I'm too tired to call her out. I want to believe what she said—that everyone makes mistakes and I should get over myself. But this feels like more than a mistake.

You can only control your own actions.

I need to tell Penny I'm not the right person to write the article. I feel like someone else should be responsible. Someone who wouldn't have said something so horrible to Marius. I should probably call her; this is the sort of thing you talk about on the phone. But I won't be able to handle it.

While we're sitting on the couch, *Living Single* playing in the background, I pull out my phone.

Penny, I text, I have to talk to you about something really important.

I wait a minute or two. She doesn't answer. There aren't even the three dots at the bottom of the screen, showing that she's typing. I'm not sure if that makes this easier or harder.

I don't know if I'm meant to do this.

She doesn't answer that text, either.

I lean back against the couch, trying to immerse myself in

the show, in Alice and Monique's conversation. Instead, I zone out. I start to think about Marius, the way he laid himself out in front of me, like I could move him however I wanted, eyes soft with trust, laughing when I poked his side.

I ruined that. And I can't stop thinking about the way Savannah teared up when we spoke to her, the painful silences when I spoke to Tallulah. Marius has been dealing with this by himself, and I didn't help him. I guess I couldn't have known, but still. I wish I could change the entire thing.

But I can't change the entire thing—not by myself. The most powerful thing I can do is finish this story. No matter what anyone else says, I feel like this is *my* problem now. Maybe it always has been. I can't just give up, even if there are big consequences. I owe it to all of them. I owe it to myself.

I push myself off the couch and walk back to my laptop.

"Josie?" Monique calls.

I open up the document with all of the stories, all of the words entrusted to me, and begin to write. Behind me, I hear Alice's quiet voice explaining things, hear Monique exclaim loudly with surprise, but I ignore it. I write and write and don't stop until there's a story I'm proud of. Finally, after what feels like hours, I attach the story to an email and send it to Penny.

It's finished. And now it's out of my hands.

CHAPTER 38

Alice and I head back to the hotel to finish packing our stuff and check out. By the time we're ready to leave for the airport, to sit around and wait for our flight later tonight, I check my phone and see I have a barrage of texts from Penny.

the story is AMAZING

remember how I said I've been trying to figure out who to send it to? I think I have an idea

okay so I sent the story to an editor at the Times that I know! Fingers crossed

I'm guessing you're asleep

okay you aren't answering bUT JOSIE, THIS IS AN EMERGENCY: KIM (the editor) SAID SHE THINKS THE STORY IS GREAT AND WANTS TO HAVE A CALL WITH US TODAY. HELLO?????

I hate talking on the phone, but nothing is more terrifying than getting on a conference call with an editor from the *Times*. Like, I can't actually picture anything any more terrifying than what I'm doing right now, especially since I'm standing in the hotel lobby.

"I just wanted to let you two know that this is such an

important story," the editor says. She introduced herself when she called, but I don't remember her name. I'm barely figuring out what's going on. "I'm so impressed by what you already have."

"It's really all Josie," Penny says from the other line. "She's super talented."

I know now is the time for me to say something. My throat is dry.

"Thanks," I say. And then there's a long pause.

"Anyway," the editor continues, "we'd really like to take a crack at publishing it. But that means we'll need you to come down to the office to work out the details."

Details? Like what? I try to swallow, but my throat is still dry.

"Details? Like what?" asks Penny, who still has her voice. "Do we need a lawyer?"

Alice pulls her suitcase over to a sofa and sits with a dramatic flourish. I stick my tongue out at her. She winks at me.

"If you'd like," the editor says. "But we have our own. I'd like to review any notes and recordings that you have from reporting the story. We'd also like our lawyer to review the story and advise us on any further steps we should take to fact-check."

I picture Penny sitting next to me, giving me a meaningful glance. I force my eyes closed and take a deep breath. I've been keeping everything in order because I figured something like this would happen—also because I know journalists need to be able to back up everything they write. But something about turning it all over to this editor, to the *Times*, makes it scarier. It makes it realer.

"So should we say three?" the editor is saying. "We'll be done with lunch by then."

"Sure," Penny says. "That works for us. Right, Josie?"

I glance over at Alice, who is now looking at her phone.

Technically, our flight is a few hours away, and we don't *have* to leave for the airport right now. And anyway, this is something I *have* to do. How long could the meeting be?

"Right," I say, but it comes out as a croak.

⁀

The *Times* building is this gigantic silver structure with the paper's logo across it in big, sparkling letters. Well, they look sparkling from across the street, but I can see bird poop as I get closer.

I'm shaking as I enter, as I show my ID and get a visitor's pass, as I wait for Penny in the lobby. I hold my bag close to my chest. She arrives only a few minutes after me, but it feels like hours. Maybe I'm just going crazy. Maybe I'm taking this too seriously. Then again, I don't think it's possible to take something like this *too* seriously.

"Do you have your notebook?" Penny asks as we walk up the steps to the office. "All your recordings?"

"Yeah," I say, gesturing to my bag. "I have everything."

"God," Penny says. "I can't believe this is happening. This is insane."

"Yeah," I say. "But it's okay. It's just going to be a quick meeting, right? I'll give her my notes and we'll be good."

We reach the newsroom. There's a bunch of cubicles all spread out, people typing away, drinking from coffee mugs, chattering. . . . I thought most journalists worked in silence, but surprisingly, this reminds me of a cafeteria. Other people run back and forth between desks, speaking intently while staring at computer screens. There's so much energy in this room. More than I would've guessed.

Penny walks confidently behind the security guard assigned to us. I follow them.

"I don't know what's going to happen, exactly," she says. "I've never done this before."

I bite my lip. I was counting on her knowing more than me. I've read about this sort of stuff, but not about teenagers doing it. Not about nervous, awkward teenagers like me doing this. I've read *All the President's Men* and *In Cold Blood*. This is definitely not one of those stories.

But being inside the corner office definitely makes me feel like I'm in a movie. There are two walls of big windows that let you see the entire city. It almost reminds me of *Working Girl*. I'm stuck in the doorway, staring, instead of going over and introducing myself, like Penny.

There are a few people in the room—a brown man sitting at a desk, a white man sitting in a chair close to it, and a white woman sitting in another chair. They all turn to face me. I force myself to shut my eyes, transporting myself back to my bathroom at home, right in front of the mirror. *I'm a journalist. I wrote this story. I belong in this room.*

I open my eyes.

"Josie and Penny," the woman says, standing up. She has big, curly hair pulled away from her face and a gap between her front teeth. She shakes hands with both of us, and I hope my hands aren't too sweaty. "It's so nice to meet you. I'm Kim."

I smile in response.

"This is our editor in chief, Tom," Kim says, gesturing to the brown man sitting at the desk. "And this is our lawyer, Stan."

I shake hands with them and try to smile, but I'm not sure if it works. I'm not sure if I'm supposed to be smiling during a moment like this. Stan has a face that makes him look like he's always smiling. Tom isn't smiling, but he doesn't look upset, either.

"All right," Kim says, clapping her hands together. "First things first—we need to go through every single line of this story and corroborate what you've written."

I gulp. This definitely isn't the quick in-and-out I thought it would be.

We sit at a circular table in the center of the room. I transcribed and printed out my interviews in the hotel business center, so Kim, Tom, and Stan go through each one, passing them around the circle.

"Where was this interview held?" Stan asks, putting on his glasses. "Were there other people there?"

"Who is on the record?" Tom asks. "Is the interview with Tallulah Port on the record?"

"How is this corroborated?" Kim asks. "Did you speak to family members? Coworkers? Managers?"

That's how I end up spending the rest of the afternoon making calls. While Penny sits next to me, trying to convince Charlotte Hart to give her the contact information of a manager or family member, I have to call everyone else. Julia is easy—she hasn't been shy about this at all. But Savannah is harder.

"What do you mean?" she asks when I first explain what I need from her.

"Like, I need to confirm that other people know about it," I say, looking around the room. It's a flurry of activity—a fact-checker has come in and started to go through the story with the others. "In order for the newspaper to publish it, they need this as proof."

"Proof?"

I wince.

"Not like that," I say. "It's just in case he tries to come back and say that you're lying. Then we have proof, a leg to stand on. It protects you."

"You mean it protects the paper," she says. "Not me."

I try my best to think of something useful to say.

"Remember how we talked about how this will help other people?" I say. "We don't have to—you don't have to do this. No one is going to make you. But remember why you wanted to do it before?"

The other end of the line is silent. Penny starts nodding at me, even though I can't hear what's being said on her call, and reaches for my pad to write something down.

"I don't know," Savannah says. Her voice is smaller than before. "I didn't tell my friends. I told my boss at the office and she shut me down. I told my mom. I told Alice. And I told you. That's literally it."

"You don't remember the person who walked in on you?" I ask. "When it was happening?"

"No," she snaps. "I just *told* you. Look, I have to go."

I bite my lip, tapping my pen against the table. Technically, Alice counts as someone who can corroborate since she knew about it before I did my article, but she's a conflict of interest because we're related. That means I have to try my best to get Savannah's old boss to talk to me. But if I call her, she'll probably run and tell Lennox.

Then again, he's gonna have to find out at some point.

"Okay," I say. "But one more thing: Do you remember the name of your manager?"

I jot down the woman's name—Anne Mullers—and start Googling it on my phone. This is the most confident I've ever felt. Well, I guess it isn't exactly accurate to say that I feel confident. But I'm not worried about flubbing on the phone or saying the wrong thing. I'm not worried about what this woman will think of me. All I'm thinking about is finishing the story.

Maybe it's unprofessional to call Anne Mullers at a personal number I found on Whitepages, but I know it'll be the fastest option. Lennox knows I'm doing the story, so if a stranger calls his office looking for Anne Mullers, they might give me the runaround, especially if she isn't working today. I know she lives in New Jersey, and this phone is probably a landline. The phone rings once, twice. I close my eyes. She has to be there. If she isn't there, I'm not sure what we'll do. We might have to take Savannah out of the story. Then there won't be any women of color at all. We can't just focus on the rich white actresses and ignore a Latinx assistant. It would be erasing part of the story. It wouldn't be the full truth.

I start to think about Marius, the way he looked when he told me what happened to him, but then someone picks up.

"Hello?"

I almost shoot straight up in my chair. All of the *Times* staffers turn to look at me. The papers are spread out around them, like they're teachers getting ready to grade final essays, and I can already see the transcripts marked with the red pen resting in Kim's hand. I can't bring myself to smile, so I just nod at them.

"Hi," I say, leaning forward. "This is Josie Wright. I'm a journalist reporting on a story for the *Times*. I wanted to reach out to corroborate something with you. Did you work with someone named Savannah Rodriguez about two years ago at Lennox Productions?"

She is quiet for a second. Penny, now done with her phone call, glances up at me.

"Why are you asking?" Anne says. "That was a long time ago. I don't know if I remember."

I resist the urge to groan. This whole back-and-forth, trying to get information out of people, it's not something I can do right now. Not without snapping at this woman and possibly tearing her head off. I guess maybe it isn't fair for me to get angry about what he did and reflect it onto her, but it's not like she tried to help Savannah at all.

"I need to confirm an allegation made against Mr. Lennox," I say. I don't know if that's something I can say or not, but none of the adults look up, so I figure it's fair game. "Is it true that Ms.

Rodriguez came to you two years ago and told you about an incident that happened between her and Mr. Lennox?"

"I'm not able to say anything about that," she says, all bluster. "And Ms. Rodriguez isn't, either."

"What do you mean?"

"She'd be breaking her agreement," she says. "We both would be."

"Like an NDA?"

"Yes," she repeats. "Like an NDA."

I frown. Savannah didn't say anything about an NDA.

"Okay," I say. "Just another question—does every employee sign an NDA?"

"Yes."

Shit. I guess that makes sense. But it would've been way more helpful if Savannah was the only one who had to sign one. That way—

"But not everyone signs *more* than one," Anne says. "I would ask Ms. Rodriguez if she still has her copy of the second agreement she signed."

Second agreement?

"What do you mean?" I ask, already jotting notes down on a pad. "Why did she have more than one agreement?"

"I can't tell you any more," she says. "I really can't. Good luck."

Then the line is dead.

Kim is staring right at me.

"Agreement?" she repeats. "Does the source have a copy?"

"I don't know," I say, already typing out a text to Savannah, asking if we can talk. "I'm going to figure it out, though."

Just as I'm holding the phone to my ear, waiting for Savannah to pick up, the door swings open. In walks Roy Lennox.

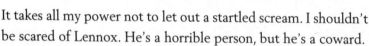

CHAPTER 39

It takes all my power not to let out a startled scream. I shouldn't be scared of Lennox. He's a horrible person, but he's a coward. Still.

As he walks toward us, my eyes grow wider and wider until I feel like they'll freeze that way. I can't stop staring at the dark scruff on his chin, at his bulldog face. He almost gets right up to me before Tom steps between us. Several security guards rush through the doorway, along with a white woman with a briefcase who looks terribly tired.

"Roy," she says. "We talked about this."

My phone is still ringing in my hand. I hear Savannah's voice, but I can't bring myself to even cancel the call. Next to me, Penny is shaking. I don't know what to do to make her feel better. I grab her hand, gripping it hard, but I'm not sure if it's more for me or for her.

"Robin." Stan clears his throat, crossing his legs. "Roy. So nice to see you both. I would've expected a word of warning before you came barging into this office."

Robin opens her mouth to say something, but Roy gets there

before she can. "Maybe you could've given *me* more of a warning," he snaps.

I can't stop staring at him. He's a small man, only a few inches taller than I am, with a big stomach like my dad's. Most of his hair is gone except for a few gray wisps. His eyes are ringed in red, and they're dark and beady, pinning me to my chair.

Roy is still talking. "I have to hear about this story from around town? About these lies you're spreading about me?"

Tom doesn't even acknowledge him. He just sits with his notepad and leans back in his seat like we're having a friendly get-together. Stan is the one who leans forward. Kim glances at Penny and me like she's trying to communicate something, but I don't want to catch more of Roy's attention than I already have.

"Roy," Stan says. "I sent a letter to your office. I called Robin. We've been in communication. Let's stop with the theatrics, shall we?"

I glance at Kim, then at Penny. I know they've been in contact about the story, but I didn't realize enough time had passed for the paper's lawyer to reach out to Lennox. I wish the *Times* didn't have to reach out to him at all. If they didn't, though, he could probably sue the newspaper. He could probably call the reporting one-sided and inaccurate. Even though I'm sure he's probably going to do that anyway.

"They aren't theatrics," Roy says. "The *Times* is trying to ruin my life."

Robin places a hand on his arm, like she's used to calming him down. Like he's not the most terrifying person in the room right now.

"What Roy is saying," she slides in, "is that we've been taken by surprise by many of the rumors going around about this story. Mr. Lennox has an excellent reputation in his field. It simply isn't ethical to publish a story based on misunderstandings from an unreliable source."

272

"As you know, the *Times* doesn't report lies," Kim says. She isn't smiling but looks like Lennox amuses her. "We only report the truth."

"Perhaps they're the truth to *someone*," Robin says. "To a bitter employee, perhaps, or an actress who didn't get her way. Maybe they're stories based on misunderstandings. Roy has a very specific way of working that can often be—"

"No one has any problems with me on set," Roy interrupts. "Who have you been talking to? Whoever it is, they've got it all wrong."

"We can't give out our sources," Kim says. I envy how calm she is.

"But you should make us aware of the allegations being made against my client," Robin replies evenly. "We're here today because we heard about this story and were concerned because—"

"It's a witch hunt," Roy cuts in. "I obviously haven't done anything wrong, not like what I've been hearing. You know, I used to have a real respect for the *Times*—got my first subscription when I was a young boy—but the state of journalism is in the gutter if you have little girls printing rumors about me on your pages instead of the actual truth."

It takes a second for me to realize that he's talking about me. I should stand up for myself. I should tell him that I've spoken to his accusers and I believe them. Every last word. But when I look at him, all I can think about is how I felt when Ryan King chased me into the bathroom.

I've never felt more like a little girl than I do right now.

"These young ladies have written a formidable story that we are eager to put our support behind," Tom says, finally stepping in. "And you know that we will put the full support of our fact-checking team behind the story to make sure everything is accurate."

"I—" Robin starts.

"Who spoke to you?" Roy says. "Who did you get on the record?"

"How about this?" Stan says, putting on a very lawyerly voice. "We'll give you twenty-four hours to respond to all allegations as soon as the story is finished."

"Not enough," Robin fires back. "A week."

Stan and Tom glance at each other. Kim cocks her head to the side, lips pressed tightly together, no longer seeming amused at all.

"I'm afraid twenty-four hours is the best we can do," Stan says after the silent conversation. "We can assure you that the story will be made available to you at the end of the day. The twenty-four hours will start immediately after that."

I glance up at the clock. It's five right now. How long will it take to finish the story? I thought we'd only be here for an hour. Looking back now, I should've known better.

"Fine," Robin says. She tugs on Roy's arm. "Let's go."

Roy lingers, noticing Penny on his way out the door, as if she's been invisible until now. She shrinks back in her seat.

"Penny," he says. "Penny Livingstone. I—"

I jerk to my feet, startling myself. My phone crashes to the floor, but I ignore it, stepping between Roy and Penny and drawing myself up to my full height so that Roy and I are face to face.

"Like she said." I clear my throat. "You should go."

Lennox's eyes lock on me. I might not be able to make my voice as loud as I want it to be, but I'll be damned if I'll let him say anything that hurts her even more.

"That's enough," Kim says. She's standing, too. "We need time to finish the story."

"My client—"

"I can speak to you and your client outside," Stan says, slowly gathering his things. "In the conference room."

"Penny," Roy says, turning to her. "I treated you so well."

I fold my arms and step to the side to block Roy's view of Penny. He turns his glare back on me. I force myself to meet it.

"Come along, Mr. Lennox," Stan says, leading them out the door. "Let me show you to the conference room."

None of us move until the door closes behind them. When I finally glance over at Penny, she's crying silently. It makes me feel like shit—even shittier than I felt to begin with. My phone is still on the floor, but I don't bend to pick it up. Kim and Tom share a long glance. I sit down next to Penny but don't touch her. She doesn't acknowledge me.

"I promise, he just seems intimidating right now because he's used to getting his way," Kim says. "He's acting like that because he's scared. That means we're on the right path."

I want to believe her. I want to call Savannah and ask her about the agreement she signed. But I feel like all the energy has been sucked out of me.

"Now that we know what we're up against, we need Tallulah on the record. The more interviews we have, the stronger we'll be," Kim says, jotting on a notepad. "And we need a copy of that agreement."

The only reason why Tallulah would speak to me was because she was off the record—that means nothing from her interview can be used for publication. I bite my lip to keep it from wobbling. How will I get her to change her mind?

I glance at Penny. She doesn't even move to wipe her tears. She just holds her arms around her center like she's going to fall apart. Kim walks to the desk, grabs a box of tissues, and hands it to Penny. After a second or two, Penny takes one.

"Let's get you something to drink," Kim says. "Yeah?"

Penny nods, rising to her feet. She and Kim walk out the door. That leaves me and Tom.

"Well, then," he says. "Let's get back to work."

I push my tears down into my chest and pick up my phone.

CHAPTER 40

"No. I told you before and I'm telling you again now: everything I said is off the record."

I resist the urge to cry into the phone. I seriously think I might. We've been in this office all afternoon and well into the night, and I already missed my flight home. I had to meet the actual Roy Lennox. Penny looks like she's going to fall apart at any moment. I feel that way, too, but I'm holding it in.

"I totally understand that," I say, tapping my fingers against the table. "But the story is moving forward really fast, and we're trying to make sure that everything can be corroborated—"

"Not my story," Tallulah says. "I already told you that. If you print anything I said, I'll sue the hell out of every single one of you."

I take a deep, trembling breath. "Please," I say. "We really need this."

"I already told you," she says. "I can't."

And then she hangs up. Actually hangs up. I hold the phone against my ear for a moment longer, maybe out of exhaustion. My eyes are burning and my throat throbs in the way it does right before I'm about to start bawling.

"We're screwed," Penny says next to me. "Completely screwed."

Honestly? I think she's right.

———

I groan as I fall out of the cab, yanking my bag strap over my shoulder, Penny following behind me. Alice is waiting for us in the hotel lobby with our suitcases. She looks between Penny and me with serious eyes.

"How'd it go?"

My lower lip starts to tremble. Penny's eyes begin to flood. With a swift nod, Alice grabs our hands, leading us to the hotel restaurant. I'm halfway through my coffee when she finally starts to speak.

"So Monique said it's okay if we stay with her for a little bit," Alice says. "Mom and Dad are probably going to kick our asses, but I told them this was extremely important. Maybe they'll have mercy when we get back home and not kill us."

The hotel restaurant is pretty much empty except for us and a few businessmen at the bar. I expected Penny to still be weepy and sad, but she just looks sort of blank.

"Yeah," I say, rubbing a hand over my face. "We have to figure out tickets back."

I don't want to think about my parents. It was such a big deal for them to let us come on this trip. Missing our flight back home definitely wasn't part of the agreement.

"I can probably do that," Alice says. "Do you know when the story will be published?"

Penny and I share a glance. Before we left the *Times* office, Kim told us she'd contact us about story details, like when it will be published. But we don't really *know*.

"No," Penny says, staring down at the table. "But it doesn't matter, since we're doomed, anyway."

This whole time, Penny has been the one leading the show. She's the one who asked me to help her. She's the one who came up with this idea. If she doesn't believe in the story anymore, I don't know who I can expect to have faith in this entire thing.

"You two need to eat," Alice says instead, pushing at the plate in the center of the table. It's full of nachos, which I normally love, but I can't bring myself to touch them. A glance at Penny tells me she's feeling the same.

I scan my brain for something, anything positive to say. My phone ringing interrupts me. Every time it rings, my entire body tenses, like it's Lennox and he's tracked me down to tear apart everything in my life that isn't already broken. It's not Lennox or his lawyer or even Kim, though. It's Savannah. I pull the phone up to my ear.

"Hey, Savannah," I say, making eye contact with Alice. "What's up?"

Alice's face scrunches up. I'm not sure what that's supposed to mean, but I brace myself for the worst. Penny picks at one of the nachos.

"I'm not sure who else to call."

Savannah sounds out of breath, like she's just come back from a jog. I grip the edge of the table.

"God," I say. "Did something happen?"

"I don't know what's going on," she says. "It's— I keep getting these calls. I think I'm getting one right now. I don't recognize the numbers. They're always unknown. And whenever I block them, they keep coming back. I think there's been five maybe every hour since a few hours ago."

Shit. Shit, shit, shit.

"I don't know what to do," she continues. She's not crying—at least I don't think I hear tears in her voice. Just panic. "I turned off my phone, but then someone called the house. My mom can't know about this—she doesn't know I told you for your article. She can't. She'll freak out."

"I get it," I say. My voice sounds small, disused, unhelpful. "Um, okay. Can you disconnect it?"

"I'm trying to keep it on," she says. "In case there's an emergency."

"Right," I say. God, I'm probably the worst possible person to handle this. "Can you tell your mom that it's just those robocalls? That it isn't anyone real?"

"I can try," she says. "But I wanna know how to fucking get them to stop."

"I know," I say. "I'm so sorry. Fuck. Um, I think maybe I can call the editor at the newspaper and—"

"Maybe?"

I don't know what to do. She must know that. I'm younger than *she* is. I rack my mind for a solution.

"I think you should go stay with a friend," I decide. "Or another family member. Take your family and go hang out with someone else. You can even bring them over here to the hotel restaurant. We checked out of the hotel—we're staying with a friend of mine—but maybe . . ."

"I can't just camp out at your random friend's house, Josie." She sighs, loud. "Jesus. I wish I never even said anything."

My stomach drops.

"I'm sorry, Savannah," I say, even though I know it isn't enough. "Can you come here? I don't—I don't know what else to do. But if you come, you might feel better."

"I can't," she says again. "I can't just—I can't."

"I'm sorry," I say. "I'm sorry—I'm going to take care of it. Did you find the NDA? The second one?"

"I'm still looking," she says. "I honestly don't even remember signing it."

I resist the urge to groan. If we could see that second agreement—the exact words he used to keep her from talking about the assault—we might find proof of Lennox's assault of Savannah. It would make our story airtight.

"Really? Because your manager—"

"Sorry, Josie," Savannah says. "I have to go."

Then she hangs up. I frown down at my phone.

Now I actually have to see if Kim can do anything about this. We don't have any proof that it's Lennox or any of his people calling her, but who else would be bothering her this way right now? We're definitely not pulling the story. Maybe . . . if the story is published soon enough, the threatening phone calls and the barging into offices and lawsuits will all stop.

Or they'll just get a million times worse.

Alice stares directly at me, as if asking a question. What does she expect me to say? Savannah was her friend first. I messed this up for both of them. I wish Lennox weren't trying to freak her out. But what can I actually do about any of this? Nothing. I don't have any power.

Penny nibbles at the edge of a chip. I slump back in my seat.

"Jesus," I say. "I wish I had a stiff drink right about now."

Alice laughs, snorting water out of her cup. Penny stares at her for a second before breaking into fits of laughter herself. I want to laugh with them. I just can't really bring myself to.

"What?" I say, looking between the two of them. "I was serious."

They're still laughing. Some of the guys at the bar glance over, but they don't look for long.

"Do you even know what a stiff drink is, Josie?" Alice asks. "You're a little kid."

"No, I'm not," I snap. "I'm almost eighteen."

"You're still a little kid," she says. "Isn't she, Penny?"

"She's not a little kid." Penny's cheeks are pink. "It's just funny to hear her say it. I've been feeling that way all day. Probably will for the next year. Maybe for the rest of my life."

She shoves another nacho into her mouth. It's the messiest I've ever seen her while eating.

"It won't be that bad," I say, but I sound unconvincing even to my own ears. "I don't know. They wouldn't publish something they don't believe in, right?"

"Still." Penny shakes her head. "I don't know. I didn't think I'd have to . . ."

Her voice trails off. I think of her face when Lennox showed up. I wish I had done something more. I wish I had said something more. I wish I hadn't been so scared.

"Me too," I say. "I had no idea what it would be like."

"But you're still doing it," Alice points out. "You guys went to that office and worked on the story and did it. How many people—not journalists, just people—can say that?"

Penny shrugs.

"Just give yourself more credit," Alice says. "Both of you."

I glance to the side. I really wish we did have wine right now. Part of me wants to check back in just to go back up to our room and raid the mini fridge again, but it reminds me too much of Marius. I'm already wobbly. I can't be even more ridiculous than I already feel.

Still. We did report this story. Even though it feels like it's falling apart, we did the work. That has to count for something.

"Penny," I say, turning my head, "we did do it. We got women to talk about what he did."

"I wanted him to be ruined." She snorts, shoving another chip into her mouth. A spot of cheese is on her chin. "I didn't want to see him again. I didn't want to feel like a fucking little ant he could squish without even lifting his foot. I didn't want it to be like this."

I frown. There's not much I can say to that. I twist my hands in my lap, ignoring the weight of Alice's gaze on me. Finally, she sighs loudly.

"I'm gonna check to see if the bartender will card me," she says, pushing herself out of her seat. "Let's hope not, for all our sakes."

That's when the phone rings again. It's Savannah. I hold the phone to my ear, bracing myself for another problem I can't help with.

"Josie," she says, sounding out of breath, "Josie, I found it. I didn't remember signing it because it was mixed in with all the paperwork I did once I quit, but—"

"Oh my God, Savannah." My chest fills with hope. "You found it?"

"He told me I couldn't tell anyone or he'd sue me," she continues. "But this NDA is insane. I wasn't supposed to tell *anyone*, not friends or family or coworkers. Not even a counselor, unless they signed an NDA, too."

"Josie?" Penny stares intensely. "What is it?"

"And this isn't the original NDA, right?" I say, rising to my feet. "You signed this one later?"

"Yeah, I signed it when I left," she says. "My manager must have explained it to me, but I didn't even—I didn't even process, you know?"

"Savannah." My voice is shaking. "If you could share that with me and give me permission to use it in the article, it would make a *huge* difference."

I hear her take a deep breath. Penny grips my hand. I look at her, my eyes brimming with tears.

"But then you'd be publishing my name," she says. "Right?"

"That's true," I say. "And, Savannah, it's your choice. Take the night to think about it—take as long as you want, even."

I pause, licking my lips.

"But I can tell you right now that what happened to you is bullshit," I continue. "The fact that he hurt you is bullshit. That NDA is bullshit. He tried to control you, but he can't. You're the one with the power here."

I squeeze Penny's hand. She squeezes back.

"You have the power, Savannah," I say again. "Not him. He's done controlling you."

It feels like I wait a lifetime for Savannah's answer, holding my breath the whole time. But then she says, "Fuck it. You're right."

And I can't help myself: I scream, right there in the middle of the restaurant.

CHAPTER 41

"Josie." Kim's voice filters into the room. "Do I have you?"

"Yeah." I swallow. "You have me."

It's morning and I'm sitting in Monique's living room, Penny, Alice, and Monique sitting beside me. We're all holding hands. I wrote an updated draft as soon as I got the NDA from Savannah and sent it to Kim last night, and I got an email from her this morning asking to talk.

"Excellent. So I won't keep you waiting. We sent the draft to Lennox at one a.m., and we've already heard back."

Penny's hand squeezes mine. I squeeze back.

"Interesting response," Kim says, voice dry. "He threatened to sue the paper."

"Jesus," I say.

Kim laughs. "Yeah, it's ballsy, all right."

I swallow. Monique puts a hand on my shoulder.

"But," Kim adds, "we've spoken about it. Everyone on our end still has confidence in the story, and we want to publish. We wanted to run it by you before we let him know and asked for a statement."

I can't even imagine what he'd say in a statement. My leg bounces.

"I don't know," Penny says, looking at me. "He could make things so much worse."

"Yeah," I say. "But he would only threaten to sue if he were scared, right?"

She bites her lip.

"I believe in this story," Kim says. "Our editorial board believes in this story. Our lawyer believes in this story. The question is whether or not you still do."

Penny stares at me. I stare back at her. I think one of us is supposed to comment, to say something first, to start it so that the other can follow. I don't know if I should be that person. After all, this isn't really about me. It's about other people's stories.

But that doesn't mean it's not important to me. That doesn't mean it's not important, period. I didn't say anything when Ryan King ripped my shirt off in the girls' bathroom, and I barely said anything when Lennox tried to bully us. I can do something now. Even if this story doesn't ruin him like Penny wanted, at least we get to fight back somehow. We don't have to yell or scream in his face. We can just let this story run.

"I think we should," I say, glancing at Penny. "I'm proud of it."

Penny swallows.

"Yeah," she says. "Let's do it."

I squeeze her hand.

CHAPTER 42

I wake up on Monique's couch late that afternoon and everything seems normal. Penny is gone and there's sunlight streaming through the window and the news playing on the TV.

There's also a lot of screaming.

I blink, rubbing my eyes, and sit up. Alice walks back and forth, a phone pressed to her ear. Every time she moves, I can see a bit of the TV. It's CNN. They keep flashing pictures of Roy Lennox and Penny and Julia and—

Oh, shit.

Underneath the pictures, in big block letters, it reads: "Director Roy Lennox Accused of Sexual Assault." I rub my eyes. It doesn't go away. I'm not dreaming.

"Oh my God," I say out loud.

I knew we were moving forward with the story. I knew Kim was going to get an official statement from Lennox and that the story would be published. But for some reason, I didn't think it would happen this fast. I certainly didn't think it would be on CNN this fast.

I reach for my phone, but it isn't on the coffee table. It must've fallen. I toss the blanket off and start feeling around, but then

Monique comes into view. I realize she's the source of all the screaming.

"Do you see this?" She jabs a finger at the TV screen. "Can you *believe* this?"

"I can't," I say, which is the truth. "I—I can't. I'm barely processing."

"Alice told me you were working on something important," she says. "I'm so proud of you, Josie. Let me hug you."

She pulls me into her arms, squeezing tight. I grin into her shoulder.

The TV's volume is up, but just barely, and Alice walks out of the way so I can see. A white-haired journalist is talking directly to the screen.

"After the article was published in the *Times* this morning, ten other victims came forward with allegations of sexual abuse," the newscaster says. It looks like he's shaking, but I can't tell if it's because he's angry or surprised. "Roy Lennox initially denied the allegations but has released an additional statement, clarifying that this was consensual sexual intercourse."

How long have I been asleep?

"Oh my God." I run a hand through my hair. "I can't believe this."

"Is it that big of a surprise?" Alice asks. " 'Cause I'm not surprised at all."

"I'm just in awe of you, Josie." Monique pulls away, eyes searching my face. "Your parents must be so proud."

"Speaking of Mom and Dad, they want to talk to you," Alice says, glancing down at her phone. "I told them you were asleep. They're worried that you might get sued."

"Oh God." My voice sounds faint. Has *Deep Focus* seen this already? They must've, if it's on TV.

I'm so screwed.

"Not you individually." Alice bites her lip, glances at Monique. "At least, we hope not. Lennox threatened to sue the *Times* before the story broke this morning. But more people—men and women and I think a nonbinary person—have been coming out, so he's had to change his statements."

The first thing I need to do is call Penny. I reach behind me, finally finding my phone, and scroll through my text messages. There are several from Savannah.

I never thought there were so many.

Thank you, Josie.

This wouldn't have happened without you.

I blink back tears. They're bittersweet. She broke her NDA, which means Lennox could sue her. But I'm proud of her. I'm glad we got to tell this story together. I'm glad that other women are telling their own stories now.

I text back: None of this would've happened without YOU.

I'm not expecting her to respond almost immediately with: <3. Also: Don't check social media for a while.

"Wow," I say out loud. I turn to Monique and Alice. Even though Savannah said not to, I immediately want to go online. "Should I check Twitter? I mean—"

"*No*," Monique snaps. "You've gotten a lot of good attention, but there are also lots of negative comments. I wouldn't check that out if I were you. Bask in the good stuff for a little while."

"Oh. God." None of this feels real, even as it's reported live.

I can't help but wonder what people are saying about me online. They flash a picture of me on CNN—the senior photo I took at the beginning of the year, cocking my head to the side and wearing a dark red cap and gown—but Alice shuts it off before we can see anything else. When I reach for my laptop, Monique wants to talk about *Living Single*.

I get that they're trying to protect me. It's just a little

annoying. I still feel myself shaking, like I just finished boxing a rhino or something, my body full of adrenaline. I need to *do* something. I can't just sit here.

Finally, Penny calls me, and I put my foot down.

"I don't need to be babysat," I say, glaring at Monique and my sister. "What I *need* is privacy."

They share a look, but I step away from the couch and into the kitchen area with my phone. Monique's apartment doesn't have rooms like Marius's does. The thought of him makes my heart ache. What is it like to see the story everywhere? I don't get a chance to think about it that much longer, because Penny's voice floods my ears.

"Oh my *God*."

"I know," I say.

"It's insane."

"I didn't think it would happen this fast," I say, shaking my head. "I didn't even— I wasn't sure the story was good enough, honestly."

"The fucking *Times* obviously thought it was good enough!" There's something breathless about her voice. "Fuck. I can't believe it. I can't believe he tried to deny it."

"It doesn't feel real." I shake my head again, a tiny laugh escaping my mouth. He tried to get me to stop, to keep me from writing the story, from *publishing* the story, but it went out anyway. "My sister and my mentor, they won't even let me check online to see how people are reacting. Is it as bad as I thought?"

"Um." She pauses. "I hung out online for maybe ten minutes and felt like I had this gigantic weight on my chest. So maybe avoid that."

"I'm sorry," I say automatically. "Jesus."

"The only person who is really looking online is Julia. Everyone else is just saying they confirm what they said in the story and don't want to be bothered. I know I don't want anyone asking me rude questions on TV. But people are starting to pull out of his movies, so there's good stuff happening, too."

"What about Marius?"

"I haven't heard anything about him, except that he was just nominated for a Golden Globe," she says, voice softening. "But I also stopped looking online a few hours ago. It was all pretty overwhelming. Like, you should just *see* the stuff about you."

"*Me?* I'm not even part of the story."

"Yeah, but people think you're interesting," she says. "They want to know who this wunderkind is. It's like you're Harriet the Spy—that's what I saw on *People* magazine, anyway. Some people are being idiots about it, though."

"Idiots how?" I glance over at Alice. She's on her laptop, looking up at the TV every few minutes. This must be what Mom is worrying about. "What did you see before you stopped looking?"

"Just stupid stuff," she says. "Stupid stuff, like that you probably couldn't have written it yourself or that your age means that you probably didn't report it correctly. But we know that isn't true."

I wrote a story so good no one believes it was me. I have to laugh.

CHAPTER 43

The anxiety is back. Wait, who am I kidding? It never really left.

Part of it is because Alice and Monique keep suggesting we watch movies or different TV shows on Netflix and I don't *care* about any of them, which only gives me more room to think about what people must be saying about me.

God, I've said so many things on Twitter that I can't remember it all. People could comb through my account and come to a million different conclusions about the kind of person I am. I'm afraid to check it out myself. If I see the notifications, I might not be able to stop myself from looking through them.

But without my computer to look at, I can't stop *thinking*. I called each of the women in the story—short, emotional conversations with lots of tears—but I wish I could take them to a private island so we didn't have to deal with the news. Instead, I'm stuck inside my head and don't know how to get out.

I wonder how Lennox felt when he saw my name in the byline. The thought of him being angry with me should be terrifying. But it isn't. When I think of Lennox, my breathing doesn't get faster and my heart doesn't race. I just want to punch him, no anxiety involved. It's kind of shocking.

My phone rings and Alice picks it up. I glance over at her as she reads the screen.

"Um," she says, "I think it might be Marius."

"What?" My stomach drops.

"That's what the phone says." She shrugs. "Do you want to talk to him or not?"

I didn't mention him in the Lennox piece, but he still must be having a hard time, just like everyone else with a story. Before I can allow myself to chicken out, I grab the phone and accept the call.

"Hi," I say.

"Hi."

His voice sounds deeper, but it's probably just the phone. I bite my lip.

"Marius—"

"Look." He takes a deep breath. "I heard about the Lennox . . . about what you wrote."

"Oh."

"And I was gonna ask my publicist to ask you," he continues. It sounds like he's rehearsed this. "But then I just . . . I thought I should do it. So I just wanted to make sure that in the *Deep Focus* profile, you didn't mention anything about what I told you. It's really . . . private. My parents don't even know."

I blink, taking his words in. My throat is dry.

"Of course not," I say, standing up. "I'd never do that. Ever."

Monique glances over. I avoid her gaze.

"Okay." He coughs. "And, um, if you could cut the parts where I talk about him, that would be really helpful."

I want to ask if he's still doing the movie. I want to ask how he's doing. I want to ask if things are going to be this awkward forever—if we'll even keep talking after this. But I don't, because part of me doesn't want to know the answer.

"Yeah," I say. "I'll talk to my editor about it."

"Thank you."

"Marius," I say. My voice is soft. "I'm sorry."

"I know," he says.

I want to say more—so much more—but the phone buzzes to let me know someone else is calling. The screen tells me it's Mom.

"Listen," Marius says, "I have to go."

"Marius—"

"But it was an amazing story." His voice goes soft. "I'm really glad you wrote it."

He hangs up before I can reply. I suck in a shaky breath and accept the call from my mom.

"Hi, Mom," I say. "It's Josie."

"Oh my goodness." Mom's voice hits my heart. I want to be back at home, want her to hug me, want to rest my head on her chest. "Josie, I've been trying to reach you for ages. Are you all right?"

"Mom," I say, because it's the first thing I can think of, "I—I'm with Alice. We're okay."

"I know, baby," she says. "We keep seeing you on the news. I can't believe it. I'm so proud of you."

Something gets caught in my throat. I'm not sure if it's a laugh or a sob. Alice's head whips around and I avoid her gaze. She's trying, I can tell, but I don't want to have this conversation in front of her. The only private place in this apartment is the bathroom. I take the two steps and close the door behind me.

"I'm freaking out, Mom," I say. My voice wavers with tears. "And it's so bad, because I shouldn't be freaked out, because this is *good*. When I was writing it, I didn't think anything like this would happen. But it's so big and so fast and I don't feel like I have any control of it at all and I'm scared of *everything*."

"Slow down, baby," she says. Her voice is calm but stern.

"It's okay to feel what you feel. You're my baby, so I'm almost as overwhelmed as you are. Understand?"

I nod. She can't see me, but I know she understands.

"What are you worried about, Josie?"

"Everything," I say again, because there's so much going on that I don't even think I can list it. "I wrote about what happened to me in middle school and I'm not sure if I should've. And people think I couldn't have written it because I'm so young."

"We know that's not true."

"It doesn't *matter*," I say. "It's what other people think that matters—that's what it feels like, anyway. And I want people to believe the women. But I don't want my life to get ruined because I tried to help. I don't want to get sued."

"Wait a second. You aren't getting sued."

"Lennox said he was gonna sue the paper, which means I'm probably gonna get in trouble," I say. My voice is hoarse with unshed tears. "And I'm only seventeen and I just want to write. I don't want to worry about that."

"Well, there hasn't been any sort of lawsuit that I've heard of," she says. I can already picture her—the same face she makes when someone comes in with an overdue library book. "Anyway, your lawyer will take care of that if it happens."

"I don't have a lawyer, Mom."

"You do now." She pauses. There's the sound of paper shuffling. "A woman named Eve called earlier. She said she wanted to make sure you had legal counsel if necessary."

"Seriously?"

When Eve said she'd help from the sidelines, I didn't think she meant getting me a lawyer. And she's paying for it with her own money. I'm pretty sure this is the nicest thing anyone has ever done for me. I let out a sigh, tension releasing from my shoulders.

"Thanks, Mom," I say, lowering my voice. "I love you."

"I love you, too, baby," she says. "We'll talk more about everything else when you get home."

"Home?"

"Yes, your father and I had to book *another* flight for you girls after you missed the first one," she says, sass pooling into her voice. "But I see why that happened now, so I'm not as angry."

Not as *angry.* But probably still pissed. I try my best not to snort. Even when I'm published in the *Times,* Mom is still Mom.

"I emailed the tickets to Alice," she adds. "Your flight is at nine. *Don't* miss this one."

The clock on the wall says it's 4:30 p.m. right now. That leaves us loads of time.

"Right," I say. "We won't. I'll see you soon."

Everything's happening so fast.

I leave the bathroom to see that Monique and Alice have flipped back to the news. It's not CNN this time but another channel. A reporter speaks while a huge block of text appears on the side of the screen.

"Roy Lennox has issued an apology to all of the people impacted by his actions," she says. "His production company, Lennox Productions, has put him on indefinite leave in the meantime."

"Wow," I say. The information doesn't fully register. I think I'm in shock.

Alice turns to look at me. Monique is on the phone.

"Hopefully it gets a lot worse for him," Alice says. She and Monique share a look. "We know this has been hard for you, but we've just been trying to make it easier by hanging out here all day."

"Well." I rub my hands on my thighs. "I was *hoping* we'd spend our last day in New York reenacting all my favorite scenes from *The Devil Wears Prada*—"

"Oh, stop. We know you're going a little stir-crazy." Monique snorts, hanging up the phone. "But Alice got a call from Lauren Jacobson, and she says she has something at the office for you. How do you feel about making a trip downtown?"

I glance between the two of them, eyebrows raised.

"Um," I say. "Would this *something* happen to be a lawsuit?"

"Not sure," Monique says. "They'd be foolish to try it, but you never know."

I think back to my phone call with Ms. Jacobson, the way she dismissed the idea that I could be writing this story. It feels like that happened years ago or in a different dimension. I still don't feel great about going to see her, but I can't spend my entire last day holed up in Monique's apartment. And despite all of the shit going on, I *do* feel a little invincible. Just the tiniest bit.

"Sure," I say, already looking for my jacket. "Let's go."

It's not like I'm expecting the paparazzi to follow us when we take the subway down to *Deep Focus*'s office, but I'm still expecting things to be *different*. I'm expecting people to look at me differently—maybe gape. But it doesn't happen. This one guy with red glasses looks at me a little longer than normal, but then I realize it's because my head is blocking the subway map.

Deep Focus is housed in a gigantic skyscraper that reminds me of the Empire State Building, or at least the opening shots of *Working Girl*.

Monique tells the man at the front desk our names, and he asks for ID before printing passes out for us. Once we get upstairs, it's like the office from *The Devil Wears Prada*—all light and open and white. I seriously don't think I see any sort of stain anywhere—and it's eerily quiet, unlike the *Times* office. There are movie posters signed by people who worked on them and celebrity pictures and magazine covers all blown up. They also have those big, clear doors that you can see everything through.

My first instinct is to loiter around the elevator until someone asks what we're doing, but Monique walks straight in. There are people sitting around at desks and typing away on shiny laptops. Up in the corner, there's a TV playing the news. It's still all about Lennox.

I can't wrap my mind around it. This is something I had a gigantic hand in. I'm not just watching someone else report the news. I *did* it.

"Josie!"

I blink before I'm wrapped in a woman's arms. She's a few inches taller than me, and her hair smells like lemon. As soon as she steps back, I realize it's Ms. Jacobson. I stumble away with surprise.

"When did you get in from California?"

"Just this morning," she says. "The magazine flew me in when we realized . . . Josie, you're so talented. The profile is *excellent*."

"Wow," I say. "Thank you."

I was just starting to forget about Marius, too.

"I read it all in one sitting. The edits are honestly so minimal. The piece really made me feel like I was meeting Marius, becoming friends with him. Do you know what I mean? I just wanted to hug him by the end."

"Oh, yeah," I say. "Um, he definitely has that effect."

"So," Alice says, breaking up our little lovefest, "what did you call us down here for? I remember you threatening Josie a few days ago."

"Alice," I hiss. God. I can handle myself.

297

"Threatening?" Ms. Jacobson looks back at me, brow furrowed. "That's definitely not what I meant to do. I wanted to give you a heads-up about . . . what was going on with Lennox. I can't believe . . ."

She stops, shaking her head. Her lips do something strange: they press together, then droop to the bottom of her face before they start trembling.

"I figured he was an asshole," she admits. "But I never thought it would've been this bad. When he called us about you, well, my first instinct was that he was completely off base. I figured it was a power trip."

"It was," I say.

"It was," Ms. Jacobson agrees. "But he was also trying to shut down a valuable piece of reporting."

I don't know what to say to that. Alice still looks unimpressed, but I can't help being touched. On one hand, I feel embarrassed and awkward when I think about that phone call. On the other hand, I can believe that Ms. Jacobson was doing what she thought was right.

"We're all very pleased with Josie's work," Ms. Jacobson says, meeting my eyes. I stare back at her, and after a second, she looks away.

"Oh!" She claps her hands together. "Speaking of Marius, that's the reason I called you over. We received a package for you a little while after you went to his fitting. Do you remember that? It's just been sitting in our mailroom. But things have been so hectic with the holidays, as you can probably understand."

Ms. Jacobson leads us to a closed-off office with huge windows overlooking Manhattan. The big white box on the desk makes my mouth go dry. I know what it's going to be before she even opens it, but that doesn't keep my jaw from dropping. It's the dress—the one I tried on when we went to the fitting. Those embroidered roses feel like they're from another time. An easier time. They're still just as beautiful.

"Oh my." Monique's jaw has also dropped. "That's an original Christina Pak."

Alice is staring at me; I feel her eyes on the side of my face. I just don't know what she wants me to say. We both know I could never afford the dress. That doesn't stop me from picking it up, letting it unfurl in graceful folds, holding it up to my body. This time, it looks like it'll fit. My eyes sting.

"Did she leave a note?" Alice finally asks. I can't read her tone. "That's an expensive gift."

"It just says 'For prom,'" Ms. Jacobson says, handing a card over. Alice reaches for it before I can. The fabric is still soft against my fingers, even as I fold it and put it back in the box. "Maybe it's something you guys talked about when you were there?"

"Yeah," I say, swallowing. "We talked about it."

I didn't think she was paying much attention to me at all. Turns out she was. Today has been full of different women being nice to me, and I eagerly soak it up, like a plant being watered.

"Excuse me," I say, picking up the box. "I have something I need to do."

If I'm going to pull this off, it has to be now, before I second-guess myself. I sneak into the bathroom and take out my phone. Like I thought, Marius is supposed to be at the Independent Infinity Awards tonight. Good.

I quickly change out of my clothes. My gut tightens, waiting for the dress to get caught on my thighs or my stomach, but it doesn't. It slips over easily. I'm used to wearing clothes that are a little bigger, just so I'll have room, but this one hugs my hips and my thighs. I look like the fat models I love. *This* must be their secret—tailors.

When I step out of the stall, I grin because I can't help it. I *feel* the dress, and it's better than anything I've ever worn. This is just like shopping with my sisters, only a million times better. It's what I *hoped* it could be. I turn to glance in the mirror, and my feelings are confirmed. My legs look fucking amazing with the slit. My hair still looks like normal, but this is more dressed up than I've ever been. Even if I weren't going to see Marius, I'd want people to see me. I look fucking great. I grin before jetting out of the bathroom.

As I push my way out of the office, I hear someone call my name. I don't look back.

I have an award show to catch.

CHAPTER 44

"Union Square is shut down."

I don't respond; I'm too busy typing. The structure I'd use for a regular article doesn't really work with this. It looks like this is just going to be a brief. It's 446 words. I can do that. I can get through 250 words before he asks me to leave.

"Hello? Ma'am?"

I glance up. I'm in the back of a taxi, en route to the award show. And he just said— *Oh, shit.*

"Can you get me as close as possible?"

The driver raises a brow but nods. Normally, I'd wonder what he's thinking about me, but it's not important right now. I email Marius, along with a text: Have something for you. Meet me outside the theater. Just five minutes. I promise.

My phone says it's already 6:30 p.m. I know Mom and Dad are probably going to kill me. I know I'm going to spend years paying back all the money I owe them for missing not one but *two* flights.

But this is important.

Marius was nice enough on the phone when I woke up from my nap, but he wasn't the same person he was before. I want to get back to that person. If I don't try, I'll regret it forever. I know I will.

I *am* anxious but still able to breathe. Maybe it's because of the dress. I feel *good* in it. It feels like I could walk down the street and make people jealous with this dress, like one of those badass spies who hide knives in their garters.

"This is the closest I can do," the driver says. Down the street, there are lines of people, probably waiting to catch glimpses of the actors and other famous people going inside. I take a shaky breath. I wish Alice were here.

I pay him before forcing myself to climb out of the cab. My phone is in my left hand. My lifeline.

The flashing lights are blinding, and the crowd seems even larger the closer I get. Lots of teen girls. I don't recognize the older couple on the red carpet. The little metal fences that security put out to keep people from getting too close block my path. I squeeze in among the fans, pushing my way to the front. Every time someone walks past, they scream loud enough to make me wince. I'm not so different from them, though. I'm just a fan in a fancy dress.

I don't see Marius. Did he go in already? My hand clenches around my phone. I could just wait here until he gets out. I wonder how long that will be. It's freezing and I didn't think to bring a jacket. But what choice do I have?

I glance back to where the taxi was, but it's long gone by now.

"That's a really pretty dress," a girl behind me says. "It looks great on you."

"Oh," I say, looking down, like there's a chance she might be seeing something different. "Thank you."

It makes me smile, even as I jump the barrier. I'm taking the long way, staring up at the theater, lingering. Security makes it hard. They're all over the place, and everyone is so much bigger than me. Maybe this wasn't the best idea.

I guess I could just send him what I wrote after the show. But it won't be the same. Marius and I will never be together again the way we were before everything happened—just hanging out in his apartment, like the outside world didn't exist. It was the only time I really felt fine with the world being small.

"Wait, wait, wait. Josie!"

I look over my shoulder, and there's Marius, running out of the theater. I whirl around to fully face him, almost tripping on the bit of the dress that comes down to my ankles. A warm, familiar hand grabs my wrist, steadying me. I look up at Marius's face. His eyes don't move. It's the first time I've seen him since Sunday. I could've looked at pictures, but every time he popped up on Twitter, my heart hurt. Distantly, I know that's how it'll feel when I go back home and all of this is over. I force the feeling down.

"Hey," I say. My voice is soft. "I thought I'd missed you."

"I just saw your message." He lets go of my wrist. His eyes dart around my face, eyebrows creased together. There's something reserved, pinched about his expression. It's like he's holding something back. "What's going on?"

"Nothing." I try to laugh, but it sounds more like I'm choking. "I came to see you."

Ever since I set eyes on him, I can't stop looking, like he'll disappear if I blink. He looks more handsome than ever in a suit that fits him like a very expensive glove and a blue tie that sets off his eyes. The nose ring is gone. Maybe his mother made him take it out. I wonder if she's around somewhere.

"Really?" The corner of his mouth turns up. "Little ol' me?"

I bite my lip, glancing at the phone in my left hand. The idea of reading the entire thing out loud is much more daunting than it originally was. A woman comes over and touches Marius's shoulder.

"The ceremony is starting," she says, side-eyeing me. "And you need to be inside."

"I know," Marius says, not looking at her. "I just need five minutes."

She doesn't look away until she gets inside. I wrap my arms around my middle, then think better of it, resting my hands at my sides.

"You're wearing the dress," he says, eyes widening. "And you look . . ."

"Marius." I grip my phone. If I don't do this now, I'll lose my nerve. "I wrote something. And I just—just let me finish it, okay?"

He nods. I see his throat bob before I glance back down at my screen and take a deep breath.

Local Girl Is Shitty

A local girl's ill-mannered antics have earned her the self-imposed label of "shitty."

Josie Wright, 17, spent more than two weeks interviewing Marius Canet, 19, an incredibly talented young actor, for a profile that will be published in *Deep Focus* magazine next week.

Marius grins, momentarily blinding me. The noise of the crowd starts to subside; they're craning to listen. I go back to reading.

Before meeting him, she didn't have much of an opinion, until she saw his performance in *Incident on 57th Street*. She couldn't stop thinking about him after that. You see, Wright hadn't even seen that much emotion from kids she went to school with in real life, let alone from a young actor in a film. He made her cry. She wanted (and still wants) him to win all of the awards.

It's too bad she messed it up. When Wright learned Canet would be working with Roy Lennox, she worried Canet would turn a blind eye to the abuse happening on set. He already didn't want to talk about the allegations during his interview, and Wright felt this was because he didn't care about anything but his career—a stark contrast to his otherwise kind and compassionate personality.

By repeatedly pestering Canet, Wright felt she was doing what she had to do to advocate for the women who had been victimized. Canet did not agree. She pushed and pushed, even though Canet was uncomfortable, because she felt her plan was more important than what he wanted. For that, she's incredibly sorry.

Wright's sister Alice Wright, 19, said Josie has a habit of being shitty.

"It's annoying," she said via text. "Josie does this thing where she keeps bothering you about something for days, even if you don't want to talk about it. I broke up with my boyfriend during junior year of high school and all she did was pester me about it for a week. So, yeah, shitty. It's a little-sister thing."

It's worth noting that Josie isn't *completely* shitty. She's smart and fun and makes cool jokes and has great taste in music. The idea of Canet having to face Lennox every day made her blood boil, and she figured writing was the only way to help. What she didn't take note of was the fact that badgering him could've made things worse.

"She's annoying," Alice added. "But she's going through with this idea, even though I kept telling her not to and she's definitely getting grounded, so I'm guessing she really cares."

Josie does, in fact, really care. She understands that Canet might not want to speak to her again, but she wants Canet to know all of these things. She wouldn't be able to go home without apologizing to him.

The crowd coos. There's the sound of cameras clicking. I look up to gauge Marius's reaction.

"Oh my *God*." He has a hand pressed over his mouth. I'm getting conflicting emotions—his eyes are watering, but something like a laugh escapes his lips. "*Josie*. Josie, Josie, Josie."

"I wanted you to know," I say. "Before I left. So that—so you'd remember me. I know you might not wanna hang out again—"

"No." His hand wraps around my fingers. I stare down at our linked hands, forcing myself to remember how to breathe. "I don't want that. I—I missed you when you weren't around."

"I missed you, too." I glance up at him. He's closer than before. "So much. Before I really knew you, even."

His lips press against mine. I melt into the kiss. I don't know how to describe it. The only thing I can think of is when I used to go on my random diets and wouldn't eat anything, no real food. Kissing Marius is like eating real food again.

I tangle my hands in his hair, pulling him closer. I want him. All the time, even when he isn't around, even when I'm trying to fool myself into thinking that I don't want him. I want his soft pink lips and his hair and his eyes and the noises he makes into my mouth and the way his eyes are still closed for a second

306

when I pull away, like he's still lost in it, even though we only kissed for a minute.

"And now you can work on whatever movie you want next."

"Yeah. I can." His voice is soft. "But I want to go to this thing first. With you."

"Me?"

The crowd breaks out in whistles and cheers, bringing me back to the moment.

"You have to go," I say, stroking his hair with my thumb. He smiles at me, easy and bright. Looking at him for too long feels like getting high. "Everyone is waiting for the future Oscar winner."

"No, no, no." He shakes his head, but his smile is bigger. "That'd better not be in your profile."

"People were saying it before I did, so I make no promises."

Marius takes my hand. Then he speaks loudly, as if announcing my entrance: "The award-winning investigative journalist Josie Wright has arrived at the Independent Infinity Awards to grace us with her presence."

"Shut *up.*" I nudge his shoulder. "Everyone is going to be paying attention to you. And I'm fine with that. That's how it should be."

"That's okay." He leans down, pressing a kiss into my neck. "They can all look at me. Just remember *je suis à toi.*"

He touches a hand to his chest before placing it on mine. I grin so hard my eyes sting. I take Marius's hand and let him lead me toward the theater. I'm not worried about how I look or what anyone thinks. Not tonight.

ACKNOWLEDGMENTS

While writing this book, I leaned heavily on my own experiences, but also on the experiences of others. I'm so grateful for every survivor who has spoken out and gone on the record with their stories. I'm in awe of your strength and bravery.

I also want to thank the journalists who have reported diligently through the #MeToo movement, especially Jodi Kantor and Megan Twohey, who first broke the Harvey Weinstein story in the *New York Times*. Their work—especially their book, *She Said*—helped me nail down so many of the details of this story.

Without writers like Sarah Hollowell, Julie Murphy, Becky Albertalli, and Renée Watson, I wouldn't know anything about fat positivity, how to love myself as I am, or how to write a character like Josie at all. Thank you for your writing and your presence. I'm so glad that I read your books and heard you speak when I was in high school. I would not be the person I am today without you.

Thank you to Katherine Harrison for your vision and your dedication when it came to this project. I also have to thank everyone at Knopf and Penguin Random House who worked on this book, including Melanie Nolan, Gianna Lakenauth, Artie

Bennett, Alison Kolani, Renée Cafiero, Amy Schroeder, Lisa Leventer, Jake Eldred, Nathan Kinney, Ken Crossland, Lili Feinberg, Mary McCue, Caitlin Whalen, Emily DuVal, Jenn Inzetta, and Mark Patti. Thank you especially to Erick Dávila and Casey Moses for the completely gorgeous cover. I feel so lucky every time I see it.

Thank you to the entire UK team, including Naomi Colthurst, Amanda Punter, Simon Armstrong, Ruth Knowles, Ben Horslen, Amy Wilkerson, Francesca Dow, and Michael Bedo. Once again, I'll highlight Emma Jones, my UK editor extraordinaire. Thank you for letting me slide into your DMs about things that have nothing to do with books!

Thank you to Allie Levick and Bri Johnson for your early excitement, notes, and work on this book, especially in the preliminary stages, where it was more fanfiction than anything else.

I have to thank my agent, Beth Phelan, who has answered far too many questions via Twitter DM than she should have to. You've been such a support during this entire process, and I'm so, so proud to call you my agent.

Thank you always to my family, especially my sister. *Off the Record* is about many things, but one of the main threads is about the messy, often difficult relationship between two sisters. I didn't want to write something simple, but something real, like what we have. I love you, and I hope you know this wouldn't be possible without you.

Tons of love to Nell Kalter for introducing me to *Almost Famous* and planting the seed for this book. Knowing you is such a joy.

Thank you to my incredible friends—you were all shouted out in my first acknowledgments, so I'll only name-check a few. Faridah, thank you for all of the texts and DMs and advice, but also for pushing me to try new things, to think, and to be better.

Christina, we're both authors now! I'm so happy that we're on this journey together. Parmida, you're one of the warmest, most lovely people I've ever met, and I'm so proud to be your friend.

Michael Waters specifically gets a paragraph here because I neglected to give him one in the first book. I don't actually know what to say, though! Go read the mushy essay I wrote about you in the eleventh grade, nerd.

I have to thank every single person who picked up *Full Disclosure*. I don't know how to describe how much your positive feedback fortifies me. When I feel insecure or down, doubting my writing and my books, being able to go back to your kind words (and photos on Instagram!) absolutely makes all the difference. Thank you, thank you, thank you.